MARK of the FAIRE

The Kell Stone Prophecy
Book Three

Dana Trantham

Wayward Cat Publishing

ISBN 978-1-938999-24-6
Library of Congress Control Number: 2015949801

Wayward Cat Publishing
Palm Bay, Florida
www.waywardcatpublishing.com

Cover art copyright © 2015 Wayward Cat Publishing
Background by KeithBishop via istock photo
Picture of swords by Olena Druzhynina via istock photo
Picture of dragonfly by Nobi_Prizue via istock photo
Picture of gold frame by naddi via istock photo

Mark of the Faire

A Fenn of the Wasteland Novel

Chapter One

1268 Autumn

Aliara woke, struggling to breathe, coughing...moving, crawling, before she knew where she was. The tent. The tent had collapsed. The child in her womb rolled and kicked. Her legs were on fire; she sat up to beat at them with her hands. Catching sight of an opening, she crawled over Rue-Anna and forced her head out, attempting a gulp of fresh air; the night was ablaze around her. Shouting echoed nearby. Horse hooves pounded the ground. She grabbed at her sister and tried to wake her, screaming her name again and again, but it was no use. She must find their men folk for help.

When Aliara stood outside the tent, she realized there would be no help. Their camp was burning, soldiers rode through smashing and cutting everything—the fine plates and cups for the wedding feast; casks of wine; her sister's wedding gown. Belfen lay motionless several yards away and a young, dark-haired guard stood over his body; he turned to her with a sly grin. When he raised his bow, she fled into the darkness away from camp.

She fell before she felt the sting of the arrow in her left thigh, crashing onto her stomach. Gasping, she caught her breath, stood and ran again. She was an esien, of the realm, kin to the maiden. She could outrun this scrawny folk any other time of life, but heavy with child, her chances were slim.

Another pang caught her in the right shoulder—she screamed but she did not fall. He was getting closer. She had to keep on. She must find a way. Then she remembered the clover and a surge of energy found her as another arrow pierced her hip. This time she fell but gave little time to suffering, darting up again, limping forward toward the patch. She could smell the clover, blooming in the warm night. Not as strong as it would be in later months, but the gemein would be there still.

Finally she felt the clover under her bare feet, struggled through, and fell to her knees. An arrow thumped into the ground just ahead of her. She lay down, exhausted, onto her side.

"Help me," she whispered. "Please."

She could see him, standing just outside the patch, and she thought she saw his smile in the dim light of the moon. The gemein rose around her as she raised her hand. The guard lifted a firearm and pointed it at her.

"Help me," she said.

Aliara watched as a cloud of bees buzzed from the clover and surrounded the folk; he dropped his weapon and shrieked, swatting at his face. He ran, his screams tore at the night all around her as she let herself lie back in the damp flowers and drift out of consciousness.

1280 Autumn

Leah Hallowsing cowered in the darkness, sobbing once again. She couldn't be sure how long she'd been lost, but it seemed weeks. She had little food left, and feared she could not fight off the cave rats again. They followed her as she crawled along the cavern floor, feeling her way, sure she'd plunge off a cliff to her death if she dared to walk; they scurried around her, occasionally nipping and pulling at her skirt. Several times now, one landed on her pack and, screaming, she battled him off. The time would come when it would be more than one. At some point, they'd have her pack and she'd have to consign herself to starving alone in the caves of the east, far from home.

She could crawl no more, she decided; she must rest. Every time she tried to sleep her mind brought her images she couldn't force away. Her father in his closet office, sitting across from her, the shadow of candle flame dancing on his face. "You are kin to the apostates," he kept saying. "What do you think of that?"

And Kirche, smirking. Watching her. She couldn't stop remembering the day she'd nearly told him about her father, about the journal of Dakenruud, about the kell stone.

"I must tell you," she heard herself say over and over again. "Something of great importance." Kirche had stared at her, almost as if he knew what she would say. And she stumbled. "I..." She could no longer remember why she'd thought to tell him the truth—could not recall what had stopped her. Was it the look on his face, the deadness in his eyes? "I'm frightened of the caves," she'd told him. It was a lie...then.

In her moments of hope, which were few of late, she'd see

Prenalin—the horror in his eyes as he reached for her other hand, just as the one slipped from his grasp. She could still hear his screams. "Leah! Leah!"

"Oh, Pren," she whispered.

They'd gathered their gear in Path, and rode hard northeast with Kirche's spelunkers, Wivel and Pike. Wivel reminded Leah of the shepherds and cowmen she'd met on school field trips. Thick with strength and tanned, he had the sharp, dark features of a man who lived for physical exertion. And his wife, Pike, as lean and wiry as an acrobat, always a thin straight line of a smile on her lips. They were eager to tour the caverns of the eastern continent and Kirche was only glad to make a quick journey of it.

He'd heard tell of a meeting in the hills between King Welk and the land pirates and deserters of Ruhm who made the place their home. He wanted to get the spelunkers to work, enjoy a bit of cave hunting himself, and then move on, leaving them to search for his kell stone while he and his entourage traveled south to find out what they could of Welk's planned meeting with the eis.

The caverns of the eastern continent rose like a giant collection of sloping ant hills, rocky and brown, surrounded by forest. They'd lost track of the spelunkers within hours, but nobody worried; they were tasked with the find and would meet Kirche back in Ruhm.

"Keep to this path here," Wivel had told them. "It circles back around. Don't go off it or you could find yourselves lost."

And so she, Prenalin, and Kirche hiked in the dim light of the upper level near their campsite, up natural steps and down, in and out of pure rock, sometimes stopping to peer up at slits of sunlight highlighting enormous boulders resting uneasily against one another above their heads.

It happened so quickly, the slip, the tiny misstep that had Leah clinging to the rock, kicking her feet in search of something beneath them to support her. Prenalin reached out and grabbed at her fingers just as she lost her grip. They stared at each other, frozen in time. All sound was muted but for her breath in her ears. Her hand pulled from his grasp like thick sap from a tree and though it seemed to take hours, she knew she only glimpsed his face and it was gone—she slid into the darkness, tumbled deep into the rock, tripping, falling, until the ground leveled beneath her. Prenalin's voice echoed far away, calling her name.

"Pren," she screamed.

He was no more than muffled noise and moving away, falling deeper into silence. She tried to climb out. For what seemed days she tried, until her fingertips and palms were bloodied and raw. She cried out; no one answered but herself.

At some point, she couldn't know how much time had passed, she feared they'd give up on her. It was then she began to move, determined to find a way out. And in her head, her own words did little to comfort her. "I'm frightened of caves."

Frightened. Leah pressed her hands against the sides of her head, forcing the sight of Prenalin's fear away. It wasn't true, she wanted to say. It was a lie. I'm not afraid. They must be searching for her, she promised herself. Prenalin wouldn't leave her to die in the dark.

Chapter Two

Dunham had assured Welk he had better sit on the throne. True, he'd thought as much himself; but now he felt silly, like he was playing at king. A heavy gold, jewel-encrusted crown sat atop his head, the purple velvet robe he wore pulled at his shoulders. He wanted to stand and readjust it, but that wouldn't be kingly. It wouldn't even be fitting for common folk. He winced, just as the representative of the ice realm began his approach followed by five others. They looked more comfortable in *their* refinements. And they glided across the stone floor effortlessly, with cold smiles on their faces.

"Luma, High Advisor to the Queen of the Eis," Chamberlain called out as Luma, pale as death, dressed in white robes, moved forward and bowed before him.

They were rather attached to formality, these eis. Prim, proper, always perfect in their dress and manner. Their smiles always barely there, as if their kindness wasn't meant to be taken too seriously. The eis were legendary for their strength, their resistance to wounds and an ability to heal. Even without the kell stone, while they could be killed, their skill with the bow and sword were formidable; their greatest weakness was in number.

In *The Book of Katze*, Welk had read as much as he'd time for about the history of the beast folk and their kell stone—a stone from which they drew not only strength and greater powers both physical and mental, but also those traits that exist, not in the *beasts* of the southern hemisphere of Kell, but in the *folk*. Katz surmised that the kell which influenced their evolution here in the north did not exist in the southern lands. Indeed, there are no eis, nor angels in the south, according to the explorers who managed to slip through Ruhm's grasp and travel to the Ruud to tell their stories. Nor any brownies, trolls, felidae, or other manner of creatures. Similar creatures that exist in the south do not appear sentient—a condition the folk who left the south and settled in the Great West long ago wished to have revisited on the beast in the north.

Without their stone above ground in the north, the beast folk had not only grown weaker and fewer in number as the generations passed, but they fell away from their Rad—the beast governmental body. According to Katz, the kell stone forced the Rad, a council the angels and the eis wanted no part of. Only the beast lord, always a felid, could free them from it. Without the kell stone, the beast folk may one day be no more than legend.

"Rise, Luma," Welk said. "You may speak."

Welk smiled inwardly as he watched Luma compose his face for his memorized speech.

"Lara of Eidolon, Daughter of the Snow, Queen of the Eis, wishes to make known her dissatisfaction with the folk of the Ruud and their kings' refusal to remove their kin from her lands. Be warned that had not a most advantageous event occurred for your sake, Welk, King of Michelruud, this emissary would be a

8

declaration of war. But fear not, you have one reprieve. Fenn of the Wasteland, child of prophecy, marked by the faire in infancy has been captured and is held for you now. If you will lead your kin out of our lands, you will have him."

Welk leaned forward, surprised. He expected a general plea, perhaps a threat, especially after the way the usurper queen's previous emissaries were summarily dismissed by his ailing father. But this? They have captured Fenn Foster and wish to ransom him?

"I must ponder this news," he said to Luma. "Please rest and join us in our mid-day meal." He held out his hand toward the set tables, the nobles all standing about watching, waiting, the wine stewards ready to pour. And as if on cue, fat chef came in from the kitchen leading a parade of tray-laden servers and the smell of roasted pig and duck wafted through the air. Surely, even eis could not resist a roasted pig.

Luma and his party bowed before the king. "I thank you for the invitation," he said, "but our queen is eager for your response."

"Very well," Welk said. He leaned back on the throne, put an elbow on the rest to his right and let his fingers scratch and play at his chin.

The boy is marked by the faire, he thought. And yet, the usurper queen would give him up. She does not fear his strength; but then why would she? The boy would have no interest in the eis; at least, not yet.

But this development would work out well for Welk. He was to leave for the hill country on the morrow. He would meet with the land pirates and representatives of those pilgrims from Ruhm and parts beyond, organize, make a stand for their rights to live on land the eis claimed, but of which they refused to take possession.

He chuckled and Luma, in his periphery, took in a deep, insulted breath. Yes, Welk thought, the usurper queen must want war. There could be no other explanation for her deigning to send emissaries to request anything, even the clearing of folk from her land. She and her angel consorts deemed the folk inferior, scum to be removed if possible, and if not, ignored. She wanted war. But without the kell stone, did the angels and the eis have enough power for it?

Welk sat upright and looked to Luma. She knows, he thought. She knows the prophecy. She expects Fenn Foster to find the stone—to wield it, destroy the Ruud, kill the kings. The *king*.

Here Welk laughed and Luma's left eye twitched. Could the usurper queen know of his efforts to unite the kingdoms of the Ruud under his throne? Thus making himself the one and only king—the only target of the prophecy? Nonsense. There is no real prophecy, he reminded himself.

"Tell your queen I will come for him," he said to the troubled Luma.

Perhaps she wants war. Or perhaps she wishes to take Welk as a better ransom. Could she be that ignorant of the tenuous relationships among Michelruud, Aaronland, and Damon Wall? Ricker and Arnot would let her have him—tell her to deal with the folk in the hill country herself, dirty her own, delicate eisen hands. No matter.

"And the folk?" Luma said, lifting his chin, no doubt wishing Welk was not above him on the throne so that he could look down his long, eis nose at him.

"Does the queen of the eis not understand that the winter folk are not from the Ruud? I'm sure she has been informed that these folk have no connection with us."

"They are folk. They are not eis nor angel. They are more

your concern than hers."

"Very well. I will come for the lad and on my way I will see what I can do about your folk problem."

Luma waited for more. But there *was* no more. Welk waved a hand in dismissal and the eis and his entourage bowed again and backed away before turning to leave.

"Dunham, you will have to send for Sorgood," Welk said with a smile. "We must pull him from the port and let him know that he is to travel to the ice realm. He should be giddy."

Dunham raised an eyebrow.

"It will be the last I ask of him, before I discharge him from the guard."

Chapter Three

Her footsteps on the spiral stair woke Fenn in the dim light of the tower. The fires were no more than embers now and he saw only shadow as she scuttled across the floor; there was a rustling to her steps, as if she wore a gown and it brushed the floor as she passed. Groggy, he rubbed at his eyes and lifted his head, but she was not on her blanket by the fire on the other side of the room. He knew she must be hidden in one of the other alcoves; but, why?

The girl was there that first morning when Fenn woke to find himself in the top room of a tower, at the back of what he assumed was the ice palace. Though the room was large and round, eight thick stone walls jutted out from the exterior, forming cubbies, three with fireplaces, one with a heavy wooden door, and the other four with windows closed off by thin boards latched with rusty hooks. Only two fires were lit, those on opposite sides of the room—his, and the girl's. He'd nodded, that first day, but she ignored him and he'd gone on to explore on his own.

The locked door faced south and he could see from the

window next to it, there was a landing outside it, and a wooden stair circling the tower to the room below. In the center of the room was a spiral stair. Pushing through a thin wooden door at the top, he found himself on a roof with a three-foot stone wall. Stacks of firewood blocked one portion and next to them were buckets, one for food, the other ice. There was a rack over his fire, where he could warm up the bits of meat and vegetables the angels left for them. He had a cup in which he could melt the ice for water.

The eisen was pale, as he'd heard they were, her hair the color of honey and her eyes the dark, angry blue of the wild burr petals that strangled out the white lilies Father Treacher tried to grow in his garden. She wore a hooded, full-length robe the color of straw, but at its bottom rim, a silky, gossamer gown slipped out occasionally and snagged on the stone floor. She said little and seemed to sneer at him when he struggled to chew the tough eleshag, or when he shivered at the icy wind whipping at him from the barely covered windows.

When she cried out in pain, Fenn sat upright, startled. She was still hidden in an alcove, away from her fire. She whimpered and cried again, though this time it was muffled, as if she were trying to hide her torment from him.

"Are you all right?" he said.

She sucked in a deep breath and Fenn scrambled to his feet.

"No," she said. "Don't come near me."

"What happened? Are you hurt?"

Here she let out a shrill scream and moaned.

Fenn took a few steps toward the shadows. "What can I do?"

"Nothing," she shouted. "Go away. Back to your fire."

He nodded and crept to the embers in his own cubby where

14

he sat and wrapped his arms around his knees, wincing at her cries.

"Speak to me," she said, finally.

"What about?"

"Anything." Her voice was weak, trembling. "A story."

Fenn's mind went blank. "I don't know any stories."

"Your story then," she whimpered. "Who are you?"

"Fenn Foster, of the wissenry in Path. In the Ruud."

"And how do you come to find yourself imprisoned in the tower?"

He told her about being awakened by Father Treacher in the early morning, weeks ago, and sent away from the wissenry. He told her about Sadie and Grayson, and about Rogget and Darnit. He told her they went into the beast forest and met Dag Voorspeld, about Kwitcher the elf and the troll on the bridge. He told her how he, Sadie, and Grayson snuck all the kids out of Steingefan and how his mark was discovered and he was sent away from the Ruud, to the ice realm, to see the maiden. He told her of the Wretched and his charm and Forbes Billing's writ and Clara. And when he woke in the dawn of the next morning, he could not remember how much he had told, and how much he'd only dreamed.

When he sat up, he found logs had been added to his fire and there in his alcove were two eleshag pelts, a loaf of bread, and a bowl of apples and berries. Across the room he saw the girl in her cubby, curled up at her fire, sleeping.

Chapter Four

Lucas offered Brinkley his extra apple and it was gladly accepted. They sat on the ground while their horses wore their feed bags and waited for the break to be ended. There was much left to do in setting up camp. More tents needed to be staked, fire pits dug—the temperature here in the east, with the spires of the ice palace in the distance, were lower than any of Sorgood's men were accustomed to, they would need to dig them deep.

They were beyond the hills, through the winter woods, on a brief plain nestled at the opening of Kingdom Pass—a path through the towering foothills of the ice realm which jutted up through the ground as if they ached for the sky. They set up camp so close to the palace, they could be seen by the eis guards in their towers, no doubt.

"They got him there in the castle," Phil said to them. "Is that it?"

"That's the word," Brinkley said. "But this meeting here... this ain't nothing to do with the boy of prophecy."

"Too true. I heard the same," Phil said. He took Brinkley's

apple from him and tore a large chunk into his mouth before handing it back.

Lucas smiled. He'd heard the rumors as well. Welk of Michelruud got the folk of the Ruud behind him by taking action to find Fenn. Then he'd ordered the freedom of all those outcast to the wastelands and demanded King Ricker and King Arnot allow it. What choice did they have? The people were now more with Welk than before.

His idea to stand with the people in the hill country against the nonsensical complaints of the eis would secure him as leader of the Ruud, whether in name or not. But what did it mean for Fenn? That was Lucas' concern. Did Welk truly intend to retrieve the boy from the usurper queen? If not, Lucas would do it himself.

"Ho, there," Brinkley said, standing. "What's this?"

Lucas stood and turned, as all the camp did, to see the Hass of Emorah, their purple robes dancing as their horses dashed across the plain, riding in from the north.

"What are they doing out here?" Phil said. "Ain't it time they went back west?"

"Lucas, what do you know about it?" Brinkley nudged him, apple still in hand.

"Why would I know anything? Maybe they want to see how the meeting plays out. There are a lot of folk out here who escaped them, snuck out of Ruhm to live free."

"You think they'll make a try to haul 'em back?"

"Welk would never allow that," Phil said. "Would he?"

Lucas moved away from them, counting the horses—ten. Two laden only with supplies, seven sat with riders, and one, free of any encumbrance. He searched the group, as they neared, for Leah Hallowing and his heart sank when he realized she was

18

not among them. But where could she be? When their horses rode into their burgeoning camp, Lucas was first to greet them, helping with their packs and supplies.

Their Lord Kirche was tired, but showed no sign of a problem. The other, his aide whose name Lucas did not know, was pale and drawn. One of the guards, a frail young man, wiped his nose and rubbed his red eyes as he dismounted and one of the porters, a woman, sobbed as soon as her feet touched ground.

"Enough," Kirche said. "You. Where is your Master of the Guard?"

Lucas bowed. "Scouting the woods nearby, sir. There."

When Kirche had stalked off in search of Sorgood, Lucas turned to the women, one wrapped around the other like mother and child.

"Can I be of any help?" he asked them. "Is someone wounded?"

"We'd like to set up our camp next to yours," the older man said.

"Yes, sir. We can spare some soldiers to help."

The man nodded and moved past him through the camp; the two guards followed, leading the horses, but the women remained, as if moving was too painful.

"Please," Lucas said to them. "What of Hallowsing?"

The younger woman sobbed again, burying her face in the older woman's bosom.

"There, there, Gretchen," the woman soothed. She looked to Lucas, her eyes brimming with tears. "We lost the dear thing in the caverns."

"Lost her?"

She winced. "Indeed. She slipped, fell into the darkness. We searched for an hour or so. But nothing. Not a sound."

"Only an hour?"

Gretchen raised her head and whispered, her voice throaty, "he wouldn't let us—"

"Hush, Gretchen," the old woman warned. "You'll not speak so. If you'll excuse us." She nodded and led the young girl to follow the others.

"That's a bad lot," Phil said coming to stand beside Lucas.

Lucas said nothing, but stood, looking to the north.

Chapter Five

Because there was nothing to do, Fenn spent much of his time wrapped in the eleshag pelts, standing on the roof overlooking the ice realm. To the south, below him, there was a small village in a little valley among the mountains, but beyond the snow-capped peaks he imagined only the sea. Behind him, east, and north, he saw only taller mountains of ice. But west he could see home. The ice palace was set at the eastern end of Kingdom Pass, the only route from the hill country into the realm. And beyond the pass was a brief plain, abutted by a wood, behind which sloping green hills rolled into the forests of the Ruud. His view of home was only interrupted by a taller tower rising up out of the west end of the palace, from which, he imagined, the angels and eis could watch the Ruud.

Sometimes when he gazed out toward home, it was a blur. Other times he could see as clearly as if through a powerful scope. He once was sure he saw Steingefan, but he struggled to keep it in view, as if his eyes had the power of great sight, but it was unused and weak.

The eisen still would not speak to him, even when he

thanked her for the pelts and fruit. But he made sure he was first onto the roof every morning to bring in their food; and he always brought in enough extra firewood for her fire as well as his. It took her a few days to recover from her night of pain and once she seemed fully herself, Fenn woke one morning before dawn to find her gone.

He crept about the room, peering into the alcoves, but they were empty. He climbed the spiral stair to the roof but there was no one there. He could see sunlight, turning the darkness into gray just over the mountains in the east and a cold wind whipped at his cheeks. He grabbed a few logs and returned below, adding them to her fire and his. He sat, wrapping himself in a pelt, and waited.

He darted awake the next morning as the door in the roof was pulled open. When he saw an angel climbing down the stairs, he closed his eyes, feigning sleep, though his heart pounded with fear and he struggled to keep his hands from trembling. When he heard the rustling, as of a silken gown against the stone floor, he let his eyes open just enough to see between his lashes and watched as the girl darted into one of the alcoves.

Sitting up, he could see her in the warm glow of the firelight, and the streams of sunlight shining through the slits in the boards at the windows. She sat, huddled against the back wall, hidden behind enormous shimmering wings. They rose and shook and she screamed, gulped for air, one hand clawing at the wall in front of her; she sobbed. Fenn stood and walked toward her, but stopped when one of the wings fell away, leaving a raw, pulsating sore on her back. The wing on the floor shuddered and warped, curled and twisted into a black rotted root while the feathers fizzled into dust. The girl cried out as the other wing broke off and crumpled on the stone.

22

Struggling to calm her breathing, she glanced behind her, catching sight of him, then turned away. Fenn pulled the eleshag pelt from his shoulders, moved forward cautiously, and covered her with it.

"I built up your fire," he said. He pulled at her, lifting her, and led her into her own alcove where she fell weakly to the floor.

"The bag," she said, her voice hoarse and troubled. "More for you."

She was asleep before Fenn looked back to the cubby. There he found a muslin bag. Inside it were two loaves of bread, four red apples, handfuls of blackberries, and several tarts. He returned it all and set it by her fire before returning to his own.

Later in the day, she woke, and Fenn watched as she pulled open the bag and turned to him. Smiling, she stood, pulling the hooded robe over her gown. She brought him the bag and sat down with him in front of his fire. She ripped off a chunk of one of the loaves of bread and handed it to him.

"In the palace," she said, "we would have flavored spreads, cheese, and fruit jams."

He nodded. "In the Ruud, too."

She ate several bites, her gaze on the floor, before she said, "I imagine you would like an explanation."

"You're an angel."

She looked at him. "Angels do not shed their wings. I am angel eisen. My mother was an eisen. My father an angel. While that much is well known...the wings...there are few who know of that. My mother taught me to be cautious. And now, if I am caught with them, I will be chained."

"Why don't you fly away, then? Escape?"

"There are more important things."

"Could you help *me* escape?"

"I cannot carry you. I'm not angel enough for that. But I will help you escape, when the time is right."

"When would that be?"

"You were brought here by my aunt, the queen. She believes you draw the folk king, Welk."

"He promised he wouldn't come looking for me."

"And yet, he comes. He and thousands of folk have gathered in the hills before the realm. Soon they will take Kingdom Pass."

"Not for me."

"Partly for you. Partly for me."

"For you?"

She nodded.

"What would King Welk want you for? He has no say here in the realm."

"It's complicated."

"How complicated could it be?"

She chuckled and ripped off another hunk of bread for him. "The queen," she grimaced, "is seduced by the angel Noromir. If not for him, she would not even be queen. He has turned her against her kind. The eis have no qualms with the folk; it is only always the angels who wish to see them gone from the eastern continent. They would like to see the folk removed back to the southlands, no doubt.

"For years, Noromir has needled her to force the kings of the Ruud to rid the hills of the folk, but her requests have been ignored. This has only succeeded in enraging him. And now, he has you, the great boy of prophecy."

"I am not."

"Of course not, but your folk are too stupid to know it."

"We're not stupid."

"They believe that mark on your arm means you're a prophecy come to pass."

Fenn unconsciously grabbed at his arm. "I'm told it's the mark of the faire, but I don't know what that means."

"It means you are chosen."

"Chosen for what?"

"It little matters now; it's not as if the angels will allow it. You've got folk blood in you. No folk has ever sat on the Rad before. It won't be only the angels who will forbid it. Your King Welk will march the pass and demand you be handed over to him, and Noromir has it in his head to fight him."

"King Welk wouldn't be so stupid as to walk right into the realm...would he?"

"Not ordinarily. I mean, it's not as stupid as it appears. Noromir will draw all his guard out to the pass to meet Welk and his army. Noromir is dumb enough to think Welk will request you be turned over to him in exchange for his promise to rid the hills of his folk. He does not understand that the folk will be ready to fight. It would never occur to him they'd be so bold as to think it, much less try."

"But they will fight? Can they win?"

"They needn't win. They only give time to my guard in capturing the queen."

"What?"

She nodded. "While Noromir is occupied, my guard will take the queen by force. We'll be marching her through the mountains to the sea before he has finished his pompous speech."

"Your guard?"

"Yes, of course. My aunt took my throne—another of Noromir's suggestions. But she never had all the guard beholden to her. It's too bad, of course, for she'll have to be brought back into the square and slit in half, once Noromir and the rest of his angels have been ejected."

"If you're part angel, maybe the other angels will fight for you."

"And if they do not, they will go the way of Noromir." She drew a finger across her neck and grinned.

"So, that's where you went at night...to your guards."
She nodded.

"When you get your throne back, you can keep the wings. I mean, it's painful, shedding them, isn't it?"

"My father told me, when I was very young, that the wings were a choice. When you choose them, they do not wish to be rejected. The angel in me, he said, will call to be awakened and it will fight to remain."

"I don't understand," he said. "They're just wings, aren't they?"

"Not at all. They are the essence of the angel. They come with more than the power of flight. See here?" She pulled the sleeve of her robe up to her shoulder and on her forearm, she bore the same mark Fenn had. "My father told me that I am chosen to represent those eis who struggle with the angel inside them. If I give in to the angel, I will not be eisen, nor angel eisen, but fully angel, and my mark will be taken from me."

Fenn was about to ask her to explain the mark—what did it mean to be chosen? But she pointed to his chest and said, "Your charm. It has the mark of the dragon."

Chapter Six

Leah dreamed there was light and the rats scurried from her, their pitter patter like a song in the silence of the cavern. A voice, soft, patient, said her name and she was lifted slightly, hair brushed from her face—she didn't care. Even when she realized it was no dream, as Lucas offered her water from a mug, she didn't care. He could touch her hair; it meant little to her, anymore. There seemed so many things of far greater importance than tiers and their sacred symbols.

"Are you awake?" he whispered.

She nodded. He lifted the lamp to see her face and she sipped more water, her hands trembling. The light was no more than a glass jar filled with lightning bugs, their abdomens glowing gold.

"How did you find me?" Her voice was rough and thick. She moved away from him to sit, leaning against cold, damp rock.

"I am felid. I smelled you out." He grinned and Leah chuckled. He stood. "Come."

She took his hand, and his offer of a bug jar of her own, and together they walked the cave.

"How long have you been without food and water?"

She shook her head. "I don't know." She wished to tell him they'd entered the cavern for a tour with food, water, and honey mead; they'd planned to stop at a spot the spelunkers had told them about, where the rock opened and a stream splashed down into a pool. There they would stop for a rest, before finding their way above ground. But she was weary and it seemed too many words, so she merely offered him a smile.

"Why were you in the caverns?"

Leah adjusted her pack on her back. "Can you not imagine?"

"The kell stone," he said. "You will not find it here."

"Do you know where it is?"

"No. But you do."

"Do I?" Each time she saw him, he puzzled her. First, spying on Kirche in the woods. She thought he was fourteen at most; but the way he caught her eye and held her gaze, even for a second—he was no boy.

"You said as much to Dag Voorspeld."

She hesitated. "Yes." And in the beast forest, when he helped lead her to safety—still thin, a few inches shorter than she, but somehow older, speaking as one might imagine a man of many years and travels.

"But you don't know where it is, do you?"

"I only said what I had to, to be free. To live."

"I don't think Voorspeld would have allowed the brownies to kill you."

"He had me fooled, then." She smiled. "Did Kirche send you to find me?"

He would not look at her, held his jar up against the darkness and continued the trek.

"They left me," she said. "How did you know I was here?"

"Your party arrived at the meeting spot of winter folk southeast of here, against the foothills of the ice realm. The women told me you were lost, believed dead."

"How long did they search for me?"

"Leah," he said, as if to a child.

"Very well. Don't break my heart."

And now. Come into the caverns to find her. Why?

They walked for what seemed hours, sometimes downward, deeper into the cave, but Leah trusted Lucas. She marveled at that feeling, a feeling she didn't have for Kirche, even for Pren. Was it that he was felidae? Had he cast a spell? She didn't care. She would follow him.

"Here," he said, when she felt her legs could carry her no more. "A place to rest."

They sat and let their packs fall from their shoulders. Lucas took her jar of bugs, held both jars up and whispered, "Calm. You may calm. I thank you." The glow dimmed, faded, until it was no more. But there was still light. She turned to see cracks of pale green, glistening through the rocks on which they sat.

"What is it?" she asked him.

"Kell," he said. "We are deep within the earth here. And yet, this is the only spot we know of where the kell can be seen. The rest is much deeper."

"I thought it was a stone. A round, smooth rock, like polished crystal."

"Our stone was made from the kell. Would you like me to tell you one of the stories of how it came to be?"

"Are there more than one?"

He chuckled. "There are a few. No one knows the truth. But I will tell you my favorite."

Leah nodded. "All right."

"It is said the beast came out of the south with a small number of folk, long ago. So long ago it couldn't be written, for there was no language. When the passage was blocked and no more could find the north, time worked its magic and transformed the beast into sentient, powerful creatures, and the folk into the angels and the eis. And as beast and folk were at odds in the south, so they were still in the north.

"Generations ago, the angel Morimar returned from an expedition to the south with news of the folk. They were developing a taste for exploration, she said, and domination. The sentients balked at the thought of such powerless creatures dominating the northern lands, but Morimar told them the folk had developed weapons that could fell a sentient from a distance. Their numbers were far greater than the sentients, and they had diseases that spread like plague and would leave thousands dead. Morimar insisted the sentients prepare for war."

"Your story does not visit well on my people," Leah said.

"There may be some bias in it," he admitted, "but it is the story, nonetheless."

"You are forgiven." She smiled and nodded, bidding him continue.

"The great felid sage Arngram, it is said, summoned all of his spirit and opened a passageway to Mutterede in Krone Mountain at the top of our world, and traveled deep into the kell to its source where he asked Mutterede for help. Mutterede told him to return to the surface and craft a scepter from an ebon tree with an open claw the size of the ancient screech raven, with a six-inch span, and bring back with him a representative of each class of sentient.

"Arngram asked Mutter how he could persuade them to

come with him, and she told him to tell them she would craft for them a weapon of such great power, they need never fear any enemy again. And so it was that Arngram was able to bring down into the kell, Morimar the angel, Lendharf, the faire eis, Kitne, the centaur, Acksen, the wolverine, Orobon the Brownie, Asphor the fairy, and Anpart the duerger.

"All the sentients in the land gathered at the passageway to await the return of their kin, their representatives, with the great weapon. But only Arngram rose out of the passage with the kell stone, a perfect sphere of emerald kell, in the scepter claw on his staff. 'But where are Lendharf and Kitne?' the sentients asked. 'Where is Acksen?' The others, Arngram told them, had placed their hands on the stone and had given their lives so that all sentients would have great power and near immortality."

Here Lucas paused and dug into his pack for a canteen. He poured water for Leah, telling her she must drink, and she obeyed, gratefully. Then he produced an apple.

"Try to eat slowly," he cautioned and went on with the tale. "And so it was that Arngram passed the scepter to the felid Witherwoof and proclaimed him Lord of the Sentient, before vanishing into a wisp of mist.

"It is said that because Arngram brought the scepter to the felidae, the felidae will always be lords of the sentient and the immortals, and keepers of the kell stone. As soon as the stone was on the surface, all of the northern continent felt its power. Every asset they had was increased tenfold including, they would learn, their life spans.

"But it is told that the angel Morimar was skeptical and withheld her palm from the stone when she touched it and so the angels gained nothing, while the greed and jealousy in her fingertips was enhanced. And the angel Loda said, 'Where is the great weapon we were promised to defeat the folk?' To which Witherwoof replied, 'Our mutterede never promised such a thing. She has enhanced our assets so we may live in peace with the mortals.' Loda, believing the angels betrayed, then attacked Witherwoof, but Witherwoof caught the angel's wing in his powerful jaws and ripped it from his body. Loda limped away, vowing vengeance."

Leah winced.

"And so it was that the angels took to the northeast and plotted to capture the kell stone for themselves, thinking they would control the others with it. The eis followed, their hearts cold and their alliance resting with their kin. The others explored their new-found strengths and awaited the folk from the south. But they did not come. For many years, they waited, and their numbers grew; they lived in peace a thousand years."

"A thousand years?" Leah said. "Why did the folk not come?"

"We had lost the angels, and so had no news. We have theories. War. Plague, perhaps."

"But we did finally come."

"In small numbers at first, and so tolerated. As their number grew, the folk told their own stories, and one was that the beast had powers given them by the evil goddess Horatia, sister of Mutterede, banished to the ice kingdoms of the severe north. Deemed unnatural, we were looked upon with great suspicion and plots arose to find the stone and destroy it.

"Legend has it that Witherwoof sought to protect the stone and still allow its powers to be felt. He traveled deep into the northern forest and placed the scepter in a crevice in boulders by a stream and spent his days and nights guarding it. We are told that one day, the angel Serena came to him and brought him a meal of fawn and honey mead. She prostrated herself before him, showed him her stripped wing, a symbol of many of the angels' desire to accept their fault and to ask for acceptance back into the world of their beast brethren. Witherwoof accepted Serena's apologies, ate the meal, and fell into a deep sleep.

"Just as Serena went for the scepter, however, she was attacked by roster fiends, and because Loda had clipped her wing in hopes of fooling Witherwoof, she could not fly and was pecked to death."

"So much violence," Leah said.

"The makings of a great story." He smiled and pulled an apple of his own from his backpack.

"What happened, then? Did Witherwoof awaken?"

Lucas shook his head. "It was the sleep of death. We are told a young folk named Keirgen ran from home to avoid marriage to one of the elites of Rhum. He traveled into the great northern forest of the Great West hoping to find adventure and instead found our kell stone in the boulders by the stream. While they could not destroy it, the folk hid it deep within the earth where we could no longer connect with it. Our number dwindled and we were driven out of the west, to settle here, near to the angels and the eis who despise us. And so the folk not only have our lands, and our power, but also our stone."

"It is a sad story."

"Yes. But the felidae did recoup the scepter and fashioned a new stone face for it here in the east. We await the return of the kell stone." He turned to look at her, a faint emerald glow glistening in his green eyes.

Leah was reminded of Dag Voorspeld and his steady gaze. There was that same question in Lucas' expression. They both wanted to trust her.

Chapter Seven

Welk sat in front of his tent. Some of the soldiers had dug out a long pit for fire and it now glowed and gave off warmth in front of him. Across from the flames sat a line of folk, representatives of the winter folk—refugees from the west—and gangs of land pirates in the hill country. Behind them mingled those not allied with any particular group, there to have their say. And beyond, miles distant, rising against the sky were the blue and white mountains of the ice realm.

"I am Welk of Michelruud," he said. "Welcome. Let us begin by introducing ourselves. There are some here who are not familiar to the others."

He motioned to the first folk seated on the left end, a well-dressed man who sat stiff and regal in his chair. He was the only folk who sat on a chair, except for Welk. The others had pulled over logs from the wood just west of the meeting place or sat on the cold ground.

The man stood, "I am Lech of the Freedom tribe. We reside at the base of the northeast mountain you call Risenpeak."

The next man stood and along down the line they stated their names. Flarneg of Brusia, in the Great West, representing a band of refugees from the Hass. Peter of Luscia, also of the Kingdom of Ruhm. A woman, Dania, fled the west with her college of women, now encamped too near the lower hills of the ice realm, two of her women already seduced and carried away by angels.

"I dare say." The next representative stood and grabbed hold of the lapels of his woolen long coat. "I am Sir Tain, of the tribe you call Breathless, though of course that is not our moniker in the Great West where we are philosophers of the highest order. We are well pleased to have been invited to this committee and, though we are thinkers as opposed to warriors, we will help in any manner we are able, perhaps strategy, if you will."

The next man rose and spoke. "I am Yriton of the lower east hills in the Kingdom of Ruhm. I would caution you not to give the floor to the Breathless philosophers or they will likely never cede it."

"I dare say, I finished my discourse and retook my seat."

"And for that we are all grateful."

"Hear, hear," Welk said. "We are all free to speak at this gathering. And I am sure we will all do well and allow our time to expire as it should." With a nod to the Breathless he turned to the other man.

"Do you have more to say?"

"We of Yriton offer Welk of Michelruud our promise to weigh his proposal with all due seriousness."

The next man rose. "Wiley of the Gnome Eaters. We land pirates are suspicious of any involvement of the Ruud in our parts." He sat again quickly.

A balding, dirty man stood and chewed on his lower lip for a second. "Scary Brutes," he said. "We's here to listen."

Clutch stood. "The Wretched have committed their support to Welk, King of Michelruud. We feel confident you will as well, when you have heard what he has to say."

"Eh." The balding man stood once more. "I did forget my name." And he sat again.

Wiley stood. "This here's Quince of the Scary Brutes."

"Right that." Quince chuckled. "I didn't mean I done forgot it. I done forgot to say it."

"Twice now," Wiley said and took his place on the ground again.

And lastly, a round man struggled to his feet from the ground and smiled at the group. "I represent the Wissenry of the Ruud." He lowered himself slowly and then fell with a thud back to the earth.

"Father Britt of the Wissenry at Cold Sea Port," Welk said. "Very well. Winter folk, those the eis wish to see removed from near their realm, I would like to know your feelings about the Great West, particularly the Hass of Emorah. Where do your loyalties lie?" He glanced to Sorgood, standing at a distance to his left with several of the guard, but the man didn't flinch. Welk was impressed.

"Certainly not with the Hass," Flarneg said.

"Certainly not, I dare say."

"We fled the Great West for the right to think and speak freely. The Hass no longer controls us."

"They're here now," Peter of Luscia said. "I saw them."

"They remain at their camp, Peter," Yriton said. "You needn't fear them."

"They can come listen for all I care," Dania said. "We are

not afraid of the Hass."

"They are at the end of the annual tour," Welk said. "They should be on their way soon."

"Back where they came from; suits us," Lech of the Freedom tribe said. "When will you stop the tribute? How can we trust the Ruud when she's still connected to Ruhm?"

"But what does the Hass have to do with this meeting?" Flarneg asked.

"I will come to that," Welk said. "Others of the hills, you are mostly of the Ruud. May I assume you have no loyalty to the Hass?"

Wiley said, "We could not tell you who they are."

"Most of us are unfamiliar with the Hass," Clutch said. "But I can speak for them. If they knew, they would stand against them."

"But this Hass...they are not with the eis are they? What do they have to do with this?"

"This is where we stand," Welk said. "The eis have been content these generations to tolerate folk in the Ruud and beyond, but now claim we draw too near. They would wish folk to move away from the hill country and into the Ruud."

"But they do not defend their lands," Peter said. "They send emissaries to you, a king of the Ruud. To us, they send threats. Why do they not attempt to force us out?"

"Oh, you don't want that," Quince said. "They's gots great powers. They can kill you just by looking at you."

"If that's so, why don't they make us leave?"

"They cannot kill you with a look," Welk said. "Though they threaten war, I believe they are too few in number. They hide there in the ice and so know little of our alliances. They are not prepared for war that might involve Ruhm. They are not with-

38

out advantages, however. Better sight, for one. They see us already from the tower against the great northern peak. They will surely see us at the base of Kingdom Pass, where we will camp before entering the realm."

They all turned to look behind them at the tops of the mountains beyond the hills and a ripple of fear agitated the group.

"They are a strong folk." Welk pulled at their attention. "Keen of hearing."

"Can they hear us now?" Wiley said.

Welk smiled. "Not as keen as that. They have superior bows and arrows. We have some good armor to repel them, though not enough to go around, as Ruhm refuses trade with us on the goods we lack. On their horses, the eis can be deadly. But if we can unseat them, we are the better soldiers. Better yet, if we can make it to the walls of the palace, their horses will be useless in the tight quarters of the outer village."

"But the angels," Clutch said.

"Yes, the have a few angels with them. Deadly creatures."

"Angels." Wiley shuddered. "They done carried off three wee ones and my man Rogget not a week ago."

Welk leaned forward. "All of them?"

"Aye. Left none but the bear."

"Why do they call on you?" Peter said with an apologetic nod to Wiley. "Why not one of the other kings of the Ruud? Why not one of us?"

"Even the eis recognize where the power of the Ruud lies," Clutch said.

"They have something I want," Welk said. "Their threat of war could be merely a ruse. Their hope is that I will force you off the land as a ransom. They believe I have some control over you."

"You must have told them you do not."

Welk looked for a moment at the speaker for the Gnome Eaters, fighting for the right words. "It has been explained to them several times that the winter folk are not folk of the Ruud. But to the eis, we are all the same. They see no difference."

"Is that why we are here, then?" Yriton of Luscia said. "You would attempt to force us off our lands?"

"I would not. I do not propose that you leave the eis lands. I propose we fight them together and let them know that if they cannot defend the outer hills, they have no claim to them."

"How are we to fare against them?"

"You will find them a worthy enemy," Welk said. "But we can show them we are willing to fight together to remain in the hill country."

"And why do you fight for us, Welk," Yriton said. "What do you want from us in return?"

"I want only good terms between our lands. We of the Ruud can offer you help in establishing law and order."

"And what if we don't want law and order?" Wiley of the Gnome Eaters said.

Many of the others grumbled and Welk raised a hand to quiet them.

"Maybe we do," Dania said. "Maybe we tire of the constant battling among the pirates and their threats against our lives and property."

"We leave you winter folk alone, mostly," Wiley said.

"Some of you do; but not all," Flarneg said. "Perhaps we need to form a government here."

"Oh, why yes," Sir Tain said. "That reflects beneficial to all so long as all our claims are secured."

"And what of our right to live free of government?" Wiley said.

"A government that allows the broadest freedoms for folk could suit you, could it not?" Welk said.

"A government may begin with the noblest of intentions, but it always ends up squelching rights and taking more power for those who serve it."

Strong words, Welk thought, for a man traipsing about the hills wearing stolen clothes. "I think we can manage a solution in which everyone may live peacefully."

"How is that?"

"Would you be satisfied if the winter folk carved out a piece of land and set up government? What harm would that cause you, except to forbid you from stealing from them without punishment?"

"Aye," Clutch spoke up. "The hills east of Damon Wall and the Plains of Glisch could be free of government, if Dania and her women's college are willing to move. Any who distrust government would still be free to live as we wish there. The settlements of winter folk and those of the wastelands could set up their governments in the hills north of Aaronland and the fertile lands north and east."

"But they'll be setting police forces against us, Clutch," Wiley protested.

"Why would we do that if you leave us alone?" Dania said.

"Well said." Welk smiled at Clutch. "Your victims have a right to organize against you."

"Aye," Clutch said with a smirk.

"So I propose we take a fight to the eis; we show them the winter folk will not move and folk do not fear them. What say you all?"

One by one, the folk stood and pledged their support to Welk, a king of the Ruud.

"And what of the Hass," Wiley said. "You were to come to that."

"If it were to come to war with the eis," Welk said, "Ruhm may offer aid, or we may find ourselves desperate to ask for it. I would, as King of the Ruud, forbid such association."

"Yes, yes," Dania said. "As much as we might need the help of a stronger power, it would only lead them to take control of the eastern continent, or at the very least, dominate us more completely than they do the Ruud now."

"But there are three kings of the Ruud," Clutch said.

"True," Welk said. "But it is not only that the people of the hills and the wastelands must unite with the Ruud against the eis; we must all together present a unified front to both the eis and Ruhm."

"And you propose we stand under your banner," Dania said.

Welk nodded. "I do."

"And what do the other kings of the Ruud think of that?" Yriton said.

"What do we care?" Clutch said.

"Where are they?" Flarneg said. "The eis deal with Welk."

"Too true," Clutch said. "And we are told Ruhm itself sees Michelruud as the dominant kingdom in the Ruud."

"I would tell you," Welk said, "to show you that my intentions are good and I mean to be only honest with you, that the other kings will arrive before we make for the ice realm. They would certainly have objections to this notion."

"It would be better to have a settlement on the issue before they arrive, I would think," Yriton said.

42

"What?" Sir Tain said. "No debate? Would we not wish to hear an offer from the others? Think mightily on the—"

"The way I see it," Yriton said, waving the representative of the Breathless away, "Welk brings us this proposal. He called on us and treats us as equals. Even the eis and Ruhm see Welk as King of the Ruud."

"I propose it, then," Dania said. "Though I can't say I am too taken with the idea of kings, I am happy to ally with Welk, King of the Ruud, where it benefits us both."

"Hear, hear," Flarneg called and the others joined him.

Welk turned to Clutch and offered the slightest smile.

Chapter Eight

Fenn grasped his charm. "It's a dragonfly," he said absent-mindedly.

"It is the symbol of forbidden love," the girl said, smiling. "You are quite young for such a thing, aren't you?" She laughed and it sounded like tinkling glass.

"What's your name?" he asked her.

"I am Brenna."

"Brenna." Fenn smiled.

"Daughter of the Snow, Queen of the Realm, Maiden Faire, if you please." She giggled.

"You're the maiden?"

"Alas, I am. It is a title I look forward to giving up. But I don't think I shall find a *forbidden* love. Too tragic."

"Father Britt told me to come to the ice realm, to see the maiden."

"For what purpose?"

"He said you might know my mother; if you hold my charm...you will know. He thought you could help me."

"Did he?"

Fenn nodded.

"This Father Britt—he is of the wissenry?"

"Yes."

"I have heard much of them."

Fenn pulled the hemp rope from his neck and handed it to her. She held the charm and the amber rock in her hand.

"Where did you get them?"

"The charm was my mother's. It was stolen from me for a while, and when I got it back, it had the red stone with it."

"I have seen the amber kell before; the angels have some. How long have you had it?"

"Not long. Why?"

"It's nothing." She let the stone drop from her palm and closed her hand around the gold charm. "Do you know the story of the dragonfly, then?"

"They have some in Aaronland, in a greenhouse."

"Yes," she said. "There was a prince of Aaronland, many generations ago, who lost his wife, as it was told. Grief stricken, he traveled to the ice realm; some say he wished to freeze to death. But instead he met an eisen who fell in love with him. Her name was Avrileis."

"Is this a kissing story?"

"I can leave out the kissing, if you like," she said. "Avrileis returned with the prince and lived for a time in Aaronland where she came to love the dragonflies he kept in his garden. But his father, the king, was unhappy with the match. Their children, he reasoned, would be folk eis, unnatural. They would be shunned and banished. And neither would their children be welcomed *here*. We do not tolerate split folk."

"Aren't you...split?"

"I am split of angel and eis. It is the folk part that is not

46

tolerated. Do not look at me that way; I didn't start it."

Fenn smiled. "I suppose not."

"Avril could not bear the thought of causing pain to her prince; she would not ask him to live in the wastelands and she would not have her children treated as unnatural. So, she returned to the eis. The prince, vowing to love only Avrileis for the rest of his life, gave her a glass jar filled with dragonflies as a parting gift. Since that time, the dragonfly has been the symbol of the forbidden love between eis and folk."

"Does that sort of thing happen a lot?"

"Much more often than you would think." She took his hand and placed his charm on his palm. "Tell me what visions the charm has given you."

He shook his head. "Only a few. I see a man, his back I mean. I see a woman's hand grasping a wissende's robe. Sometimes I see her face. I hear her pleading for her child."

"It is as I suspected," Brenna said. "The charm is not your mother's."

Chapter Nine

How long was I lost?" Leah asked Lucas on the evening after their first ride toward the meeting place.

"About six days," he said. "I left to get you as soon as your party arrived at the encampment. It's a good three days' ride, though I made it in less time. I only had the one horse and didn't have to stop as often."

Leah stopped poking at the fire and looked at him. "Did you at least stop to sleep?"

He shrugged. "I will sleep tonight. I feel I owe you an apology; I could have gotten to you faster. Even as folk, felidae are fast. If I hadn't brought the horse..."

"Could you not have taken your felid form?"

"I have not entered that time of my life, no. The felidae once lived all their lives as folk, only to transform when their time was done. My parents wished that tradition for me."

"So you brought the horse because I would require one?"

"That, and it would have taken a week to get back on foot with you in tow." He grinned at her.

"I can run," she said, "but I'm no match for a felid."

They slept in an open field of grass sheltered against the cold autumn winds by blankets Lucas had brought along. Leah lay awake for hours after Lucas' soft breathing told her he slept, staring at the clear night sky full of pinpoints of light. There was a story told to her at the Hass school in Ruhm. The lights were the spirit eyes of the greatest followers of Rett, watching, always watching, ready to choose who among the living would be worthy of joining them in the afterlife. And what was it her father had told her?

"Eyes? Nonsense. Have you not peered into the night sky with the scope? Go out again this evening and watch the twinkling lanterns in the dark sky. Whisper a greeting. For somewhere, on one of those lights, a pretty little folk such as yourself is looking up, and wondering what your light might be."

"Hello," Leah whispered to the sky. She put a hand to her lips to stifle a homesick sob.

As the land passed under the horse the next morning, Leah found herself wishing Kirche, thinking her dead, had left for Ruhm. She didn't want to see him again, nor Prenalin. They would read her face, see there her doubts—more than that, her rejection of the Hass. It had been seeping in, somehow, since the meeting with her father in his little office before she left for the eastern continent. Those adoring eyes with which she'd looked upon Kirche every day had dimmed over time and now she knew there would be no love left in them. Perhaps Kirche wouldn't notice; he rarely noticed anyone but himself. But Prenalin would know. As soon as he caught sight of her, he would know they'd lost her.

"We will arrive tomorrow, I should think," Lucas told her by the fire their second night. "I believe the Hass is still in the Ruud, but if not, I will get you to a boat."

She nodded. "I thank you, again. For everything."

"It was no trouble."

"You jest. I would have died in the caverns if you had not come for me. I will never be able to repay you."

"What price your life, Leah? There is no payment due, but that you live."

"I do have something for you," she said. "A small token."

"I will accept no payment."

"It is but a story."

He smiled. "That I will take, gladly."

"When I was a little girl in Ruhm, my parents allowed me to attend the Hass school. I never knew why, really. All of my friends attended the common school. The Hass school only took those students who could pass a rigorous test of intelligence, as rigorous as one can be for small children." She looked across the fire with a grin. "But none of my friends even tried the test. I do not remember asking to take it, or to attend the school, but my father has told me over the years that I begged to go."

"You sound doubtful."

"I am, but then, I am finding myself unsure of so many things of late. It spreads, this doubt, like a vine. Anyway, I went and was thoroughly, I think, indoctrinated with admiration for all things Hass, most especially our Lord Kirche."

"I can see where he would turn a girl's eyes."

Leah picked up a tiny pebble and tossed it at him over the fire. "I didn't mean that." But she couldn't force the smile from her face. "I studied diligently and behaved impressively, I must say. And I told my instructors I wished to be not just an historian of Ruhm, and work in the libraries and museum, but *the* Historian of Ruhm. I wanted to oversee the libraries and the museum. I thought being named Aide to the High Priest was the first step in that direction." Her voice faltered.

"And now?"

She shook her head. "Before I left to come here for the annual tour, my father sat me down in his office and told me a truth that has changed everything. I wonder now, if he knew it would—if he knew what I would find here in the east."

"Can you tell me?"

"Yes. And it is my gift to you." She gazed at him and was reassured that she was right to tell him. "I am kin to the great wissende, Michelruud, who left Ruhm generations ago with the kell stone."

Lucas sat straighter, his brow knit together and he looked as if he were going to speak, but he let her continue.

"I'm told Michelruud retrieved the stone from the mines of Galdred, where it had been hidden, and was planning to return it to the beast here in the east."

"Our grandfathers felt it returned to surface; they believed it would be found. But they were weakened by the generations without it."

"And of course, Michelruud did not return it to them. I didn't know why until I read the history book at the stationer's in Path."

"The big book on the front table?"

"No. I found another, in an office. I wasn't supposed to be in there, of course. I didn't mean to pry. I'd no idea what I was reading."

"*The Book of Katz?*"

She nodded.

"I confess to you, then," he said. "I have also read the history, though it is a forbidden book. And so, you know that upon arriving here, the folk, fearful of the beast, and of being so far

52

from Ruhm, begged Michelruud to be their king—to protect them from my kin."

"Yes."

"And you know about the devices they constructed to capture and murder my kind?"

"But still they could not defeat you and needed help from Ruhm. In exchange for an army and weapons, Michelruud was to give the kell stone to his brother, Dakenruud, who had remained loyal to the Hass."

"This is why my folk have long believed it to be hidden once again in the west."

"Perhaps. My father told me Daken was commissioned to travel Kell and hide the stone; he was to tell no one where. When he returned home, he first went to his family and gave his brother Abueruud a journal of his travels. Two days later, he was taken by the Hass and never seen again."

"They couldn't let him disclose to his family where he'd hidden it."

"It's worse than that, I'm afraid. I heard it from Kirche that he was tortured. He would not tell even the Hass its place of hiding and he never did. They murdered him."

They were silent for a moment and Lucas lifted his face to the dark sky before looking at her. "The journal," he said. "You think he confessed it."

"I believe that was what my father was trying to tell me. I can feel it now, just as I did when I spoke with him, but didn't understand. He was trying to see how much he could reveal to me—how loyal I was to the Hass. In the end, he knew better than to reveal all."

"Do you know where the journal is?"

"I do not. But my father must know."

"When you told Voorspeld you would find it and return it to us, is that what you meant to do? Go to your father, find the journal?"

She shook her head. "Not at the time. I only wanted to get out of the forest alive."

"But he believed you wanted that."

"Yes, of course. I forgot. I'd already decided that if I could find the journal, and retrieve the stone for Kirche, my place as historian would be set. So, I suppose I did want to find the stone."

"What will you do now? It's a dangerous thing to be so close to the Hass and betray them."

"Perhaps my chances of finding the stone are better in my position. What if my father intended it all along? Maybe he knows where it is, but only a member of the inner circle can retrieve it."

"Would your father put you in such danger?"

She shrugged. "I confess, I cannot say. I thought I knew him—thought I knew myself—but I feel as lost and confused as I did deep within the earth in the darkness."

"You know what the kell stone means to me and to my folk. But I would not have you risk your life for it."

"Especially as you've gone through so much trouble to save it." She smiled.

"True enough," he said with a laugh. "The stone is ours to find."

"No," she said. "My folk stole it from you. It is our place to rectify the crime we committed."

"Then I will help you. I will follow you to Ruhm."

"Am I to allow you to risk *your* life?"

"You can't stop me, if you must know. And now I will give you a gift in return. No"—he held his hand up to stay her objection—"it is a trifle thing to folk, but I hope you will use it."

54

"You have already given me my life. Nothing you give now could compare."

"Nonetheless, I give you my name. I am called Frieden."

Leah blushed. "Frieden." Sighing, she shook her head and turned to the darkness surrounding them. "And once again, I am indebted to you." When he laughed, she looked at him across the fire. "It is your plan to keep me thus; I see it now."

"I confess; I am enamored."

Laughing, Leah searched the ground at her feet for another pebble.

Chapter Ten

Dunham brought two covered plates of roasted pig, vegetables, warmed bread, and gravy into Welk's large tent from the kitchen set up several yards away and set them on the small table where Welk sat across from Clutch. "Thank you, Dunham," Clutch said with a nod.

"You are welcome, Sire." Dunham bowed and left them to eat alone.

"You won them over, Welk," Clutch said as he pulled apart his bread. "But you do not give them all the facts."

"They do not need all the facts. You know as well as I we ought to keep as much to ourselves as possible. But I will tell *you*, at least, this: I will aid the maiden against her aunt."

"You are sure she has not been killed?"

Welk chuckled. "The usurper dare not enrage her eis folk doing such a thing. The maiden lives in the palace under guard. My spies tell me Lara has been seduced by the angels and is overconfident in her power; but even so, it's unlikely she would harm her own kin."

"So it is only the usurper queen we fight."

"Perhaps. I believe the maiden, unlike Lara, is ready for peace and compromise. But it is Lara's relationship with the angels that is most troubling."

"They are the source of the problem?"

"They were always cruel, bitter creatures, even before folk came to the east, so I have come to understand."

"But what of this business with the boy? Do you not want the others aware of him? When the eis attempt to hand him over, will the winter folk not feel as if they've been used ill?"

"You may be right. Why don't you spread a little rumor that the boy is what the eis hold from me. Certainly they would not begrudge me possession of the child of prophecy; he's better off with us than with the immortals. The soldiers know of the boy already, of course. They may do the job for you."

"You are a sly one."

"I learned much from my father."

Clutch leaned back and laughed hard. "Indeed, more so than I. Should you ever have children, I hope you will not emulate him. It was because of him we found ourselves in the hill country together thieving and warring."

Welk smiled. "Those were the best times of my life."

"What?" Clutch laughed again. "You don't prefer the warm soft bed, the fire in every room, the lavish meals?"

Welk looked at the plate before him. "Ah, well, maybe so. But there is a pressure in being king that is not welcome."

"Come now," Clutch teased him. "If it is so stressful, why did you enlist the loyalty of the winter folk in gaining control of the entire Ruud?"

"I confess," Welk said, "it is a ruse."

Clutch's smile turned and he furrowed his brow. "What's this?"

"Do you remember what I said to you when we met at Steingefan last? On our parting."

"Remind me, for I've no idea what you're going on about."

"I told you I was no more a king than you are."

"I know you are the king; there is no doubt."

"That is not what I mean."

"No?"

"I cannot say why I said it to you. I wasn't thinking it. But after the words were out, it began to gnaw at me. A vision of a different way of living."

"You see visions, now?"

"Do you not?"

Clutch shook his head. "Visions are for kings and boys who were prophesied. Not tramps and pirates."

Welk shook his head. "You chose your lot."

"I did. And when I did so, I forsook visions. Tell me yours."

"For the Ruud. Do you not ever see it? One whole, unified realm. Stronger, healthier. No more bickering among cousins. All working toward a common goal."

Clutch chewed silently for a moment eyeing Welk with something of a smile. "No. I never had that vision. But, it was not mine to have, was it? I was not first born. I was not to be a king. I am only a pirate and a rogue."

Welk sighed. "By choice."

"And what were my options? No, this is the best life I could have chosen for myself."

"And now you are a legend."

"I am not that folk, anymore, and I will not embrace a good legend. A protector of travelers, of all things. I would try for something much more sordid. I want to be remembered for my evil ways." Clutch smiled broadly.

Welk laughed. "You aren't as vile as you like everyone to believe. No, I think you'll be stuck with being remembered as a good sort of folk." He sighed, saddened. "I did enjoy our time together here in the hills."

And for a long time they were both silent and distant.

Finally, Clutch spoke again. "But you said that was a ruse...a unified Ruud."

"The ruse is that I wish to be king."

"If not you, then it will be Ricker or Arnot."

Welk shook his head. "No one."

"No king? Why would they abide that?"

"I could see to it."

"But why?"

"Because we were not meant to be kings. We were once wissendes, not rulers."

Clutch stared at him, his fork raised almost to his mouth, a piece of meat dangling from a tine. When he dropped it onto his plate and fell backward with laughter, Welk couldn't help laughing with him.

"Well, I cannot stand against that," Clutch said, wiping his chin with a cloth. "I despise rulers, after all."

Welk's face fell as the words reminded him of his father, Evan, and the evil thing he'd done. He turned his gaze from Clutch and tried to force Rue-Anna's face from his mind; it only ever brought suffering. But she refused to yield, and he thought he felt a change, however slight.

"They would be happy for us now, I think," Clutch said.

Welk shook his head. "I do not wish to speak of them."

"It still pains you."

"Yes. Does it not you?"

Clutch shook his head. "I think, no. I found my peace with

it. They were not like us. They were too perfect, too fair, too delicate for the likes of rogues, be they pirate or king. And the life I have chosen...I can freely live with her memory and never need consider marriage again."

Welk's jaw hardened. Clutch's meaning was clear. As King of the Ruud, Welk would have to marry and produce an heir. He would forget his beloved Rue and bind himself to another.

"Another reason to abolish the kingdom," Welk mused.

"I did mean to tell you something—"

Welk held up his hand. "I do not wish to speak more of our losses. Let us move on to another subject. I have a story to tell you."

"A story? Very well, regale me."

"Did you know that the history of the Ruud we spent so much time trying to avoid reading—"

"I believe I managed to avoid learning to read just to avoid it."

Welk chuckled. "Well, that history is false."

"False?"

"I have recently come into possession of the true history of the Ruud."

Clutch poured more wine into his goblet, sat back in his chair and said, "Ah, then, it was well and good that I did not bother with reading it. Tell me about it."

"It would seem much of what we know is not true. For instance, folk were not the first creatures on the world, not put here by Rett, the god of the Hass, or any other god."

"We never worshiped gods here, but we did assume we were first."

"According to the history, it was Michelruud who discovered the truth that the beast was first in the land and folk emerged

61

from one of their ancestral lines. He learned this from sources he found in trades with a tinker, one of those who often brought treasures of books and discoveries to the wissendes. I haven't time to tell you all now; the important thing is, it was that truth and his refusal to recant it, that forced Michelruud from Ruhm. And believing the beast to have been wronged, he first intended to restore to them their kell stone, but once he tasted the same sort of power that drove him from Ruhm, instead he allowed the capture, torture, and murder of thousands of them."

"The kell stone is real?"

"Indeed. But not here in the east; at least we know Michelruud bartered it back to Ruhm in exchange for their help in forcing the beast into the forests and outskirts of our realm."

"Do we know what power the stone gives them?"

"It makes everything about them stronger, better, apparently. Gives them longer life; makes them more fertile. Their numbers have dwindled over the generations without the stone. I am certain *that* alone was enough to set them at our mercy."

"If the stone is returned to them, it could be the end of folk."

Welk mused for a moment and took a sip of wine. "Perhaps. But if that be so, we no doubt deserve it."

"And the boy with the mark? What is his part? Is there really a prophecy?"

"Of course not. But folk have a funny way of doing things they are convinced they will not do. I don't know why I fear it, but I do. I'm afraid he will find the kell stone and return it to the beast. I fear he is indeed on a prophetic mission, certainly not by design, but by choice, or by coincidence."

"He's just a boy."

"From the stories I am hearing, I am not the only folk who

believes he will do this. The beast lord, Dag Voorspeld is it still? I hear he has set a spy to follow the boy. And the eis. Yes, I am certain they took him, not to ransom him, but to see if he is who they think he is."

"But if there is no true prophecy—"

"The future cannot be foretold."

"Why would the beast and the eis believe this?"

"He has the mark of the faire. A mark that until I read the true history, I thought only designated him as one of them."

"What more could it mean?"

"Did Aliara never tell you?"

Suddenly there was a roar from outside.

"Oh, yes," Clutch said. "I forgot. What shall we do with the bear?"

A gunshot, a yelp, and another roar ended their conversation.

Chapter Eleven

Brenna refused to tell Fenn more of the charm, pleading the need for rest.

"I will tell you the story of the charm when I have more strength," she said. "You must give me time."

He spent his days on the roof. With the warmth of his charm and the eleshag pelts Brenna had given him, he was able to spend longer hours there, watching the gathering of folk at the base of the pass. When he first spied them, he nearly waved, assuming they could see him as well as he saw them. But he realized, as he learned to focus his eyes closer and farther, they were too far away. This must be an eis gift, he decided. Clara was right. Despite what Brenna said, his mother must have been an eisen.

One day he was particularly tired and irritated. Brenna spent her time lying by her fire, sometimes it seemed she whispered poetry to herself, other times she stood at one of the windows and spoke quietly. But she refused to tell him the story of his charm. She hadn't disappeared again and he was glad. The pain she endured in shedding her wings was difficult for him to bear;

he was unable to help and he hated the feeling.

He looked out toward the encampment of folk and cried out, "Sadie. Grayson. Where are you?"

"Fenn?" He heard Sadie call from below, as if from within the tower. Then, "Fenn?" She was at a window, shouting out into the cold afternoon air.

"Sadie?"

He walked the perimeter of the roof, looking down, until he saw her.

"Fenn!" She laughed and called to Grayson and his head appeared.

Fenn let out a whoop of joy; how glad he was to see them. Sadie's brown hair hung down, dangling beneath her as she smiled up at him.

And Grayson, his dark hair and eyes, blacker it seemed against the backdrop of the ice, laughed and called out to him. "How long have you been up there?"

"I'm in the top room, just below the roof. Been here for at least a week. Maybe two. I've lost track."

"We've been here nearly the same," he said. "They took us first to the queen. She badgered us something awful."

"That's the truth," Sadie said. "Threatened to chain us in a dungeon if we didn't tell her everything we knew about you and the prophecy."

"What did you tell her?"

"Everything of course," Grayson said. "We were no match for her, I'm afraid."

Fenn laughed. "It's all right. There isn't much to tell. What of Rogget?"

"We don't know," Sadie said. "He and Wiley fought off the angels, but it did no good."

66

"It was the strangest thing, Fenn. I knew I should care, but I didn't."

"Same here. It's some sort of angel spell, I think."

Fenn realized Brenna was beside him. She leaned over the wall of the roof and said, "What's this?"

"My friends. The ones I told you about."

"Why were they brought here?"

"They said the queen questioned them."

"Who is that with you?" Sadie said.

"Brenna's a prisoner, too."

Fenn nearly told them Brenna was going to free them and only stopped himself just in time. They told him about their guards, who live in the tower and traveled to their room daily with food and water, but refused to speak to them or answer any questions.

"Do you think we'll be kept here forever?" Grayson called up to Fenn.

Brenna put a hand on his arm and he nodded to her, knowing he had to be careful. "Not forever," he said. "Maybe just until the prophecy thing blows over."

"It's not so bad," Sadie said. "The fire is warm and the food is good."

"Why don't the guards bring us the food and water?" Fenn asked Brenna. "Why do angels leave it on the roof?"

"My aunt believes I am too powerful for her eis guards. You, however...are a puzzle. Unless she knows you are split."

"Would that mean I'm powerful?"

"It would, indeed. But just as I did not know of my wings until my father taught me how to grow and shed them, you are likely not to know of your skills until they are required of you."

"What are you two going on about?" Sadie called out. "Let's

think up a game to play, to pass the time."

"I know," Grayson said. "Choose and guess."

"Choose and guess it is," Fenn said. "Do you know how to play?" he asked Brenna. And for a long time, Fenn forgot he was trapped in a tower in the ice realm; he forgot King Welk would march the pass and demand the queen hand him over; he forgot that Brenna told him his charm was not his mother's.

Chapter Twelve

Leah struggled to decide if this was the reception she'd expected. For while she told herself as she and Lucas approached the encampment that Kirche, even Prenalin, had proven they cared little for her by spending so little time in search of her, and not sending anyone after her, she still found herself surprised at their easy acceptance of her appearance before them.

Kirche, after acknowledging her return with a nod, leered at Lucas, as if he'd rather the boy hadn't rescued his aide—as if he was not happy with his actions at all. Prenalin seethed with some emotion, but he controlled it well enough that Leah dared not assume it was relief or pleasure. Only Gretchen, Zelda, and Xavier let their happiness be known.

Leah allowed Gretchen to take her hand and lead her to a tent. She cast a glance at Lucas and he offered her a smile before he left. The tent was empty, only just erected. She was given a bed roll and a pillow and told to rest, but she could not. Instead, she asked for her things, worried they'd been left off somewhere on the trail from the caverns, or sent to Path to be packed in her trunks and shipped home to her parents. The latter was clearly the better outcome, but Leah wanted little more at the moment than to have her journal in her hands. She knew there was more in it that she should have removed, but she didn't expect to be lost from her party yet again and was too trusting that no one else would see it.

When her luggage case was brought to her, she rummaged through it, disappointed, then fearful. Her journal was gone. Just a fluke, she told herself, nothing to worry about. Gretchen probably took it for safekeeping, that was all. But when she found the girl at the kitchen tent and questioned her, she would only cower and shake her head.

"Leah."

She startled and turned to find Prenalin, his face still constrained.

"Kirche wishes to see you."

He turned abruptly and she followed, dread rising up in her throat. She hurriedly ran over her journal in her mind. What had she written? Certainly, she'd mentioned Daken; that much she'd have to own up to. But Daken's journal. Had she told that?

Kirche sat cross-legged on a large pillow in his spacious tent and motioned for her to sit opposite him, while Prenalin remained standing at the door flap. As soon as she put her hands in her lap to hear what Kirche had to say, he pulled her journal from behind him and she tensed noticeably.

"You are wanting this," he said, holding the book out for her.

She took it and felt her face grow hot; she could not look at him, nor Prenalin, only at the book in her hands.

"There are two things I must speak to you about," Kirche said.

70

She nodded, preparing to beg forgiveness for keeping this decidedly important information from him, knowing she must convince him she was still loyal to Hass.

"First, I imagine you have been left wondering why you were chosen as Aide to the High Priest. It is unusual for one with so little experience to have the position."

"Yes, my Lord," she whispered. No, she'd believed she was chosen because she'd shown herself to be worthy. She cringed at her own arrogance.

"It was because of your father, I'm afraid."

Here she looked at him. His blue eyes were cold and unreadable as usual. So leveled and simple he was. But was there turbulence beneath the bland facade?

"When I was named High Priest, I set out on a mission to unite Ruhm. She has lived with a schism since your ancestor, Michelruud the Betrayer, left us for the eastern continent. There have existed within our midst those still loyal to him, and to the ways of the wissendes he represented." He paused, as if expecting a reply of some kind, but Leah had nothing to say. "My thought was to bring these divisions together—to unite them through a common bond. We are as feuding families who only need two young lovers to force them to see reason, to see that we do better united, than torn." Again, he waited. Leah nodded, but could not fathom what he might wish her to say. "And so you were chosen to be my bride."

She sputtered, her eyes flying open as if they'd been closed tight and now hungered for sight—as if she'd slept and now was startled awake. "Your what?"

"Ancestor of the betrayer and the High Priest of Hass."

"I don't understand." She turned to Prenalin but he would not meet her eyes.

"It is so simple, you see," Kirche nearly purred. "You will speak for those who followed your father, those who still work against the Hass. As your father's heir, they will look to you for guidance. And you will lead them, with my help, to turn away from their treason, turn back to Hass. With your help and theirs, those who will not return to Hass will be found and purged."

"Purged?"

"Hass cannot lead the folk to paradise when there are demons in our midst."

"Demons?"

"They steal from us the hope of our folk. They spread deceit and turmoil, nothing more. Surely you agree that if we are to have peace, those who work against peace must be eliminated."

"But marry you?"

"As your father's heir, your willingness to embrace Hass, to extol its virtue, will convince them of its benefits."

"Lord Kirche, begging your pardon, but, even if my father has followers, why would they turn from him to listen to me?"

"Ah, well, that is the sad part. But we must get to it. I have already sent word that your father is to be arrested."

Leah gaped at him, forgetting herself. "On what charges?"

Kirche chuckled. "For possession of Dakenruud's journal. He won't tell us where it is, of course, but you will persuade him. Once you have the journal, your father will release a statement recanting both Michelruud's blasphemy and his own—"

"I am unaware of any such—"

"And he will name you his heir and ask his followers to honor you."

Leah giggled and shook her head. He was mad—lost his mind. She turned again to Prenalin, stared hard at him until his eyes met hers. He knew it, too; she could read it there on his face. The High Priest of Hass had gone to the wilds.

She looked back to Kirche. "My father has no followers. Daken's journal may be nothing more than legend. If my father cannot tell me where it is—"

"Then he will be hanged."

Her face froze, her breath caught in her throat. Still his face betrayed nothing, no kindness, no compassion, but neither hatred or cruelty.

"And if I do not marry you, will you hang me as well?"

Here he smiled, but it was not a pleasant sight. "You have no choice in that matter, I'm afraid. And now, to the second point, the boy Lucas. I care not why he left here to rescue you from the caverns. Whatever his motivations, they are no longer to be a consideration for you."

"I'm sure I don't know what you mean."

"You will not see or speak to him again."

"But why?"

"As my betrothed, it would be unseemly to encourage him in this matter."

Leah tried to shake herself out of her confusion, but nothing changed.

"Of course," Prenalin finally spoke and she turned to him, hopeful. But he only said, "The boy will be rewarded for returning Kirche's betrothed to him. If he had not acted, our plans would have taken much reworking."

Everything in her seemed to fall and she suddenly felt trapped— a mouse in a child's maze. If Prenalin would not help her, where would she turn? Perhaps, Lucas...

"You understand," Kirche said, "if you do not return to Ruhm as my wife, your father will be tortured in your presence. He will know his agony is your doing."

The tent spun around her and her nod felt out of balance. She stood, still holding fast to her journal, and forced a curtsy before staggering out, into the cold, sunlit day. There was a commotion at the other end of the encampment, south, and she made her way to the crowd, dazed, needing to find herself lost in the throng, somewhere away from Gretchen or Zelda. Even Xavier would try to pry from her what made her ill. And she could not speak it.

A trumpet sounded and the gathering of soldiers and winter folk all fell to a knee, leaving Leah standing, looking upon the sight of the king of Michelruud facing west. And approaching him, were Arnot and Ricker, uneasy, clearly anxious, their own soldiers standing back. Not desiring to be noticed, she knelt, but raised her eyes to watch as the other kings of the Ruud seemed to grow smaller and smaller as Welk spoke to them, until—Leah let out a gasp—they bowed before him.

The trumpet sounded once again and the crowd stood and roared its approval. Confused, Leah turned, only to find Kirche and Prenalin standing only yards distant, watching. Kirche had lost his calm demeanor; he turned briskly and stalked away.

Chapter Thirteen

When the sun found its way behind the peaks, it was too cold on the roof of the tower and Fenn had to say goodbye to Sadie and Grayson. He and Brenna built up their fires in their room and he sat huddled beneath warm pelts noshing an apple, the heat of the flames giving his cheeks a blush. When Brenna came to sit with him in his alcove, she reached out her hand and asked to hold the charm once again.

"Will you tell me its story now?" he asked.

She nodded.

"How do you know the charm didn't belong to my mother?"

"I'm not *certain*," she said. "But you clearly have the gift of touch; you are receiving visions from the charm. And yet, they are brief and without context. If this were your mother's charm, you would see more. Much more."

"What would I see?"

"You would see what I see."

He stared at her, confused, and waited for her to explain.

"This charm was carved by a folk," she said, rubbing her

thumb across the grooves of the dragonfly on its front. "And given to an eisen. Their love was kept secret from their families for many months. They planned to marry, on the plain of Nergens, without consent. There is happiness and joy, laughter..." Brenna wrapped her hands around the charm and brought it to her chest; she shivered.

"What else?"

"Then there is darkness and glimpses of things not meant to be seen."

"I don't understand."

"There are none who can see anything of an object without connection to its owner. If you were the child of the woman who wore this charm, you would see her. With the kell stone, it was different, so I'm told. When the stone was with us, those of us with touch could glean much from any object we held, with no connection at all. Some say it was quite maddening and many are happy to be without the burden."

"But I do see stuff...I think."

"You may have a distant connection to the charm. Or perhaps your touch is in its infancy. I can't be sure that is not the case. And yet, I cannot fathom you would not be able to see what I see, if this did belong to your mother."

"What connection do you have to it?"

"Many years ago, we lost two of our eisen to murder. One was marked by the faire, heralded as the heir to the throne. Her name was Rue-Anna. She slipped out of the realm to meet and marry her lover, a young folk of the Ruud, we believe. This is her charm." She opened her palm to look at it. "He must have made it for her. It's crude; but I can feel that she cherished it."

"What happened to her?"

"I'm told the guards saw the flames of her encampment and

76

felt the call of her spirit."

"Are you sure she couldn't have been my mother? My nurse, Clara, told me my mother had the charm with her when I was born."

Brenna shrugged. "Perhaps the party who raided Rue-Anna's camp were thieves."

"You're saying my mother was a thief?"

"I only know the charm is not your mother's and therefore not yours. If anyone has claim to it, it would be me."

"You?"

She nodded. "Rue-Anna was my sister. I was five years old when she was killed. I woke the morning of her death with the mark of the faire."

Fenn reached out and took his charm from her hand. "You could touch me. And you would know...if I was related to you."

"I have touched you. Just a moment ago, on the roof. But no, I cannot sense your kin; I see only the wissendes who raised you. I would know if Rue-Anna had a child. Or, if you had known her, I would be able to know it. But you were raised alone. I can't feel anything in you but what you know."

Tears pooled in his eyes and Fenn pulled at them with his fingertips then pressed the heels of his palm to his lids.

"Do not despair," she said.

He surprised himself with a laugh. "How can I not? This all seems so pointless. I don't know what everyone wants of me. The fairies told me to go to the wasteland and that did no good. Father Britt told me to come here, but you're no help either."

"What help are you seeking?"

"I want to know," he said. "I *need* to know who I am."

"Yes, exactly. You are split—part eis. That much I can say is certain. And the first thing a young eis must do to begin to live by the seven great principles, is know who he is."

Fenn shook his head, confused.

"We must find out who we are," she said.

"I've tried."

"No, Fenn. Who you are has nothing to do with who your parents were."

"It doesn't?"

"No. It doesn't have anything to do with where you were born, where you have lived, what skills or talents you possess, whether you are beast or folk. Who you are is right here." She poked him hard in the forehead.

"Ow."

"Who you are is determined by how much knowledge and experience you can fit into your head. Who you are is how much you know. It is the decisions you make, the actions you take, based on that knowledge. Who you are is what you think. An eis strives to work past what he believes, what he wishes to be true, to rely only on what he can know. That is who we are."

"That doesn't sound easy."

"It's not. But you must do it. Find out what you know to be true. Then you will know who you are and all decisions will come easy. Your path will be evident as if it's already been worn down by your feet. It will be lit up as a fairy parade at midnight. All will be clear and all will make sense."

"Do you know who you are?" he asked her.

"The greatest principle is one we eis strive for always."

"Oh, that's great," he said. "So what you're telling me is I have to do something that I will never do."

"Never perfect, perhaps. But trust me. You will come to know who you are."

"Where do I begin?"

"Begin with what you know."

"I only know what everyone else thinks I am."

"The child of prophecy, yes. The kell stone."

"I don't know what the kell stone is."

"Of course you do. *It is a place to start.*"

"You think I should look for it?"

She shrugged. "You sought the truth of the prophecy in the beast forest and found there was none. You sought your mother in the wastelands and found you were an eis. You sought the eisen maiden here in the realm and found that despite your mother being eisen, the charm is not yours. What is left for you to find?"

"I could find a place to hide and forget it all."

She laughed and it echoed on the stone walls around them. The fire lit the left side of her face and hid the right in shadow, as if there were two sides to her, one dark and one bright, one kind and one deceitful. But it was just a trick of the light.

"Where would you look for the kell stone," he asked her, "if you went in search of it?"

"I would sprout my wings and fly to Ruhm. The angels tell us it is there; they claim to feel it."

"Why haven't *they* found it?"

"Angels cannot go beneath the ground."

"How do you know it's underground?"

"If it were not, we would draw strength from it, even were it in the Great West."

"So, I should go to Ruhm."

She nodded, hopeful.

"What if I found it, and did what the prophecy said I would do? What if I killed King Welk and destroyed the Ruud?"

Brenna turned her face to the fire.

"That's what you want me to do, isn't it?"

"No," she whispered. "But there are few who would agree with me."

"Then why do you want me to find it?"

"I want it returned to my folk. I want us to live as we were meant to. But I would wish to live in peace with the folk of the Ruud. Think on it. The eis in you would have you seek the stone. You are the only one who can. For you are neither eis, nor angel, nor felidae. You are folk. Only you can get to the stone without being noticed and captured by the folk of Ruhm."

Fenn sighed and shook his head. "I'll think about it."

"Look to yourself, Fenn. Not to anyone else. Know yourself."

Chapter Fourteen

Leah found she was captive as soon as she returned to her tent, though it seemed Kirche was loath to part with Redd and Kipling too often and so it was Xavier who spent most of his time watching her.

"What do you make of it?" the boy asked when she emerged with her shawl. "The other kings of the Ruud, I mean. Have they abdicated?"

"That's unlikely, isn't it?"

He followed her through the encampment, winding around tents and well-tended fires, laundry lines, and make-shift kitchens. The sky was a powdery blue, dotted with puffy white clouds, and the sunlight shone timid, as if from hiding.

"Where are you off to?" he said, skipping to catch up to her.

"You don't have to come along." She breathed in the aromas of the camp—kaff, beans, roasting rabbit.

"But I do. I'm charged with keeping an eye on you."

"Is that so?"

"You're not allowed to leave the camp, nor see that young

fellow what rescued you."

"Can I take a walk?"

"There's a bear somewhere about," he said. "I heard tell. Could we find it?"

Leah stopped, turned to him and smiled. "That's a plan, isn't it?"

Together they roamed through the camp, Xavier on the lookout for a bear, Leah simply trying to breathe. Every part of her told her to run, but to where? Home to Ruhm and her father? Could she save him? When they came to the northern edge of camp where there was a patch of woods to the northeast, set against the backdrop of the icy mountains of the eis, Xavier let out a whoop.

"Two bears," he cheered.

At the tree line was a camp of six tents, and there, just as Xavier said, were two bears rolling in a patch of grass.

"Can we ask to see them do you think?" Xavier said, his face lit with the smile of a child.

And so they walked several yards to the camp and were met by a group of what Leah could only describe as vagabonds. Grimy, every one. Three played at cards; two others napped; and one stood to greet them as they neared.

He introduced himself as Wiley of the Gnome Eaters.

"Do the bears eat gnomes?" Xavier asked.

"Not so far as I can tell," Wiley said. "What group are you with?"

"We are with the Hass," Leah told him.

Wiley's face hardened, but when Xavier beamed and said, "Can I touch one?" the man chuckled and led the boy to one of the bears as it sat up to greet them.

"Where did you come by bears?" Leah asked.

"Gambling. That there's Darnit. Our friend Rogget won him years ago. And this here is Petunia. One of the Wretched won her to the Port a little while ago and our man Tanner just took her off him yesterday."

"They ought to be together," Xavier said.

"Aye, I think that's why he won him so easy. She wouldn't stay with old Grindel, anyway."

Leah watched for several minutes, uncomfortable, while Xavier nuzzled the bear and scratched behind its ears.

"Why is it so friendly?" she asked Wiley.

He shrugged. "I can't be saying for sure he'd be friendly to everybody."

"We should go now, Xavier."

"Aw."

"It's all right," Wiley said. "Looks like Darnit's taken to you. Come back anytime you like. So long as me or one of the boys is here."

"Tomorrow then?"

Wiley nodded. "I'll be with the delegation to the ice palace day after tomorrow. After that, ask Tanner there if it'd be okay."

Xavier leaned down to hug Darnit.

"The kings of the Ruud," Leah said. "They've united?"

"Against the eis, yes."

"You think there will only be one Ruud, soon?" Xavier said.

"I imagine so. King Welk is the stronger of the three and he's got the people behind him. Ricker and Arnot gave over soldiers to him for confronting the eis and angels, and now they've gone off home."

"Would they give up their thrones so easily?" Leah said.

"Oh, I imagine there will be a fight. But I suspect Welk has more to bargain with than he lets on."

"What do you mean?"

"What? Ain't you heard? The eis have got the boy of prophecy
—the one who's to destroy the Ruud. I saw him took up by an
angel myself and carried off there. If Welk can get hold of him,
all the Ruud will be behind him. It don't look too good for you
folk."

"What have we got to do with it?" Xavier said.

"Ah, now, don't be pretending you don't know your Hass
isn't wanting to come over here and start a fight of their own."

Xavier laughed. "If Ruhm wanted this little slap of land,
she'd have it. It would take more than your little army of folk to
run us off."

"Hush," Leah told him.

"But, it's true. If we wanted the Ruud we'd have had it a
long time ago. We've got an army twice as big as anything you
could come up with."

"And what have they been doing over there in Ruhm, eh?
Patrolling for stray beast folk? Marching in parades? You think
the winter folk who run off from the Hass and settle over here
don't talk? You got a big bunch of pretty folk in costume, that's
all. Out here in the hills, we been fighting up close for years—
real fighting, something your dressed up fancy boys haven't had
to do."

"But we have firearms. Lots of them."

"And you don't think we do?"

"We know you don't."

"You think you know."

Xavier took a step closer to Wiley and Darnit let out a roar.
The boy jumped and backed away.

"That's right," Wiley said. "We got bears, too."

Xavier was happy enough to leave after that, and Leah

scolded him on their way through the camp.

"I'll tell Kirche what he said. We'll have them all searched."

"It would take an army just to do that."

"I'll tell him, even so."

"Your pride's been hurt, that's all."

The boy grumbled behind her and Leah pitied him. After all, she'd been in that frame of mind not too long ago, she realized —thinking Ruhm the best at everything.

"Leah?" A woman called to her. "Leah Hallowsing?"

She stopped in front of a large tent where several women stood wringing out wet clothing, hanging it on ropes tied to tall stakes sunk into the ground. An older woman came forward with a timid smile.

"Is that you?"

Finally, Leah recognized the face. "Madam Roths?"

Her smile widened. "I am called simply Dania, now." She glanced at Xavier. "What has brought you east?"

"She's the Aide to the High Priest of Hass," Xavier said.

"Are you now? And on the annual tour, no doubt."

"But what are you doing here?" Leah asked her.

"I represent the College of Women. One of the kings of the Ruud called us to meet regarding the eis."

"But what are you doing here in the east?"

"Hah," she laughed. "I suppose when we left, the Hass made up some story about our disappearance."

"You retired."

"That's as good an excuse as any. Did you know Byn Always is here, as well?"

"Madam Always?" Leah shook her head. "Here?"

"Well, not here at the meeting. She's back at our camp, some thirty miles south. There near the foot hills."

Leah turned to look. "So close."

"I imagine you would not be allowed to visit."

"No."

"Will your party be following when we confront the eis? Or waiting here in the hills for our return?"

She looked to Xavier, then shook her head. "I'm not sure why we haven't moved on as yet, but no. So far as I know, we will not join the march."

Madam Roths seemed to wish to say more. She took Leah's hands and frowned, squeezed them slightly and tried to smile.

"I wish you luck on your journey home," she said.

Chapter Fifteen

Welk woke from his dream with a start, the cold night air sending a chill through him. He sat up, reached for a log and tossed it onto the fire, stoked it, and sat for some time letting the warmth ease his mind. The camp was quiet now; even the card players and revelers nodded off. The crackle and spit of the fires echoed, and smoke whirled upward into darkness.

He heard it again. The voice, calling his name. In his dream it was Rue-Anna and he'd dared not answer, for even in sleep he knew she was dead and only a demon or a doppleganger would have called to him. He couldn't bear the heartache, even imaginary, of losing her again.

"Welk of Michelruud," the girl said.

Behind him, he found her standing between tents fifty yards north. An angel.

"I am still asleep," he mumbled. But he stood, wrapped himself in his cloak, and walked toward her. When he came near, she turned and made her way through the camp, out into the open field where the fires could not warm them and only the moonlight showed her face.

She could be Rue-Anna, he thought. Younger, taller, her hair a touch too much like honey, not enough like gold. Her eyes darker, like Rue-Anna's sapphires with a flare of anger to them. Another version of Rue, he thought, and realized he was not dreaming.

"I am Bren-Aian of Eidolon. Daughther of the Snow. Queen of the Eis."

Welk looked around them at the darkness. "Where is your entourage?"

"I come alone."

"I was not aware the queen of the eis was an angel."

"I am angel eisen."

"What does that mean?"

"My father was an angel."

Welk let his eyes gaze into hers for as long as she would stand it. He could see them both in her. Aliara's lips, always pursed in confidence. Rue's brow, curved with concern. But they were not angels. Of that much, he consoled himself, he could be sure. For no blur of mourning could erase wings such as those. Their shoulders rose to her ears. Thick with blinding white feathers, the tips of which danced with each breeze. When a strong wind whistled from the north, she lifted them, opened them slightly, and sent the wind off, shielding him.

"The queen has no plans to turn the boy over to you. She will attempt to take you. But her guard has dwindled low these past months, without her knowledge. She and Noromir have grown lazy. You will find a majority of the guard will turn against the others, once you make it clear you mean to fight."

He nodded. "Your emissaries told me as much."

"I wish to know when you march the pass."

"Day after tomorrow. We are hoping our delay makes her Highness restless."

The girl smiled. "Be assured you will make it to the first gate of the realm freely. Once a skirmish is raised, my allies will act swiftly. We will retake the realm."

"But this news is not why you came," he said. "You could have sent another of the eis on horseback."

"Yes," she said. "I would ask something of you."

He hesitated. "You may."

"I wish to touch you."

Welk flinched and drew back, unprepared for such a request. "Why?"

"You will know."

With that, Welk knew already; she needn't touch him at all. But he let her place her hand on his forearm. She closed her eyes and Welk fought to keep his open—to watch her lip tremble when she learned the truth of her suspicions. Why hadn't she known it was him? Did Rue never speak of him?

She lowered her head and her hand dropped to her side. "Thank you," she whispered.

"You are her kin," he said.

Her eyes seemed to sink to black there in the night when she looked at him. "I must know," she said. "Could she not have lived?"

Welk's jaw set hard and he fought to keep from grinding his teeth. "If she lived, she would be by my side."

"You're certain?"

"I watched the eis burn their bodies on the pyre."

She flinched when he spoke, as if his anger were thorns flung from his lips.

"You saw the bodies for yourself," she said, her chin raised, refusing to be cowed by his venom.

"I—" Welk realized the truth. "I did not."

He broke. He could feel the split in his heart. How could she do it to him? How could an eisen not be wary of his pain? It was unlike them—unlike Rue and Aliara, and so he thought all eisen—to purposefully cause harm. But there the eisen stood, forcing him to have hope where there could be none.

"Why?" he asked her.

She shook her head. "I cannot say."

"She is dead. They are both dead."

"Yes," she said.

"Then why do you question me?"

"It is when they died that is uncertain."

Chapter Sixteen

When he handed her the bow, Prenalin offered Leah a worried look, but she was still too angry to give him any solace. They followed Kirche, Kipling, and Redd into the woods west of the encampment and trudged on in silence for some time until she gave up and deigned to speak to him.

"He doesn't intend to find brownies here in this small wood, surely," she said.

Prenalin seemed to breathe finally, as if he hadn't had a decent intake since the day she'd returned from the caverns with Lucas—since Kirche made his vile threat of marriage.

"Merely rabbit." Pren tried to smile, but he only half managed. "I wish you to know," he whispered as the two of them fell farther behind Kirche, "it was not my doing that it happened as it did."

"The proposal you mean."

He nodded.

"But you knew he intended to marry me?"

"It was his plan all along. Yes."

They hiked the woods for two hours before Kirche let out a strangled growl and stomped off toward the camp. Not even a squirrel showed itself.

"How can one manage a decent hunt with all that racket?" Kirche said. "Do they carouse all day? What sort of army could they hope to make?"

When they exited the wood, Leah hesitated, watched their backs as they all left her there and disappeared among the tents. She flung her bow onto her shoulder and walked the edge of the wood to where Sorgood's guard were camped, hoping to see Lucas. He'd spied her twice since their return, both times nodding, smiling, not approaching, as if he understood she was under guard and warned against him. It wouldn't surprise her, as she found him much more intuitive than any folk of Ruhm. Perhaps it was the felid in him, she thought.

As she neared the last of the tents, she caught sight of him entering the wood twenty yards ahead and, thinking it best not to be seen following him, took to the woods there where she was. It was too bad she wasn't a felid herself, so she could smell him out, she thought with a smile. But better to search while hidden in the woods than get into trouble with Kirche.

As small as the wood east of the encampment was, it still had its dense, dark patches, and once caught within one, Leah couldn't help being reminded of the beast forest of the Ruud. Her heart quickened its pace and she caught her breath.

"Calm down," she whispered to the wind in the trees above her. But she began to fear, sure she was walking in circles. Perhaps the wood was not so small after all. When she felt a sob begin to rise in her throat, she startled at the sound of a strange voice.

"If you did not wish to die," the folk said, "why did you wander off from your fellows."

Leah shuddered, fearful now of being caught up in something grisly. She moved forward slowly, let a hand reach for a thick pine to steady herself, and peered out from among the branches and shrubs.

"I do not seek you out," Lucas said and Leah's eyes widened. She could see the back of a folk, tall, thin but heavy with strength; he must tower over young Lucas. She strained to see the boy but could not.

"You must have sensed my presence."

"Hence my turning back to the camp."

Lucas was impatient, but fearful, she was sure; but the folk was cruelly playful, toying with him.

"No matter," the folk said.

Leah watched in horror as the folk raised a bow and she saw Lucas dart away; the folk rushed to follow. Without thinking, she pushed through the trees and shrubs after them. She caught sight of the tall folk as he glanced back at her. He smiled and continued after Lucas; she heard him chuckle, but Leah knew this could not be a game.

When she came upon him, stopped in a brief clearing, his bow raised, she pulled hers from her shoulder, nocked an arrow without thinking and let it fly. He jerked forward, stumbled, and turned toward her, frustration in his brow. He was set to shout at her, scold her like a child, but Leah nocked a second arrow and sent it into his throat before he had the chance—he fell. Once at him, she thrust her foot into his chest and glared, another arrow ready for his eye socket, her breath coming in raging gasps now.

"You are an eis," she said.

He nodded, shuddering.

"You will heal well enough, then."

His mouth opened and closed, but only blood flowed from it.

"I should kill you now."

"No," Lucas came through the trees, his hand held up to stay her. Leah didn't take her eyes from the eis at her feet. "Let him go."

"He was going to kill you."

"But he won't now. Not today."

Leah kicked at the eis and sucked in a deep breath, calming herself. "We should leave before he is healed."

Together they walked through the woods at a pace until they found their way into the encampment and Lucas faced her with a smile.

"How did you know he was an eis?"

"I studied them in school. I could have killed him, you know. An arrow in the brain will do it."

He shook his head and chuckled. "I had no idea you were so violent. And yet you shudder at my stories."

Leah finally let herself tremble from the fright and had to laugh at herself. "I am not violent," she said. "But I will do whatever is necessary to protect a friend."

"Now you have to say our debts are balanced."

"Would you care to tell me why an eis is intent upon killing you?"

"Would you tell me why you have been under guard since your return?"

They stood looking at each other, smiling, for several seconds until she laughed again. "I suppose neither of us is willing to burden the other."

His face softened and concern grew in his eyes. "Will you come with me to the ice palace? You don't have to tell me there is something wrong for me to help you. Come with me; your Lord Kirche needn't treat you this way. I will keep you safe from him."

Leah's heart lurched and settled back. How easy it would be to run from Kirche—run with Lucas. Even King Welk, no doubt, would protect her. And there lay the problem. She sighed. "I cannot ask our troubled truce be overthrown because of a dispute over me. For you know Kirche would blame the Ruud for my defection. He may say I was kidnapped, stolen, indoctrinated."

"Then tell me I am not to worry. You will be all right?"

"I will be," she said, though her voice quaked. "But will you?"

"I will. I promise the eis is no match for a felid." Here he offered a wily smile. "Will your party still be here when the delegation returns from the palace?"

"I think not. Kirche was not happy to see the other kings give up soldiers to Welk. He plans to return to the port on the morrow, though our ship is not due for a fortnight."

"Very well, then," he said. "I will see you at the port; I will find you there, before you sail."

"You still plan to follow me to Ruhm?"

He nodded.

"It is dangerous; much more so than an eis assassin, I'm afraid. If anything were to happen to you, I would feel...responsible."

"Then do not believe I go on your account. See me as concerned only with the kell stone. It's all I am after, I assure you." He smiled and put a hand on her arm. "I care not for you one whit."

She laughed and watched him take a path through the tents; he smiled at her, before disappearing from sight. When she turned to walk the edge of the wood back to her own camp, she found Redd and Kipling striding toward her. A pair of handcuffs rattled at Kipling's side.

"You leave him no choice," Prenalin said to her when she was deposited in her tent, chained to the center post.

Leah glared at him.

"He will release you, he says, once the boy is dealt with."

"What does that mean?"

"Don't concern yourself with the details."

"Tell me, Pren. What will he do? He can't harm him. Can he? It was my fault. Please tell Kirche not to blame Lucas. It was my doing, not his. Please tell him."

Prenalin lifted the flap of her tent to leave; he frowned at her. "I will tell him," he said, but he shook his head slightly before he was gone.

Chapter Seventeen

I t is time," Brenna whispered. "The folk are gathering to confront the queen's guard."

Fenn nodded and winced. She was still weak from her last shedding, he knew. And when she returned the last time, she seemed changed—defeated somehow, saddened.

"How do we get out?" he asked her.

Brenna smiled and held up a long gold key. "Give me a lift," she said, beckoning him to the window in the cubby next to the door.

"Out the window?"

"There's a small ledge; trust me."

As Fenn cupped his hands for her slender foot and lifted her up, he thought of the children of Path, wondering if all tower walls might be clung to for daring escapes.

Her key tinkled in the lock and she pulled open the heavy door; a cold, thick wind rushed at Fenn's face.

"Did you have the key all the time?"

"For a while," she said.

"What about the guard?"

"We've done our best to keep those loyal to the queen out of our plans."

Outside there was a wood landing with a low rail, barely reaching his hip, and thin planks serving as steps circling the tower.

"Is it safe?" Fenn asked, shaking.

"There's no time for fear," Brenna said. "Hurry."

He followed her down the narrow stairs, around to the other side where there was another landing.

"These hardly seem like the sort of stairs a folk would find in the ice palace," Fenn said, his teeth chattering in the cold.

"This is a prison tower," she said, pulling open the door. "They're not designed to help you get down."

She pushed him into the dimly lit room where he saw Sadie and Grayson huddled in front of a fire. They jumped up, surprised, and Brenna held up a hand.

"Quiet," she said. "We do not know which guards are with us and which are not. Be wary."

"Oh, no," Sadie moaned as soon as they were out of the room and on the landing. "Isn't there a better way?"

"The only other way down is in the arms of an angel," Brenna said.

"Well, come on," Grayson said. "Let's get it done."

"To the next level," Brenna said. "There is another in your party there."

"Rogget?" Fenn said.

"A huntsman by the look of him."

They hugged the cold stone walls of the tower and stepped quickly, but gingerly, down the stairs. Fenn's legs trembled wildly. Finally, they wound round to the next door and found Rogget inside the room there. He grabbed them all into his arms

98

and Fenn felt the man shudder with tears.

"You've all gone too thin," he muttered. Suddenly he tensed.

Fenn turned to find Brenna staring at them, her eyes wide in frustration.

"We must hurry."

"This is Brenna," Fenn said. "She was with me, on the top floor."

"We have no time for greetings. This way."

Together, they made their way down the stairs, around the tower, until they came to their fourth landing where Grayson begged for a rest. Fenn was glad to oblige. His legs wobbled as if he had no bones and his heart refused to calm. He decided, despite his rescue of the children of Path at Steingefan, he did not like heights.

"We come to the tenth floor," Brenna said. "You can go inside there and take the spiral stair in the center of the tower to the bottom."

When they neared the landing, the door swung open and three guards walked out, talking heatedly. As they headed up the steps, they looked upward and stopped abruptly at the sight of the three children, Rogget, and Brenna, staggered on the stair above them.

"What's this?" the taller of the eis said with a hint of amusement. He glared at Brenna and tilted his head. "Is this an act of treason?"

"It is." She smiled. "Who is with me?"

The younger guards drew their swords. "I am not," one of them said.

The other shouted, "bring them into the ante chamber, we'll cuff them there."

But the taller guard drew his sword and faced them. "I stand with the true queen. We will help her in her quest."

"You will die," the other guard said.

Fenn watched in horror as the three guards began to fight—their swords glinting in the sunlight, clashes echoing off the tower walls.

"Quickly," Brenna said. "We must move past them."

"It's all right," he heard Rogget say from above him on the stairs. "Move carefully."

But as they stepped onto the landing and Fenn reached to grab Sadie's arm, he was knocked over by one of the guards. Sadie fell over him and struggled to stand.

"Sadie," Grayson yelled, just as another guard's arm flew back and knocked her over the low railing.

Sadie's screams echoed all around, bouncing off the peaks. Fenn could see her hands grasping the low bar of the railing. Climbing to his knees, he was grabbed by one of the young soldiers.

"The ransom must not escape," he said. "You deal with these, let them loose if you have to."

The guard dragged Fenn toward the door, but Rogget grabbed the eis around the neck.

"Let him go."

The guard hung on tighter. Sadie screamed again and Fenn struggled to free himself. Brenna said something, in eis, and a sword fell to the ground at his feet. Finally, the guard's hold on him failed and Fenn stepped away from him as the folk slid sluggishly to the ground against the door. Fenn grabbed the heavy sword and called to Grayson.

"Do you need help?"

"I've got her," Grayson cried, kneeling on the landing and pulling Sadie up so she could grab the higher rung on the railing.

Fenn turned back to the door where Rogget was dragging

the lifeless soldier out of the way. Brenna was backed into a corner, behind the tall eis who battled the younger guard. Fenn lifted the sword he'd claimed, closed his eyes, and stabbed toward the young guard.

"Ahh." With a terrible, shrieking gasp, the guard sank to the ground.

Fenn shuddered, opened his eyes and panicked. He dropped the bloodied sword to the floor of the landing and staggered, nauseated.

"Quickly," the older eis called.

Sadie climbed over the railing and Grayson grabbed her and pulled her toward the door. Fenn, shaking, took Brenna's hand and led her away from the corner.

"It's all right," Rogget was saying as they ran across the ante chamber floor and down the spiral stairs. "They aren't dead."

"Are you sure," Fenn said breathlessly, "I didn't kill him?"

"You got him in the side. He'll be fine."

But Fenn thought Rogget was only trying to make him feel better.

"Look here," Rogget said.

There against the wall were their knapsacks, their supplies strewn about the room. They gathered up their things as quickly as they could—blankets, tin mugs, Sadie's maps.

"What in Mutterede's name?" Rogget said.

Fenn stood and turned to the door; he gasped. Sadie and Grayson let Rogget step in front of them and he drew his knife to protect them.

"Step over here," Rogget told Fenn.

He shook his head. "It's all right, Rogget."

Brenna stood before them, her heavy white wings lifted and shuddered. "I have to leave you now," she said. "You must make your way to the front of the palace. Once out of the tower, the path winds through the gardens. It will take you to the eastern door. You will find it unlocked."

"Thank you," Fenn said. He reached his hand out to grasp hers, and she looked at it, hesitating, before taking it. In the brief moment they touched, she looked into his eyes and he thought he saw something familiar and warm there. But she released his hand before he was sure what had happened. They went to the door, stood on the landing, and watched as she let herself drop out of sight. Then she soared above them and flew into the sunlight.

"She was an angel?" Grayson said, his voice hollow.

"Angel eisen," Fenn said. "Split."

"All right then," Rogget said, sheathing his knife. "No time to dally."

They nearly fell the ten flights of spiral stairs toward the ground. Fenn struggled to keep tears from welling up in his eyes. He never thought he'd stab someone. He feared himself—wondered what other awful things he might be capable of. But he pushed that thought away; he must think only of getting to the bottom of the tower.

As they took the path through gardens and courtyards, the palace was abuzz with panic. Eis ran with them, passed them, crossed their path, but ignored them as they made their way, exhausted and panting, to the outer wall where the door stood, ten feet tall. Fenn put his hand on the latch, ready to pull it open.

"Listen to me," Rogget said, huffing and puffing, still not finding his breath. "You all run down the pass, you hear? They won't notice you."

"But what about you?" Sadie said.

"I'll run. I'm not saying I won't follow. But I'm bigger. I'll get noticed. If I should stop, you keep running."

"We will," Fenn promised, knowing it would never be that easy.

He pulled the door open and they found themselves in a mass of folk, on the opposite side of where they ought to be. To reach the pass, they'd have to make their way through a sea of white-robed eis who had filed out of the palace gates to meet the hundreds of soldiers of the Ruud, many on horseback, who had gathered at the walls of the palace.

Fenn followed Sadie and Grayson as best he could through the throng of white, but he knew at some point they'd be noticed, or fighting would break out. The thought of insanity ran through his head. But hadn't they done stupider things? Suddenly trumpets blared again and he heard the full throated, yet airy, voice of one of the eis.

Chapter Eighteen

Hundreds of eis had gathered before the first gate of the realm. Beyond it rose the towers and spires of the palace. All along the pass, Welk had expected an ambush, but Bren-Aian had fulfilled her promise; he detected not even a scout.

"This is not as the queen demanded," the tall, glowing eis who'd come forward bellowed.

Welk dismounted and let Sorgood's first lieutenant take his horse. He wrapped his arms across his chest and looked up slightly at the eis. Sorgood's men were gathered behind Welk, many on horseback, squeezed together in a long line from one end of the marbled wall to the other—a distance of some hundred yards. Many of the soldiers had dismounted on orders and attempted to flank the eis.

The eis guards stood like statues, their strong jaws set rigid, and their stares focused on something in the distance behind the folk. They were more disciplined than the guards of the Ruud, Welk knew; but he wondered if that discipline would make them vulnerable when faced with feverish young folk eager for battle.

"You agreed to sweep the land at our border of its refuse," the eis said. "Instead you bring it here."

"I never promised I would force folk from the hill country," Welk said. "I met with them and have heard their complaints."

"They must be removed from our lands," the eis roared. "It is the queen's command."

"Then the queen will have to move them off herself."

"If you wish to have the bairn, you must fulfill your part of the bargain."

"I made no bargain."

"Then the boy will remain with us."

"You do not have the boy," Welk said.

"He is this moment being shackled and brought out to a balcony where you may see him."

"You are mistaken."

The eis guard's eyes closed up a bit and he sneered. "Are all folk of the Ruud so ignorant? Or is it just your kings?"

Welk laughed. "We can debate which species of folk is the stupider another time, but I assure you, you no longer have the boy."

"How could you know?"

"Because he is there." Welk pointed to the boy in the crowd of angels and when the eis guard turned to see him, Welk grabbed him from behind and forced him to the ground. The sounds of confusion and pending chaos broke out all around him.

"You will send a message to the maiden," Welk said. "Seize the boy!" he called out to his guard. A shot rang out and the eis began a loud scream in unison as they moved forward toward the folk, their bows drawn. Too sudden, Welk thought, but it was done. If Bren-Aian was truthful, his folk would have little trouble getting the boy and leaving the eis to their own battle.

106

"Tell the maiden we are with her," he said to the guard. "She has but to call on us."

The eis, on his knees, struggled in Welk's grasp. "The maiden no longer has power here. It is the queen you must deal with. She will not ally with folk."

"Your false queen is too easily seduced by angels, my eis friend. And her throat is pricked by the point of sword as we speak."

He pointed to the balcony on the second floor and made sure the eis saw the young maiden standing there watching them.

Welk heard her voice, even from afar. "The throne is restored."

"No," the eis raged, pushing Welk off him and fumbling to his feet. He turned and drew his sword. "The eis will never ally with folk."

Welk smiled at him. "I have no time to fight with you. But I'm sure you'll find any number of soldiers willing."

Welk pushed through the throng after Fenn. The skirmish had billowed out from the gate, filling in the craggy grounds all the way toward the small pathway of the pass. Folk battled eis, eis battled eis and folk; it was a muddled, confused affair. He found Sorgood on the ground with his arm raised above his head as a shield.

"Get up," he said and dragged Sorgood up by his collar. "He's there, hurry."

He could see Fenn and the huntsman in the distance, struggling through the battling soldiers for the pass. He made his way forward, keeping his eyes on the boy.

Chapter Nineteen

Keep going," Fenn called to Sadie and Grayson. They'd stopped, panicked, amid the chaos. "Run!" he screamed. They ran through the crowd, shoving their way around both folk and eis, none of whom appeared to care about their escape. Just as he let himself believe they'd made it out of the chaos, when he could see the road ahead leading away from the palace, that would take him through the pass and back into the hills, he heard a shout, and behind him, King Welk stood, his sword drawn, the tip red with blood.

The king grabbed him, first by his knapsack, yanking him to a stop, then by the back of his tunic. Fenn called out to Rogget but the huntsman was running with Sadie and Grayson, making for the pass.

"It's not safe," the king said to him. "Stay with the guard."

Fenn turned to look at him, confused, and caught sight of Lucas darting from the edges of the chaos, running toward him. Relief washed over him—Lucas was safe—but it was tinged with hurt and he realized then that he couldn't be sure if Lucas was coming to help him get away, or to help King Welk turn him over to Sorgood. He struggled against Welk's grasp, but Lucas was on them both within seconds, grabbing Welk from behind, surprising him, forcing him to let go of Fenn; the king's sword fell to the ground. Without thinking, Fenn picked it up. It felt strangely comfortable in his hand.

"Lucas?" he said.

"Run, Fenn. I cannot hold him long."

But Fenn stood there, his eyes wide, frantic.

"The boy should stay with the guard," Welk said, struggling free of Lucas' grasp.

Amid the shots and clanging of swords, the shouts and orders, one powerful bang rang out nearby, causing Fenn to jump. Everything went silent. Rogget caught hold of him as Fenn watched Lucas' face, his eyes wide, his mouth open as if he gasped for air. As Rogget pulled Fenn away, Lucas fell to his knees and Fenn's hearing returned.

"Lucas!" Fenn started forward, but Rogget lifted him off his feet. "Lucas!"

Lucas fell face down onto the ground; his back soaked in blood. Standing only a few yards behind him was Sorgood with a firearm, smiling, nodding. Fenn raged and pulled free of Rogget's grasp. Rushing toward Sorgood, he lifted Welk's heavy sword over his head. Sorgood, surprisingly, turned and ran, but Welk grabbed Fenn's arm. Struggling against the king, Fenn felt Rogget's huge arm wrap around his body once again, lifting him off the ground. He was pulled from Welk's grasp and dragged away. He watched a cluster of white-clad, glowing angels surround Welk.

"The King!" someone shouted.

Fenn saw the dagger, white and icy as the angels themselves, lifted high and brought down against the king's back. Welk

110

caught Fenn's eye as he jerked with pain. A sadness washed over his face before he fell.

Rogget set Fenn on his feet and pushed him forward; he ran from the battle, down the road away from the ice realm, passing folk who'd followed to watch the scene.

"Lucas," he gasped as he ran behind Rogget. "They killed Lucas."

Chapter Twenty

1268 Autumn

Aliara was awakened by thumping footsteps in the clover; the geimen buzzed around her, telling her all was well. She opened her eyes to see an old, plump folk, in a brown robe, tied at his middle with a pale hemp rope. He stood just outside the clover patch, reached to the ground, and lifted the firearm her attacker had dropped. Her breathing quickened.

"All is well," the geimen sang. "All is well."

When he turned to her, he smiled and said, "You live," as if he hadn't expected it.

He tucked the firearm under his arm and walked into the field of clover to where she lay; he knelt at her side and cast his gaze along her body. She wondered how much blood there was to see.

"The geimen called to me," he said.

When she woke again, Aliara was in a hut built of tree branches, slits of sunlight danced between them spotted with specks of dust like fairies. Women, old as the wissende, haggard and gray, dressed her wounds. She was helped into a gown and the oldest of them offered a toothless grin.

"The finest we could find, my lady," she said.

Aliara opened her mouth to speak but no sound escaped; it was then she realized how quickly she was fading. The hag placed a hand on her engorged belly and nodded.

"The child lives; but you must fight."

She awoke and stared at the hut, at the collection of artifacts strewn about, hanging on the walls and from the ceiling. Utensils, ticking timepieces, shoes without mates, bunches of dried flowers, and yellowed, peeling pages full of writing and drawings. The wissende entered and took a seat at her bedside; his eyes were rimmed red.

"I will take you to the midwife, but the journey is long. I have secured a wagon."

Aliara reached for him, her hand trembling violently until it found rest on his knee. Her brows knit together and she sucked in a ragged breath.

He seemed to understand and frowned, a sweet quiver at his lower lip. "There was a massacre," he said. "I find no evidence of survivors...other than you, my lady. I can send an emissary to—"

She closed her eyes and shook her head. Finally, she managed to speak. "No." The darkness invaded her once again as she told herself she must live.

1280 Autumn

Leah woke to a hand clasped over her mouth; she startled and struggled to sit, realizing she was cuffed and chained to the post in her tent.

"Quiet," Xavier said. "Kirche and his guard sleep."

Groggy, unsure of what was happening, Leah watched as Xavier carefully—so as not to let the keys jingle in his grasp—found the correct one and unlatched her cuffs. She rubbed the raw spots on her sore wrists. Her hands had not been unbound since the day Kipling found her speaking to Lucas.

"This way." Xavier led Leah from the tent and they crept past the fire, now only embers, and the empty bedrolls of the porters, to the kitchen tent where Gretchen and Zelda stood, nervous and fumbling.

"This is for you," Zelda whispered, putting a pack on her shoulders. "Food, drink, clothing, blanket."

"But this is madness," she said. "Where can I go?"

"You must go to Ruhm," Gretchen said. "Warn your father."

"I can warn him when I arrive with Kirche."

Gretchen shook her head.

"Hurry," Xavier whispered. "Kipling is returned from the woods."

"He means to have your father hanged on Founding Day," Gretchen said.

"What?" Leah nearly called out loud. "But he said—"

"This is a man who threatens to torture your father if you do not obey him," Zelda said. "Can you believe anything he says?"

She stood staring at them in the dark, her mouth open, her stomach turning. Nodding, she felt the sting of her fingernails digging into her palms.

"Very well," she said. "Thank you." She hugged Gretchen, then Zelda, whose strong grip took her breath away, and then Xavier who she knew blushed heavily though she couldn't see it in the dark. "Mutterede's blessings be with you," she whispered and darted through the tents to the south.

Chapter Twenty-one

They hiked Kingdom Pass and in the night skirted around the guarded folk encampment and headed south toward the Plains of Glisch, camping at the base of a hill. Fenn wouldn't talk about the ice realm, or the battle, even when Rogget asked him. Lost and disoriented, he didn't think he could answer any questions if he tried.

He woke in the early morning sunlight, warmed by Rogget's fire, and wrapped his blanket around him. "It's gotten colder," he said quietly, taking a mug of hot bitters from Rogget.

"Sorry," Rogget said. "It's all I got for us until we can barter more food and drink."

Sadie nodded, took a mug and shivered.

"We'll head south to the coast," Rogget said. "It'll be a bit warmer there, especially if we can find a bit of forest."

"When can we go home?" Grayson asked, looking around at each of them. "I mean, any idea?"

They all seemed to look at Fenn for the answer. He needed to focus. He got up and walked to the top of the hill and peered across the slopes, to the plain beyond, reaching to the horizon.

Then he turned back toward the mountains of the ice realm. The southeast tower rose high into the sky. He squinted, hoping he would see Brenna, standing in the tower, watching him. But she wasn't there.

He rejoined the others by the fire and sipped his bitters.

"Well?" Grayson said.

"Well, what?"

"What are we supposed to do now?"

"How should I know?"

Grayson sputtered. "How should you know? You're the whole reason we're in this mess. If you don't know, who will?"

"That's hardly fair," Sadie said. "It's not Fenn's fault."

"It is so. He had the mark all along. If he'd just told us, we might not be in this mess."

"Why? Would you have run to the village and handed him over to the guard?"

Grayson pouted and looked to the ground. "No."

"It wasn't Fenn's fault Father Treacher sent him through the tunnel. And it wasn't our fault we were sitting there when he came out. It just happened. And don't act like you haven't been having fun."

Grayson rolled his eyes. "Great fun! Traipsing all over the Ruud. Roster fiends. Angels and arrows flying through the air."

"Well, it wasn't Fenn's fault. You could be back in Banished, you know. Nobody made you come along."

"That's enough," Rogget said. "Bickering don't change anything."

They were silent for a moment while Fenn tried to think of what to say. Finally, he set his mug down by the fire pit and said, "Well, I don't know what to do now."

"No clue at all?" Grayson said.

"Did you see the queen, like we did? Did she tell you about your charm?"

Fenn shook his head. "That's a story to tell. It turns out the eisen you met wasn't the queen. It was Brenna all along. She is the maiden."

"But she's an angel," Sadie said.

"Angel eisen," Grayson corrected. "You showed her the charm then?"

Fenn nodded. "She wasn't much help." He couldn't bring himself to tell them that Brenna said the charm was not his mother's. He didn't understand it, still. He was deeply connected to it. Why would it not be his mother's? "She said I ought to go into the Great West."

"What for?" Rogget said.

Fenn shrugged. "Seems like nobody knows what I'm supposed to do and they don't want to deal with me, so they just tell me to go as far away from them as they can think of."

"Aw, come now," Rogget said.

"Father Treacher told me to go to Father Britt and he told me to go to the ice realm, and the maiden told me to go west. They're just trying to get rid of me."

"You really think so?" Sadie said.

Fenn nodded.

"We can't get a ship west," Rogget said. "We'd have to make our way back to the port and I don't think that's a good idea."

"Sorgood and a lot of the guard were at the battle," Grayson said. "Maybe there won't be many in the port."

"Father Britt said they don't have any control there," Fenn said.

Rogget shook his head. "I don't know."

"I thought there was another port," Sadie said, "east of Cold

Sea, where the winter folk landed."

"Aye, but it isn't just the immigrants who use it. They're plenty of pirates and scalawags about."

"That's no different from Cold Sea," Grayson said.

"Well, if we can get into the Ruud and to the wissenry at Cold Sea," Sadie said, "Father Britt could find us a safe passage."

"You're all talking like we're going west," Fenn said.

"Do you have any other ideas?" Sadie said.

"Do we have to go anywhere?" Grayson said.

Fenn nodded. "Exactly. Why don't we just sit here?"

"Sit here?" Sadie said, raising her eyebrows. "For how long?"

"Forever. Let's just sit here and do nothing. I don't know what else to do. I should just go back and find King Welk and turn myself in already." Fenn felt a pang of regret at his words and put his face in his hands.

"What is it?" Grayson asked.

"I saw the king. Just after Sorgood shot Lucas, the angels attacked him. He was stabbed."

"Aye," Rogget said. "But I'm sure he lived."

"You can't know that."

They let Fenn sit in silence for a while, warming themselves at the fire, sipping their bitters.

"Well, we can't just sit here," Sadie said.

"Why not?" Fenn mumbled.

She growled and stood up. "We need more supplies. We lost too much when we were taken to the ice palace." She stomped a foot. "Stop acting like this. You're not the only one having trouble here, you know."

"Really?" Fenn looked up, his face streaked with tears. "Are you an evil bairn of prophecy? I didn't think so. Did you stab

120

somebody yesterday? No? Did you see your brother killed yesterday? No, again."

"Lucas was your brother?" Sadie said.

"They're wissendes," Grayson said. "They call each other brothers."

"He was my brother; we grew up together."

"Okay, I'm sorry." Sadie looked around. "But we have to go somewhere."

"Aye," Rogget stood as well. "We'll see if we can't find a camp of winter folk who'll take us in for a while."

"How does that sound?" Sadie said to Fenn.

"Stop asking me, like I'm the leader."

"Fine." She rolled her eyes.

"Enough bickering," Rogget's voice boomed over the hills.

They were silent as they put out their fire and packed their sacks and made the long hike over the hills toward the Plains of Glisch.

"There," Fenn said later in the day, pointing southeast. "I see an encampment."

Across the plain, nestled up against the lower mountains on the far south side of the ice realm, he could see huts and tents and smoke from a fire.

"Where?" Grayson said.

"It's there."

"There's nothing there," Sadie said. "Just the blur of the mountains on the horizon."

"It's right there," he pointed.

"We can't see it," Rogget said. "Fenn's got the eyes of an eis—when he can control them."

Sadie and Grayson gaped at him, as if they didn't believe Rogget. But one look from the old huntsman and they accepted it. They hiked toward the encampment until dark, and made camp again.

The next afternoon they approached the little make-shift village and were hailed by a guard who limped hurriedly toward them with his hands raised.

"State your whereabouts," he said.

"We're standing right in front of you," Grayson said.

"Oh, aye. I mean, uh." He fumbled in his trouser pocket and pulled out a piece of thick parchment paper. "Uh," he mumbled to himself, "halt, where are you heading." And then he looked at them, "Where are you headed?"

"We came to see if you could spare some food and lodgings in exchange for another hunter," Rogget said. "I'm good with the bow and knife, though mine have been taken from me."

The guard looked back at his paper and scanned it. "Uh, state your business?" He looked at them anxiously.

"We're traveling," Sadie said. "Probably over to the west."

"The west, eh? Well, you're going the wrong way, aren't you?"

Sadie looked at Fenn, confused, and Fenn smiled.

"We're of the Ruud," Rogget said.

"Ah, our brothers of the Ruud. We were told much about your kind back home. Yes, yes, join us and tell us of this Ruud." He beckoned them to follow toward the encampment. "We hear you live amongst the beasts and have learned their magic."

"Really?" Grayson said. Then he turned to Fenn with a smile. "This could be interesting."

The guard led them into the small encampment where women set about their chores. Several large pots were hung over fires and they stood with sticks, stirring clothes in the hot soapy water. Some pulled pieces of clothing out and set them through

122

wringers, others took them and hung them on lines to dry in the cold air.

They all smiled at the visitors and said hellos.

"Found some travelers, eh, Wally?" a young woman said and winked at him.

"Where's Byn?" Wally asked.

She pointed behind her. "Cooking the rabbit."

Fenn could smell the stew and cider already. They approached a long house at the back of the encampment and entered. Three fire pits were lit down the middle of the rectangular hut and a woman sat at each, stirring. Around the fire pits were logs for sitting and along the sides of the house were tables for preparing meals and more logs.

Another woman stood over to the side at a long table with a short axe. She lifted it and brought it down quickly onto the thick wood table. Thwack!

"Madam Always," Wally called out and the woman with the axe turned the them. "Visitors from the Ruud." Wally's excitement beamed on his face.

"Come, come," the woman said and as they approached, she dipped her bloody hands into a pot of steaming water and wiped them on her apron.

"I'm Byn Always," she said. "Assistant to Dania Roths, head of the college."

"The college?" Sadie said.

"The Ruhm College of Women. Lena, would you be a dear and finish chopping the last bunny for the stew?"

Lena got up from the middle fire, smiled and bobbed her head. "Pleasure, madam." She seemed happy to take the axe and grab the skinned rabbit on the table. Thwack!

"This way." Byn ushered them over to the middle fire. "Sit,

we'll get you something warm to drink. This pot's full of cider."

She ladled hot cider into mugs and handed them around and joined them on the logs.

"Yes," she said. "We come from the the Kingdom of Ruhm. Dania was head of the college for women there; but we were forced out. Women in Ruhm these days are not able to learn beyond level nine. Do you have any schools for women in the Ruud?"

Sadie shook her head. "We don't have schools at all."

Byn tilted her head and her brow furrowed. "But how have you continued the path of the wissenry?"

Grayson frowned. "We have not."

"We just found out our first king was a wissende," Sadie said. "Had no idea."

Byn sighed. "That is a shame, truth be told. But perhaps we now have a calling, if the king of the Ruud would permit us to teach. I will bring it up with Dania when she returns; she may have questions for you. But she has gone with your King Welk to confront the eis."

"We've just come from there," Rogget said. "There was a battle, I'm afraid."

"Was it a good little skirmish?" She smiled unexpectedly. "We had a rider just an hour ago tell us they'd marched to the palace. We expect some losses."

"Why did they go to the ice realm?" Sadie asked and Byn looked at her with a frown.

"To show strength. The eis have been pestering us, saying we're on their land. But we do not plan to leave. We want an end to the bickering and the king of the Ruud organized a bit of a confrontation. He said it would solidify us in the eyes of the ice realm and they would either fight us, or leave us alone. I prefer

124

the latter. Leastwise, anyway, that's what Wally tells us. He took Dania overland to the meeting. Hard to say with Wally and all, though. Such as he is, the dear man."

"Why do you say, 'king of the Ruud,' like there's only one?" Fenn asked and looked around at them all. "Weren't the other kings involved?" His eyes fell on Rogget who was looking back at him as if he'd just discovered something.

"The skirmish with the eis unites the outlanders against the eis," Rogget said. "But it also unites them with Welk."

"Do you think he will try to unite the Ruud?" Grayson said.

Rogget nodded. "I'm not sure it's a bad idea, knowing of the Great West and all."

"What do you mean?" Sadie said.

"Welk isn't the first to try to make the Ruud into one kingdom and rule it for himself," Grayson said. "Alfred of Michelruud tried to do it ages ago. But he was betrayed by his wissende and killed by Prince John of Aaronland. And Alfred's wife, Osara, had John captured and beheaded as revenge. These thing rarely work out well."

"It might turn out better for Welk," Rogget said. "Think on it this way. If the ice realm and the winter folk recognize him as king, he's already got an advantage. They'll deal with him more and more and not with the others. And then, well, I hate to scare you all, but if Ruhm made a bid to overtake us—"

"You think they plan to do that?" Grayson said.

"We have no proof of it," Byn said. "Rumors, however." The woman's face went pale and her mouth fell open slightly. "If you'll excuse me." She bowed slightly and left them to the fire.

"I'll see what I can get for some hunting," Rogget said. "Then we can be on our way."

Fenn turned to watch Madam Always grab hold of a woman

at the front of the tent. They embraced and he was sure they were both crying.

Chapter Twenty-two

Leah first bristled at the contact, being pulled into a tight hug; such intimacy between unrelated folk was quite forbidden in Ruhm. But she missed her mother so deeply, and remembering fondly Madam Always' clean soapy scent, she relaxed and let herself be comforted.

Madam Always led her through the camp to a small fire outside her private tent, where Leah gladly accepted a mug of warm kaff, though her hands trembled so much it was difficult to drink. She sat on a thick stump at the fire while her old teacher from the Hass school back in Ruhm, looking surprisingly at home camping in the wilds of the east, stoked it and added another log.

She'd run as much as she could, but was forced to walk much of the way, through the first night and another, guided only by hope and the general direction Madam Roths had pointed out. And though she was flooded with relief upon seeing Madam Always and finding herself safe in her encampment, she still feared Kirche would send someone after her.

"I didn't know where else to go," she whispered. "I'm glad I've found you, but I cannot stay here."

"You must tell me what has happened. What brought you to the eastern continent?" Madam Always sat next to her on a thick log.

Leah set her mug on the ground at her feet and wiped tears from her face. "I am aide to Kirche now."

"Of course, the annual tour. But what happened? Do speak of it quickly, my dear; you're frightening me. Are you ill? Was your party attacked?"

She shook her head and new tears filled her eyes. "We were camped with the others. Welk of Michelruud called a meeting with what they call the winter folk, those of you who live here in the hills."

"Madam Roths was there."

Nodding, Leah said, "That is how I knew to find you here. Some time after they marched, I was freed."

"Freed from whom?"

"Kirche."

Madam sat back, her head tilted and a question on her lips, but she held quiet and waited. Leah thought over the last several weeks, wondering where she should start her story. She shuddered and let out a sob.

"I'm so ashamed. So ashamed."

"What could you have to be ashamed of, my dear?" Her voice was so kind, gentle, it only made Leah weep all the more.

"I was so happy to be named Aid to the High Preist of Hass. I thought you would be proud of me."

"I am, indeed. Quite an honor."

Now there was a tone in Madam Always' voice that Leah didn't quite recognize. Certainly she wasn't lying, but something else.

"I truly believed I wanted it." She wiped the tears from her

128

face, ashamed of them.

"Yes," Madam said, frowning. "You were always fond of Hass."

"I was enamored. But, oh, I'm so ashamed to say it."

"Leah Hallowsing, there is no shame in feelings, in truth, in owning up to our faults."

Leah flinched a bit. This was not the general practice in Ruhm. Blasphemous thoughts were to be kept to oneself, pushed deep and forgotten.

"You do not sound like a citizen of Ruhm," she said. "Not like my teacher."

Madam Always smiled and laid a hand atop Leah's. "But I'm not in Ruhm any longer, am I? Now, go on. What has you so troubled?"

"Oh, it's awful. I...I thought he liked me."

"Who?"

"Lord Kirche. I know, it's so stupid. I've behaved like a child."

"But you are still a child, my dear. Do not regret your innocence."

"Innocence, indeed! I was so wrong. Oh, Madam! Lord Kirche gave me a diary and told me to use it to parse my thoughts on...on..." Here Leah could not bring herself to tell Madam Always the truth about the kell stone. "And he stole it and read it. He read my most personal thoughts. Worse, he read what I wrote about my father. About something he told me, in confidence. Oh, how could I have been so stupid as to put down on paper such a secret? But I didn't know. I didn't realize what I was writing. And now Kirche has sent a message to Ruhm. My father will be arrested and he insists I—Madam it's too awful to say."

She waited, her hand giving Leah a patient pat.

"He wishes me to marry him."

Here Madam Always sat upright. "He what?"

"He believes a marriage between us will unite the Hass and its skeptics in Ruhm. He claims my father leads a contingent against Hass and once we are married...oh, I don't know. Madam, I am not meant for intrigue. I only know I was going to marry him because he told me Father would be tortured and hanged if I did not."

Madam Always was silent for several seconds before she whispered, "I'm so sorry, Leah."

"But the porters, Gretchen, Zelda...they say he will have Father hanged on Founding Day, before we return to Ruhm, whether I marry Kirche or not. They told me to run. And I did so." Leah broke into sobs. "I'm confused. I do not know if I have done the right thing."

Madam Always' body seemed to deflate, her face softened into deep concern and she shook her head.

"Never fear, Leah. Your father would not blame you."

"But it is my fault. I think I must get home. If I could get to him before Kirche's message..."

"Yes, of course you must try."

Leah stood suddenly. "I must go, then."

Madam Always pulled her to sitting again. "We will get you to a boat in time, I assure you. But the boat that could take Kirche's message does not arrive for days."

"How could you know?"

She smiled. "We have porters who barter with the captains; we send and receive news of Ruhm."

Leah sighed in relief. "Another boat, then."

"Leah, you can't get on just any boat and expect the captain to do your bidding."

130

"But he must."

Madam shook her head sadly. "I understand your pain, my dear."

"How could you?"

"Trust me. You have time. Try to relax a bit; we will get you home. But I have information that will help you to help your father."

"You do?"

"Indeed. Leah, you say your father told you some secrets. Did he tell you why he sent you to the Hass school?"

"What?" She waved a dismissive hand and sipped her kaff. "He said he wanted me to have a good education. And I wanted to go so badly."

"You were recruited, of course."

"Recruited?"

"Dania and your father needed a way to meet regularly without arousing suspicion. And so you were brought into the Hass school—against your parents' wishes. Your mother was staunchly against it. But your father realized it was the only way."

"The only way for what?"

"For Dania to have access to your father's library."

Leah shook her head in several tiny jerks and her eyes fluttered closed and opened. "What are you talking about?"

"There is a hidden cache of blasphemy at the stationer's. It was necessary to examine it, make copies of pertinent parts for distribution and—"

"Distribution of blasphemy?"

"Leah, you are young."

"Stop saying that. Stop calling me a child. I am the Aide to the High Preist of Hass."

"Are you now?"

"I mean..."

"You are a strong young woman. Strong enough to know the truth."

Madam Always hesitated and Leah watched the woman's eyes; they were kind, tender, sad. They were the same as her father's—burdened with knowledge that no one dared to learn. She nodded for her to continue.

"The Hass is a lie."

"A lie," Leah repeated.

"You thought Lord Kirche liked you? You were enamored of him? And now you see he is not as you thought he was. Good. Because Kirche represents all there is to the Hass. It's a pretty, vacuous lie."

"They are the keepers of the moral laws of Rett."

"Rett is a lie."

Leah's mouth fell open.

"It's true."

"I know," Leah said.

"Do you?"

She nodded and looked to the fire. "I saw the flaming tree of Rett, just like the one on which he was hanged and burned."

"Where?"

"There is a forest in the Ruud, where most of the beasts live. Deep within it, I saw the tree—I touched it; it was real. The story in *The Book of Rett* must be a lie. They did not all burn to ash."

"I would very much like to see that tree someday. Perhaps, when this has all come to fruition, you and I will travel there."

"Is everything a lie, then?"

"In *The Book of Rett*? No, of course not. There is just enough truth, just enough goodness, for the lies to pass, to be dismissed."

132

"Father knew this."

"Yes. And more proof is there, in the secret cache."

"And now Kirche knows about Daken's journal." She gasped and put a hand to her lips. "He was right about Father."

Madam nodded. "Your father will not tell them where it is; he will not give them the books that remain—for he and Dania have sent most away over the years. And he will not tell them where the kell stone is."

"You know about the stone? Of course you do."

"Yes."

"Does Father know where it is?"

"Dania told me your father has read the journal, yes. But she did not tell me what it said about the stone."

"Tell me everything you know."

Madam Always nodded and poured more kaff into their mugs. Leah first wanted to tell the woman to quiet down, whisper, but remembered they were not in Ruhm; there were no Hass spies here—no Hass to arrest them.

"Long ago," Madam Always began, "the wissendes were honored in Ruhm. They were discoverers, inventors, problem solvers. Our leadership looked to them for guidance. But the followers of Rett and his devotion were concerned over some of the changes in the land. Folk don't like change, in general, you know. And they have always been fearful of the beasts. Since we migrated from the south and encountered them, we've been trying to find ways to avoid them."

"There are few beasts in Ruhm."

"Now. But long ago, they were many. And the wissendes began to tell us their power was harmless to us as long as we lived in harmony with them."

"Why would anyone object to that?"

133

"Ah, because the beasts were stronger, smarter, faster. The folk wished to control them, as they had controlled the nonsentients on the southern continents, but they could not. So they clung to the ideas of Rett, as the newly emerging Hass extolled his virtues. The Hass told the folk the wissendes were liars. That their ideas about the folk being kin to the beast were vicious untruths."

"Kin to the beast?"

"The wissenry studied and learned and gathered evidence. The beast, they said, were not evil—not the product of Horatia any more than folk were the divine creation of Mutterede."

Leah's eyes widened.

"Yes, you see. Blasphemy. But it wasn't blasphemy so long ago. It was simply two competing world views: one of learning and discovery, and one of dominance and ignorance."

"But why would anyone choose ignorance?"

"To avoid change. To avoid fear."

"And so they banished the beasts and the wissendes."

"The beasts, yes. Once the kell stone was stolen from them, over time they were easier and easier to drive away. The wissendes were forced to recant their blasphemies and they continued for some time trying to work within the Hass to change things. But eventually, Michelruud sailed here to the east and the rest of us remained in darkness."

"But...Father, and Dania."

"Oh, yes. There remained always a small cadre of revolutionaries, determined to keep the truth safe. We have bided our time, secretly and smartly spreading our knowledge. The seeds of revolution are fomenting in Ruhm. Your father and Dania had a difference of opinion, I'm afraid. Dania fled before she was caught and I went with her. She tried to persuade your father to leave years ago, but he would not. He insisted on continuing there, goading the Hass into lighting the wick that will incite the revolution."

"What sort of wick?"

"Leah, sometimes it takes an act so vile, something so clearly wrong, to make the people finally wake up and take action."

"I don't understand."

Madam Always patted her hand again and smiled weakly. "I know."

Chapter Twenty-three

Where is Sorgood?"

Welk's voice was barely a rough whisper and when he coughed, sharp biting pain stabbed at his lungs. He'd allowed himself to be lifted onto a horse and led through the pass, but halted his party before they turned toward the encampments. Lucas' frail body, wrapped carefully in a blanket, lay draped over another horse, and when he was helped from his own, Welk took the reins and guided the steed northwest.

"Sorgood's run off, Sire," one of the young soldiers said.

"Footman Wolf, isn't it?"

"Yes, sir. Sire."

He tried to chuckle, but found his lungs had little enough in them for a sigh. "Here," he said, motioning to a spot on the grass where he dropped to his knees and let himself fall, lying with his face to the warm sun, the cold breezes of the ice realm wafting over him.

Clutch knelt beside him.

"I'm all right," Welk waved him away and forced himself to sit, grinding his jaw against the pain.

"Angel blade," one the folk said.

Welk nodded. He looked at those gathered with him. Clutch of the Wretched, several of Sorgood's men, a dozen soldiers wearing the colors of Arnot and Ricker. Good, he thought.

"Wolf," he said. The young guard stepped forward and knelt, bowing his head. "Who of Sorgood's men is loyal to me?"

The boy blustered. "Why, all of them, Sire."

"Who would choose me over Sorgood?"

Here the boy raised his face to Welk, his brow furrowed. He nodded slightly. "Not Lieutenant Drake, Sire. No. But Sergeant Cotton, yes."

"Very well. Wolf, you are to find Cotton. Tell him, with these soldiers here as your witness, that he is to arrest Sorgood for murder. Cotton is to take charge of the Michelruud guard." Welk forced a cough and winced in pain.

"Yes, Sire," Wolf said. "But sir, I saw that boy, the one with the mark. Will you set a party out to find him?"

"You will lead that party, Wolf, when the time comes."

The look on the young footman's face was nearly unbearable —pride and fear. Welk knew he must look pale as a linen sheet; he could feel the lack of blood in his own face. He struggled to regain some composure, to look alive and not of death.

"I'm taking young Lucas' body to the caverns just north. I'll need four men."

All but Footman Wolf stepped forward and Welk smiled. Suddenly, a jolt of energy surged through him and he pressed his shoulders back in a painful stretch. The wound would heal over and the pain subside, he knew, but the poison would work within him, over time, debilitating him. He'd heard tell of angel blades, stories spread by adventurers and hunters who dared travel into the ice for rare pelts and prizes.

138

He picked his four men and sent the rest on to the encampment with a promise to meet his guard in Michelruud as soon as he could. "We have done well in the ice, my allies. Tell of it when you reach your peers. The usurper queen is unseated and we must now pledge to help the maiden; she will forge a peace between the eis and the folk of the Ruud."

The small gathering raised a meager cheer.

"Go then. I will be home again soon and we will plan for Ruhm, if she dares to come."

Another cheer and the folk hesitated, and slowly by twos and threes, drifted toward the camp.

Clutch reached a hand to help Welk to his feet. "Why the caverns?"

"There is a bit of exposed kell there. Belfen told me of the ceremony, when there were no folk here in the east, the felidae often carried their dead to the kell. I will do for Frieden what Belfen and Vreni would have done."

"And what of the boy?"

Welk shrugged. "The angels will try to get him back, I think; he makes a fine pawn. I will take a new approach as soon as I've dealt with Frieden. Don't look at me so, Clutch. I can't bear it."

The rugged folk's face was softened, sad. "How long?"

Welk shook his head. "I could live for years."

"Or?"

Welk put a hand on his shoulder. "What would you do if I died today?"

Clutch flinched and took a step back. "I do not wish to contemplate it."

Welk chuckled, glad to be able to breathe freely once again, though there would always be pain now. "Perhaps you should begin to think on it."

Chapter Twenty-four

L eah went to Madam Always' tent before she was to meet the young folk and travel back to the Ruud with them. They all fled the ice realm, she was told, and were to get to Father Britt at Cold Sea. They seemed an odd assortment: a huntsman and three children. When she asked Madam Always whom they fled and why they'd been in the ice realm at all, Always smiled and said, "Your father and Dania would have differing opinions on that, as well." And she'd told Leah about the prophecy and King Welk chasing the boy all over the eastern continent. They both laughed over it and Leah confided in her that Kirche, too, was after the boy.

"He told King Welk that if he had the boy killed, he could turn his memory into a devotion and create something like the Hass out of it. Pren dismissed it; he said Kirche didn't mean to insinuate Rett was killed on purpose, just so a devotion to him could be used to give a moral law to the folk."

"Ah, and what do you make of that now?"

Leah had frowned and shook her head. "It seems a difficult thing to attempt. And I find myself wondering now, if Rett ever lived at all."

Madam Always smiled and held up a finger. "You are not alone in that suspicion. And you will find, I hope one day, your father's library holds the key to that question."

"But the boy," she'd said. "Welk couldn't seriously consider killing him?"

"So young to be so important," Madam Always said. "You must protect him. See that he gets back to the wissenry where he belongs."

"They sent him away."

"Indeed, and they'll likely do it again. Just help him get there and perhaps Britt can find you a boat."

Now, hesitating by the fire, hiding the kitchen knife behind her back, Leah gathered her wits and called for her former teacher.

"You must learn to call me Byn," the old woman said with a smile when she emerged from her tent.

"That, I think, is appropriate, considering what I am about to ask you to do for me."

"Why, what is it, dear? Why so grave?"

Leah showed her the knife.

"Who are you going to kill with that?"

"I should tell you of my meeting with an eis assassin recently."

"Oh?"

"I'm quite violent, as it turns out. But I mean no one harm. None but myself."

Madam Always crossed her arms at her chest. "Explain."

"I wish for you to cut off my hair."

The old woman gasped and put her hands to her mouth. "I could not."

"You must." She pulled her toward the fire and sat down on

142

the stump in front of her. "I will return to Ruhm, but I cannot be in the upper tier. I will be an ordinary girl, and go unnoticed." She held up the knife. "Cut it all."

And as the woman sawed away at her hair, Leah drew in a ragged breath and wiped the tears from her face. As soon as the long mane fell, a heaviness lifted from her, more than the weight of the hair, more even than the weight of her station. She had a plan—a vision. She would save her father, take him far from Ruhm, but beyond that, she must continue her father's work. She must find his library, the journal...and the kell stone, if for no other reason than to keep it from the Hass.

She met the young folk and curtseyed, trying out the greeting she never would have offered to someone below her in Ruhm. The three children were about twelve in age, she was told. Rugged, as most of the eastern folk were. Fenn had sharp, dark features against a pale face, hardened by experience, she thought. Grayson was dark, but in a softer way. His eyes hinted at intelligence more than heroism. And Sadie...she lifted her chin upon meeting Leah and looked suspiciously at her. But she smiled when Leah ruffled her own mop of newly shorn, curly hair.

"What do you think?" Leah asked her. "I need a woman's opinion."

This brought a laugh out of the girl and Leah relaxed. Even the huntsman Rogget didn't frighten her. He called her *ma'am* and *miss* at every opportunity and nodded his head as if she were a noblewoman and he, her servant.

They were off, and after some hours hiking, Grayson pounded his feet against the cold ground, and kicked at the browned grass of the plain, grumpy and tired. Occasionally he mumbled something sour and Sadie turned to Leah with a smile.

"You've been traveling long with these male folk?" she asked the girl.

"It's not so bad."

"Sadie's hardly a girl, really," Grayson said.

Leah gasped. "What a rude thing to say about a girl."

"I didn't mean... I mean. Sorry Miss Hallowsing," Grayson said.

"Call me Leah, please. I do not wish to be miss or madam any longer."

They all agreed, but she knew they'd be back to it soon enough.

"I only meant Sadie's not like some of the other girls in Path. She's strong and brave and doesn't bat her eyelashes at the older boys."

Leah laughed. "I think you'd be surprised at how many girls are strong and brave and just don't think you need to know it, until they're ready to show you."

Grayson blushed.

She enjoyed her new company so much more than that of Kirche and his party, though she missed them, she had to admit to herself. Gretchen's babbling would fit with the young folk moving from topic to topic without a care. Zelda would be able to mother Sadie; goodness knows the girl could use it—all them could, even Rogget. Xavier, though only a boy, was always quick with a joke. Leah felt a pang tug at her heart. She missed even Kipling and Redd. And Alphonse. She thought back on the last time she'd seen him, in Timber, at the edge of the beast forest, just before he was trampled.

"Are you all right?" Sadie said, wrapping a hand around Leah's elbow.

"I miss my folk, I suppose."

"But you ran from them," Grayson said. He blushed again.

144

"I'm sorry, Miss Hallowsing. I shouldn't tell tales."

"We heard it back at the camp. Is it true?" Sadie said.

"That I ran away? Yes. I'm afraid I'm in some trouble."

"So are we," Fenn told her.

"It's good that way," Sadie said. "We'll all understand one another."

"What sort of trouble are you in? I mean," Leah faltered. "Madam Always told me about the prophecy story. The king of Michelruud is after you. The angels, too."

"Do you suppose they still are?" Grayson said.

"Ard," Rogget said, "count on it."

"But why the angels?" Sadie said. "Fenn said Brenna was going to oust the usurper queen. She wouldn't send them after us."

"Brenna said they wanted the kell stone," Fenn said. "Maybe they think I can get it for them."

"I learned a lot about them angels while I was in the guard," Rogget said. "They're beautiful creatures and full of themselves over it. They spend a lot of time looking at their reflections. I know 'cause I saw one."

"You did?" Sadie said.

"Aye, I did. But don't tell anyone I said that. I was on a secret mission for King Evan and no one's supposed to know we went to them."

"What did you do? What was the mission?"

Rogget laughed. "I haven't the faintest clue. I was just a guard."

"I'm told angels are evil," Leah said. "But none too bright."

"But they seduced the queen," Fenn said, "or Brenna's aunt. Don't you need smarts to do that?"

"Well, that's their danger really," Rogget said. "They know

how to charm you. They make you feel so good you do whatever they want you to do willingly."

"That's scary," Sadie said.

"Aye. We'll keep our eyes open. You especially Fenn."

Leah sighed and shifted her pack; it was heavy and growing heavier. The women's college sent them off with bedrolls and enough food and water for the journey straight across the Plains of Glisch, through Damon Wall to the port. The ground was flat at least; to her right she could see the hills sloping gently higher and higher toward the mountains. She expected to see horses riding toward them, and Kirche's mitre glistening against the muted autumn sun, and the thought had her always searching for a place to hide. The grass on the plain was knee-high in some spots and she wanted to crouch down in it and crawl her way to the Ruud; though there were small, brief bits of wood on the plain, she wouldn't feel safe until she was in the forest of Damon Wall.

On the second day, in the afternoon, they approached a small encampment of a half dozen tents surrounding a fire pit. A cheerful folk called out to them, "Salutations!" He waved his arm back and forth above his head.

"What's he saying?" Sadie said.

"It's like hello is all," Grayson said.

Gray smoke from the fire swirled toward the sky, and as they neared they smelled roasting meat, kaff, and cider. The folk who'd waved at them was short and round with black hair cropped closely except for long strands falling over his forehead. He smiled broadly when they met him just outside the circle of tents.

"Welcome unwonted viators." He took Rogget's hand and pumped it up and down. "You have no rantipoles along, I assume?"

146

Rogget sucked in a breath prepared to respond, but stared at the beaming folk with a curious look until he let his breath out without replying. Leah stifled a laugh.

"Did he say he didn't want us here?" Grayson whispered.

Leah shook her head. "I can't say for certain, but he doesn't act like it."

The folk rubbed his large belly, looked at the kids and shook his head. "Ah, well, we'll submit to providence then. Come, come. Join us. I am Walter, a bona fide philosopher. Here you will meet my brother Ned, a philosophaster. But don't speak of it. And we also have Sir John; you'll find him full to the brim with gasconade and I do say I often suspect him of being something of a footpad. So, you will be careful, won't you? But come, come."

Rogget gave Leah a worried look, and she shrugged and shook her head.

"Can't you translate what he's saying?" Fenn asked Grayson. He turned to Leah, "Grayson reads a lot."

"I see," she said with a smile.

Grayson shook his head. "There aren't many language books at the stationer's."

They followed the folk to the fire where two others sat on logs drinking out of tin mugs.

"Viators," he said to his fellows and they waved hellos.

"Salutations, I'm sure," the oldest man said, his hair gray and his face lined.

"This is Sir John," Walter told them. "And here, my brother Ned."

"Good afternoon," Sadie said with a slight curtsy.

Leah followed her lead while the boys, shuffling their feet, bowed slightly. Rogget merely grumbled.

"She's in fine fettle, I dare say," Sir John said looking Sadie over. "And you've brought us a hobbledehoy as well," he said turning to Fenn.

"I'm a what?" Fenn said.

Grayson nudged him sharply in the ribs and gave him a scornful look.

"Join us, join us," Walter said showing them to a few logs at the fire.

They all removed their packs. Sadie, Grayson, and Fenn sat on one log and Rogget labored to the ground beside it, while Leah took a short log next to him. Ned handed them mugs filled with steaming hot cider and Leah grasped hers with both her palms, warming them, and breathed in the wonderful smell. Rogget had kaff and the strong odor competed with the delicate fruity smell of her cider. She turned to see young Fenn with his nose in his mug. She smiled at him.

"I don't like the smell of bitters," he said. "It's mucking up my cider."

She laughed. "I quite agree, though I don't mind the smell of kaff."

"Tis quite hiemal, this land, is it now?" Sir John said to Rogget.

"Aye," Rogget muttered.

"We're immigrants ourselves. We flee a kakistocracy, seeking eunomy. Have you much illth in the area?"

"Uh," Rogget looked to Leah and she raised her shoulders, wide-eyed, helpless to suggest a response. "Er..."

But no matter; Sir John went on talking. "We locomote from afar to seek out our brethren. They denominate themselves Breathless."

"Oh, no, Sir John," Walter broke in, "they write that they are designated Breathless by the querimonious ruddy folk hereabouts. We can't imagine why."

148

"Nonetheless our brethren have adopted the moniker. Have you heard of them? We will felicitate them on their success in this land, to be sure. It is said they have garnered much. We do not at all suspect them of improbity, I dare say. No, no, we do not."

"There is much improbity in our mother land," Ned said.

"Indeed, indeed." Sir John nodded. "Such ipsedixitism, such hypermimia, such farrago, and pseudodox all about."

"Stop, Sir John," Walter said. "You're infecting me with horripilation."

"Oh, don't be such a mythomane."

Walter turned to the kids and said, "From whence do you roam? Tell us of your interests."

They stared at him for a moment, until Grayson, as if in a daze, said, "My da owns the inn."

Sir John gasped. "Do tell us all about it. You must, then, be quite expert in xenodocheionology. Why Ned here claims such knowledge, but he's all bluster and polylogy."

Ned snorted. "Least I don't brabble grandiloquence."

"Do you attempt to fustigate me, young Ned? I dare say your fetor and ozostomia do nothing to recommend you to our vulgus guests."

"Is that it, now?" Ned said. "You must resort to ad hominem attacks? Your logorrhea isn't enough?"

"I dare say!"

"Now, now," Walter said. "Let's not engage in ruction in front of our hebetudenous guests."

"Jackanapes," Ned said.

"Pygalgia," Sir John said.

Slowly, and with much grunting and gasping, Sir John and Ned stood, and began to swat at each other. Sadie gasped, but

Grayson chuckled. Fenn looked at Rogget who just stared at the folk, confused. Leah put a hand to her mouth to keep from laughing aloud.

Walter tried to wedge himself between the two fighters, squeaking, "You're both grobians. Abdominous, amentiatic, anserine, blatherskites."

Finally, all three men stood apart and breathed heavily for a long moment.

"I dare say," Sir John said to Walter, "that was quite unnecessary."

"You have become rather incondite of late, Sir John," Walter said, returning carefully to his log. He looked at his guests and said, "Just a velitation, my comrades. Nothing serious; do drink up." And he looked over to Sir John.

"Indeed," Sir John said.

"Uh..." Ned said.

Sir John spluttered, "My friend, you have lapsed into monepic utterings."

"I believe, I mean, I daresay, I see something of an ursiform in the distance."

Walter laughed. "Ursiform? Don't be duncical." To Rogget, he said, "You don't have bears about, do you?"

Just as Rogget turned, Sir John fell backward to the ground in trying to jump up, and screeched in a high-pitched voice from where he lay, "Bear!"

"Ah, I think we'll be going now," Rogget said, standing. "We've enjoyed your hospitality and the bitters."

Leah caught sight of a bear loping toward them from the north. She recalled the two bears at Wiley Arbus' camp and wondered if one had escaped.

"But the bear," Walter said, beginning to sweat and ignoring

John on the ground.

"It's only Darnit; he's nothing to worry about," Rogget said. "He won't come near your camp."

Walter wiped his forehead with his sleeve. "I daresay I was clamoring for additional engrossing conversation, especially as relates to the boy's expertise in xenodocheionology, but I'm afraid our trio is quite ursaphobic."

"Do they have bears where you come from?" Grayson asked.

Ned, who hadn't moved, but kept his wide gaze glued to Darnit, now pacing in the distance, said, "Indeed. Godless execution machines. They're soulless, I tell you. No souls!"

"Ah, yes. As I said. We thank you for your hospitality. But..."

"Yes, yes," Walter said. "I agree it would be for the best. Could you take the bear very, very far away?"

"Of course," Rogget said. He walked around the circle and held out a hand to Sir John, still lying on the ground. "Let me help you up."

Sir John whispered, "No, no. His visual acuity is motion sensitive. If I just lie here I'll be fine. Pretend you don't see me. Move along. Move along."

Leah, having lost control, laughed out loud and turned from the sight so as not to embarrass herself further. Rogget, too, let out a laugh and a loud roar escaped Darnit. Startled, Leah watched the bear, now standing, his back to the group. Looking beyond him, in the distance, against the mountains, she saw a glow.

"What is that?"

"Angels," Fenn said, standing and moving to her side.

Darnit lay on the ground and curled up as the angels flew over him toward the tents, their great white wings flapping easily in the air. There were three—glowing a pale subtle blue, wearing loose, stark white gowns shimmering in the sunlight, so long it looked as if they had no feet and could not walk on the ground. And they were singing.

"I'd forgotten how beautiful they are," Sadie said. Her face lit up and she smiled, walking toward them.

"No—" Fenn grabbed her arm—"Don't go near them."

Leah felt Fenn's other hand on her elbow.

"They won't hurt us," Rogget said.

"Are you crazy?" Fenn said.

But Rogget's face was also bright with a smile.

Fenn turned to Grayson. "You're not going to get all angel mushy are you?"

"No." He smiled. "But they do sing nicely, don't they? Let's have these folk offer them some bitters or something."

"You can't offer them bitters. They're here to catch us again, or worse, take us into the ice mountains and leave us there."

"Well, I daresay," Walter said, coming forward. "I do not believe I have ever witnessed such a luminous display. Angels, you say?"

"They're dangerous," Fenn said.

Leah watched them, her heart rising to rejoice, to sing their song. Their faces, pale and sharp, reminded her of the carved heads of the premiers of Ruhm on the Hall of Hass. Like gods. But sensing their deception, she winced against the desire to follow them. Though Sadie, Grayson, and Rogget, she realized, were falling quite in love with the creatures.

"They're evil," Leah said. "Get down."

"Oh, now that's harsh," Rogget said.

"But don't you remember what Wiley told us?" Fenn said. "Don't you remember when they took us and left us in the tower?"

"What is that refrain they're singing?" Sir John said, rolling this

152

way and that on the ground trying to get up.

"Stop listening!" Fenn said.

Just as Sir John was on his knees ready to stand, the angels dove toward the campsite. Leah felt a smile tugging at the corners of her mouth and warmth floated up from her feet.

"Stop!" Fenn screamed.

She jerked awake and turned to him. "We should look away," she said.

Walter, Sir John, and Ned held out their arms and began twirling.

"Positively gleeful," Ned said.

"I daresay," said Sir John, "I've lost all fright of the bear."

The Breathless folk stopped spinning and walked toward one of the angels; Ned shouted up at him, "Shall we go with you? Will you take us away?"

Leah, unable to keep from looking at them, watched as a luminous young male floated down to the huntsman. Rogget merely stood before it, as if waiting to be carried off. The angel slipped its hands under his arms and picked the man off the ground as if he were weightless.

"Don't," Fenn said, grasping Rogget's leg as he floated away.

Rogget looked down at him and smiled. "Maybe if you use the fire," he said with a laugh, "you could scare them away."

Leah was awash with confusion—the desire to run, a yearning to leave with the angels, to fly, but more, wanting to protect the children. She grabbed for Fenn and dug her heels into the ground as she and the boy were pulled along with Rogget.

"Sir John," Leah called. "Take the children."

The three men paused, watching her hang on to Fenn by his waist while trying to keep Sadie and Grayson from the other two angels hovering over them. Then, as if she'd poked them with an iron from the fire, the men leapt forward, grabbed Sadie and Grayson, pushed them to the ground and fell atop them; there they remained huddled.

"Stop!" Fenn screamed.

He was lifted off the ground and Leah pulled hard, forcing the boy to let go of Rogget. Together they fell backward to the grass.

"No," Fenn cried, watching his friend being carried away.

The other two angels came for them, but Fenn dodged them, ran to the fire pit and threw his hands at the flames as if batting them away. Leah ran from the flying creatures, crouched low with the Breathless, and watched the boy swat at the fire, again and again, until he cried out in frustration. Finally, he swooped his hands deep, nearly to the burning logs, and with a great audible whoosh, flames flew in a torrent like a wave at the two angels hovering above their camp. Their soothing song erupted into screeches.

"Make it stop," Sadie called.

Fenn threw his hands at the fire again, swinging his arms in a circle, sending flames into the air. One angel twirled toward the sky, screaming, batting at his gown. Fenn attacked the fire again and again until finally, the last angel rose into the sky in a cloud of blue smoke. They both soared away, their angry cries ringing out across the plain.

Leah struggled to stand and made her way to the boy, now lying on the ground, gasping for air, trembling.

"Rogget," he said.

The Breathless folk stood and helped Sadie and Grayson to their feet where they watched Rogget, in the angel's arms, far in the distance.

"I daresay," Ned said, "the pennate beast is removing your

154

compatriot to the sea."

Fenn stood, shakily, watching Darnit race toward Rogget and the angel. Seething with rage, he ran, too, reached his hand toward the sky and shouted, "Let him go!"

The angel stumbled in the air, dropping toward the ground.

"Now," Fenn ordered.

Rogget fell from the angel's grasp onto Darnit and they both tumbled to the ground. The three angels hovered in the distance while the huntsman and the bear hobbled back to the tents. Leah moved to stand next to Fenn and put a hand on his shoulder.

"Leave us alone," he said.

The angels shrieked, turned, and soared northeastward toward the mountains.

"The sooner we get you to Father Britt," Leah said, "the better for all of us."

Chapter Twenty-five

Fenn trudged forward, across the grassy field overlooking Cold Sea Port, toward the wissenry on the hill. He followed behind Sadie, pulled by Grayson who had tight hold on her hand. Her head was bowed and she stumbled often; Fenn reached out and lifted her back to her feet a few times without thinking.

"We'll sleep when we get there," Grayson told her again and again.

Darnit grumbled as he was set off into the woods behind the wissenry. Rogget yawned and nearly lost his balance. Leah Hallowsing had kept them going—the whole time—herding them like dazed sheep, telling them they mustn't stop, must keep walking, must get to safety.

"Come on," Grayson would say every few minutes and pull harder at Sadie. There was fear in his eyes—a fear Fenn didn't recognize. Not the fear of the beast forest, or the beast lord. Not the fear of the Wretched. Not of the battle in the ice realm or the angels.

It's me, he told himself. They're afraid of me.

Fenn remembered eating, but there lingered a nagging emptiness in his middle that made him want to vomit. His legs shook and his hands trembled as they walked up the steps to the back door and he knocked. The smell of roasted chicken wafted out a window to his nose and he reeled and almost lost balance completely. Sadie sank onto the first step and Grayson knocked again. Finally the door opened and Fenn was sure he fell asleep where he stood.

When he woke, Fenn found himself in the hidden rooms below the wissenry, in the same bed he'd slept in weeks before when they'd come to Father Britt for help. Sadie was in her bed, pale, but sleeping. Grayson sat at the table eating, slowly, as if he didn't enjoy it. Fenn sat up, put his feet to the floor and rubbed at his eyes.

"Where's Leah?"

Grayson shrugged and held out a biscuit. Fenn went to the table and accepted it; sitting, he sliced it in half and slathered butter on it, topped it with honey. He took a bite and closed his eyes. How long had it been since he'd had a fresh-baked biscuit? Sadie sat up, her brown hair twisted atop her head. She tried to smile but only half made it, before she yawned. Father Britt knocked at the door and smiled at them as he took a seat on Grayson's bed.

"Well, now," he said, slapping his knees with his hands, "tell me."

"We went out to the hill country," Grayson said. "Fenn told us he was to go to the ice realm, but he wanted to find out about his mother." He turned to Fenn and offered a bit of a smile. Fenn nodded to him, letting him know it was okay. Better *he* tell it. Father Britt was less likely to scold him. "So we went over to the wasteland. He found his mother's nurse, but she wasn't much help. Then Fenn was caught by the Wretched and they tried to give him over to King Welk."

Father Britt nodded. "I know all of that."

"You do?" Fenn said.

"Some I heard from Treacher—still wandering about in disguise teasing out the folk's whim with regard to you. The rest in the hill country where I traveled to join the league of folk organizing against the ice realm. There was much talk of your exploits there. While you are feared and hated here in the Ruud, you're all quite celebrated in the hills."

"You were with King Welk," Fenn whispered. "So, you know about Lucas."

Father nodded again and Fenn was relieved that at least that much of the story would not have to be told.

"What happened after you escaped the battle at the palace?"

"We first went to an encampment south," Grayson said. "We weren't sure what we should do, I think. We met up with Miss Hallowsing; she's going back to Ruhm. We all crossed the Plains of Glisch but were attacked by angels. Fenn cast fire at them. It was amazing."

"How did you do it?" Father Britt asked.

Fenn whispered, "Rogget told me to throw fire at them. So I just did it."

Father Britt smiled. Fenn balled his fists tight. There was nothing in the wissende's face hinting at sorrow for the loss of Lucas. Was this the demeanor expected of a wissende? It couldn't be, he thought. Father Treacher wouldn't be so callous; he'd let his emotions show—Father Treacher had a heart.

"We have reports," Britt said, "that the angels are furious. The usurper queen was taken prisoner. One of their own was on the side of the maiden and carried her aunt into the mountains; we are told she was left there to die."

"That's awful," Sadie said. She wrapped herself in a robe Tom had given her when they arrived, made her way to the small table against the wall and took a chair.

"It may not be true," Father Britt said. "And even so, it would be better than a public execution. But it is true enough that after the skirmish at the palace, there has been a great increase in the number of attacks on the people of the hill country. Many dozens have been carried off."

"So they weren't after me," Fenn said.

"It seems not."

"What about King Welk? I saw an angel stab him with a weird knife. Is he...is he alive?"

Father Britt sighed.

"The king is all right," Grayson said, as if saying it would make it so. "And he knows Fenn isn't the bairn of prophecy."

"Is it all over, Father?" Sadie said. "Can we go home?"

"I wish I could send you all away and not have to tell you what I know, but, alas, I cannot. My heart will not allow it."

"What is it?" Sadie said, worry on her face.

Britt slapped his hands on his knees once again and said, "Very well, I will out with it. We don't know where Welk has gone or if he lives; he's disappeared. Some of his guard approached Sorgood in Michelruud, attempting to take control, but Sorgood overcame them, had them hanged as traitors."

"What?" Grayson said.

"Aye, it is a gruesome business. There hasn't been a hanging in the Ruud for nigh on to two decades. I'm afraid there is more. Your parents were guests in Michelruud castle, we are told, but are now in the jailhouse. Sorgood has sent out a missive saying they, too, will be hanged, unless Fenn gives himself up."

Father Britt paused, as if waiting for them to speak, to ask questions, to sob. But they all sat very still. Fenn looked at Sadie and Grayson, but they wouldn't meet his gaze.

Finally Grayson nodded and said, "We won't let him have Fenn."

"Very well. Now that the wasteland has been emptied of those who wished to return home, we think it best you all make your way there. We can secret you back into the hills with Rogget."

"What about the kell stone?" Fenn asked him.

"The stone is not your problem."

"Isn't it? Father Treacher told me when he first sent me away...he said no matter what, I shouldn't go looking for it."

"Because of the prophecy," Grayson said.

"I don't think so," Fenn said. "Tell us the truth, Father."

"I'm not sure I know what the truth is."

"Try."

Britt sighed again and rubbed his hands through his short hair, leaving it sticking up wildly around his head. "A wise young folk told me recently that I could understand much if I took the time to read my own books. I've read more in these last weeks than I have in all my life, I'm willing to say. And I've learned much. But, alas, I've gained more questions in the process."

"You mean, you hadn't read all of the books before?" Fenn said, surprised.

Father shook his head. "Some. Bits and pieces. But not all. The wissenry is something of a brotherhood, you see. Our traditions and knowledge are passed along one to another; it's in the books, to be sure...as we are told. But it never seemed necessary to read it for ourselves."

"What did you learn?"

He gazed at the wall behind them as if he saw something far in the distance and wished to touch it. "I learned that folk are cruel and small." He turned to Fenn. "I learned that we have wronged our brothers. But knowing everything I know now, I still cannot say it would be wise to return the kell stone to the beast folk."

"Why not?" Sadie said.

"We are too entrenched here. Our lives are here. With the stone in their midst, the beast would rise once again—their power doubled, tripled."

"What power?" Fenn said.

"Strength, life span, intelligence. They would continue the path of evolution on which they were so speedily racing along. They would oust us."

"You don't know that for sure."

"Would we want to live here among such powerful creatures?"

"You mean...creatures we treated so badly?" Grayson said. "I read about it. I know. We tortured them, murdered them, forced them off their land."

"And where would you have read such a thing?"

"That's not important," Fenn said.

"No, it's okay," Grayson said. "I read some of *The Book of Katze*."

Father Britt's eyes widened. "You what?"

"I did. And if we ever get out of this mess, I'm going to read the rest of it. Everybody should know the truth of what we did."

"And you think knowing that, the folk of the Ruud would allow the kell stone returned to the beasts?"

"They have no choice," Fenn said.

"Indeed, they do."

Fenn's jaw hardened and he fought to keep himself from grinding his teeth. "You know where the kell stone is, don't you?"

Britt sputtered. "I told you it was not your concern."

"How can it not be?"

"If I knew where it was, I certainly would not tell you. No. Your part in this story is done. You will take to the wasteland, or farther north. Stay out of Sorgood's way and let us deal with this mess."

"You know I can't do that."

Britt shook his head and closed his eyes. "Very well, hear this: we have found out where it might be"—he held up his hand to dissuade interruption—"but we do not know for certain. And we have learned there might be a way to destroy it."

"Destroy it?" Fenn said.

"The wissenry has decided this is the best course of action. We are searching now for a suitable candidate to travel to—to its place of hiding. We will secure it, and see to its demise. Surely you understand it would be unwise to give the beast folk enough power to bring us ruin."

Sadie and Grayson turned to Fenn. He hesitated, holding Britt's gaze, then nodded. "Give us a day or two here, to rest," Fenn said. "We'll go north and let the wissenry handle this."

Father Britt seemed to deflate; he let out a nervous chuckle. "Wise, my boy. You will indeed make a fine wissende one day. And you'll see—when this is all done and told, you three will be welcomed home and this sordid ordeal will be put behind us." He clapped his hands together and pulled them each into a jolly hug before leaving them to rest.

"Back to the wasteland?" Sadie said.

"Maybe," he said. "Let's think about it."

"Aren't you mad at him?" Grayson said. "They keep sending you away. Are they protecting *you*, or themselves?"

"I am angry, yes. But it won't do any good to express that to Britt."

Chapter Twenty-six

When the boy found her room, Leah was putting the last of her few things in the pack Madam Always had given her. An apple, two pieces of jerky, a locket of her own hair, bound in a length of blue ribbon. "For your mother," Madam had said.

"I saw you before," the boy said, standing in the doorway.

She sat at her small table and invited him to take the chair opposite. The hidden rooms in the wissenry were dark, chilly, but comfortable. She was grateful for Britt's hospitality, and sorry to have to sneak away, but the less he and Tom knew of her whereabouts the better for them, she reasoned.

"I think you'd only just arrived," Fenn said. "You were with the Hass. Grayson told me he recognized the flaming tree symbol one of you wore on a chain."

She nodded.

"You passed us on the street and looked back. Your hair was very long then."

"I don't recall," she said. "But my arrival here was rather exciting; much of it is a blur in my memory."

"Why did you cut it?"

She tilted her head at him; it seemed an odd question. "In Ruhm, only those of a higher station may wear their hair long."

"So, it's almost like a disguise."

"Yes." She smiled.

"Is the Hass after the kell stone?"

She chuckled. "That was rather abrupt, was it not?"

"No sense wandering down side roads. Father Britt doesn't want it returned to the beast folk."

"I would imagine not."

"He says the folk of the Ruud would agree."

"But you think differently?"

He turned to look around her room, hesitating. "I don't know what to think. Except, if I found the stone—if I gave it to King Arnot or King Ricker, or maybe...destroyed it—everybody would stop chasing me, stop thinking I'm going to do something awful with it. The kings of the Ruud would oust Sorgood from Michelruud and I could go back to the wissenry in Path. Sadie and Grayson could go home."

"But what of King Welk?"

He turned to look at her and his dark eyes reminded her of someone she couldn't place. She'd seen those eyes before, she was sure; but they were playful where his were filled with worry.

"You didn't know?"

She shook her head, fearful now of what he would say.

"He was stabbed by an angel; I saw it myself."

"Madam Always told me you fled the ice realm; she didn't say you were in the battle."

"I was," he said. "I saw Welk stabbed, just after Sorgood shot Lucas. They say—"

"Lucas? Shot?"

166

"Did you know him? He was my brother...at the wissenry in Path."

Leah could feel her face pale and she swallowed.

"He's dead," Fenn said. "And Welk has disappeared, probably dead, too. Sorgood took over Michelruud. You see, if I can get the stone, give it to King Arnot, say—"

"Or destroy it."

"Exactly. Sorgood would be ousted, if not by the other kings, then by the folk of Michelruud. They're only allowing all of this because of their fear of the prophecy and the stone; I'm sure of it."

"But if you destroy the stone, how would they know? Would they trust your word?"

Here he flinched, barely visible, and he suddenly looked less a child and more a...again, she couldn't quite place his eyes. He has cunning in him, she thought.

"That is a concern," he said. "Maybe I can bring it to them in pieces, or melted down, or..."

"How do you intend to find it?"

The boy got up from his chair and went to her doorway. Peering out, he looked this way and that, returned to the table and whispered, "I snuck into Father Britt's room this morning while he was at the port. He's been reading; he told me so, and all the most important books were lying open on his desk. It was easy enough to find the book with the location of the stone in it."

"What book?" Her heart sped at the thought that Daken's journal could be here in the Ruud.

"It was a book of wissenry interviews and biographies."

"I see." She let herself breathe with relief. "And what did you find out?"

He leaned back in his chair. "How do I know you aren't with the Hass any longer?"

Leah tried not to smile; patronizing the boy would be cruel, sure enough, but also inappropriate. After what she'd seen of him at the Breathless camp, the way he threw fire at the angels and commanded them, she knew he was at least split folk, if not an eis. How much should she tell him? And should she tell him about Lucas? Was Lucas' identity a secret? It must be; if the boy lived with him at the Path wissenry and yet, didn't know, then it was not her story to tell. It was a shame; she could see how saddened he was by the loss. Nonetheless, there was much she *could* reveal.

After offering the boy a mug of cider, Leah told him of her travels with Kirche, of his cruelty to the brownies, to all the beast folk. And she told him, candidly, of Dakenruud's journal.

"That's as much as I found out," he said. "In Britt's book, several wissendes speak of a journal that can be found at the stationer's in Ruhm. The location of the kell stone is in there. Is that why you're going back?"

"No. I only ever wanted the stone to prove my loyalty to the Hass. My only concern now is my father. Kirche plans to have him killed."

"Because of the journal?"

She nodded. "I'm leaving now," she said. "Or I was until you came to see me."

He peered at her, as if he were trying to read her thoughts. He leaned forward, over the table and reached his hand across it, almost to her arm. "May I touch you?" he said.

A bit frightened, Leah nodded and he put his hand atop hers. His was warm and pulsed slightly. She looked up at him but his eyes were closed. After a few seconds he removed his hand and opened his eyes.

"What is it?" she said. "What did you do?"

He smiled timidly. "Apparently, I'm part eis; many of them have the power of touch."

"And what did you learn of me?"

"That you're honest, caring, frightened. Worried."

She sighed a ragged breath. "That I am."

"You have a boat?"

"No. But I know someone I could ask."

"Not someone from Ruhm?"

She shook her head. "A young woman at one of the inns in the port."

"Can I come with you?"

"You're determined to destroy it?"

He shrugged. "Not completely, no. But I'm going to find it."

"Very well, then. You'll have to hurry."

Fenn hid in the bathroom while Leah invited Sadie and Grayson to visit her room. She felt silly, showing them nothing. Her room was the same as theirs. Just as empty, just as ordinary. Nonetheless, she feigned excitement, telling them they could visit one another while they stayed there at the wissenry. When she imagined Fenn had enough time to pack up his things and sneak out of the hidden rooms, she yawned and said she must nap, shooing them out. Then she tied the top of her knapsack and snuck quietly up through the cellar, pilfering a few more apples on her way, into the main rooms, and out the front door, marveling at how easily she could engage in stealing, as well as lying.

She found Fenn waiting just down the hill and together they walked the long, steep path into the port and to the Snapping Turtle Inn.

169

Chapter Twenty-seven

It was dark when they went to board *Tansey's Sorrow*. They wouldn't sail until just before dawn, but Leah insisted they were safer on the boat than at the inn. Just as Fenn stepped on the gangplank, he felt a twinge of guilt at leaving the others behind. And just as that twinge welled up in his chest and threatened to become a sob, he heard Sadie's voice behind him.

"I can't believe you thought you could leave us behind."

"We had a pact," Grayson said, walking past him and onto the boat. "You know what a pact is, right?"

"What are you three doing here?"

"Leah sent Wanda for us," Rogget said. "Wanda said Captain Olgut promised there'd be plenty of room, if we're willing to work our passage."

Fenn hopped off the plank to the deck and caught Leah smiling at him. "But...Father Britt?"

"Wanda was clever," Grayson said. "She told him Leah had forgotten a message for us. Britt had us come up to the main floor—didn't want to give away the hidden rooms, I suppose."

"And she told him," Sadie said, "'Why Father, it's private,' so he had to leave us alone with her."

"Oh, he was listening from the hallway," Rogget said.

Sadie laughed. "He didn't hear a thing."

"Does he know you're gone?"

"Not yet," Grayson said. "We just snuck out a bit ago."

Sadie, Grayson, and Fenn had a small cubby in the hold, as Olgut said they would not be allowed with the sailors like Rogget was; there was plenty of room as he'd sold his lot at port. The captain was a tinker by trade, carrying whatever goods he thought profitable, and legal, from Ruhm to the Ruud. They were grateful to have a spot of their own after they met the crew—a rowdy bunch, but eager to be polite. Their chores were easy enough: laundry, helping out in the mess, swabbing decks, cleaning Olgut's cabin, and telling stories of the Ruud and Ruhm. Olgut gave Leah his own cabin, insisting he enjoyed sleeping out on deck.

The first night in their cubby, when Leah was on deck watching the darkness, as she put it, and Rogget snored away down below, Grayson said, "What's the plan, then? Why Ruhm instead of north?"

"I want to find the kell stone," Fenn said. "I want this to be over."

"But Britt said—"

"I don't trust him, nor the wissenry."

"Why would he lie?"

"I'm not saying he lied. I looked at his books. It's true; they know a place to look for the stone and they had some ideas about how to destroy it. But I have to do it myself."

Sadie shook her head. "I understand we've done great things, Fenn," she said. "We rescued the children of Path from Steingefan and saw the beast lord. We fought the Wretched and...I even held a firearm on a king. But finding the kell stone and destroying it?
172

Shouldn't we leave that to the adult folk?"

"But that's just it. It's the adult folk who started all this. Think of it. A wissende—not the sort in the Ruud, but a real wissende from the old days in Ruhm, when they were folk of logic and reason—he couldn't bring himself to give the stone to the beast folk. And now we should trust them?"

"But you're not planning to give it back, are you?"

"No, I didn't mean that. It's just...I won't be free of this unless I know for myself. I have to be the one to do it."

Grayson nodded. "But, folk have been looking for the kell stone for centuries; what makes you think we can find it?"

"I think they've only just started looking. The beast folk have looked longer, sure, but you said they've been weakened without it; they can't search for it without risking folk catching and killing them."

Grayson's frown cast a clownish shadow on his face in the lantern light, rocking slightly with the boat. "It looks as if you're doing what the prophecy said you'd do."

"I don't believe in prophecy. And anyway, I'm not going to destroy the Ruud. It's my home."

He watched them both carefully as they tried to avoid his gaze.

"Well," Grayson mumbled. "We made the pact. We stick together."

"You could have gone home," Fenn said. "Is the pact more important than your folks?"

"If we went to Path without you," Sadie said, "Sorgood wouldn't believe we didn't know where you were; we'd be put in jail, too. And my mother would be angry with me."

"It's true enough," Grayson said. "As much trouble as we've caused our folk, they'd want us safe, and as far from the Ruud as we can get."

Fenn's heart sank just a little and he felt as if he'd lost something. They'd come along, really, because they had nowhere else to go. "Well, I'm glad you came," he said, not sure he believed it himself.

Chapter Twenty-eight

Welk allowed Krup to carry Lucas' body into the caverns in the north, far beyond the Plain of Nergens — where he felt the spirit of Rue-Anna calling with each gust of wind—over the field of lilac clover, and through the northern forests. He would not allow Clutch to join them; the man had too much to do—the folk of the hill country had a lot to consider. And so Clutch sent along Krup, his stoutest man, in his stead. And it was Krup whom Welk had chosen to enter the caverns with him, for as he traveled farther from the Ruud, as his fears for Lucas grew, he felt less kinship with the soldiers of his guard and more for Clutch, and any folk he trusted.

Every time he was forced by the wound on his back, just at his left shoulder, to stop and rest, Welk watched Krup pull Lucas from over his shoulder, cradle the young felid in his arms, and lay him gently on the rocky floor before kneeling behind Welk and checking his bandages.

"Something about you surprises me," Welk found himself saying, his hollow voice echoing in the chamber.

Krup lit Welk's lantern and set it in front of him. "What's

that, sir?"

"You suffer from a deplorable lack of curiosity."

"Do I?"

"Don't you?"

"Clutch tells me to go with the king of Michelruud, I go." The man wiped his face and stroked his beard, pulling at a knot. "The king of Michelruud tells me to carry a body into the caverns, I carry."

"And you care not why?"

"I think I know why."

"Tell me, then."

"Only for you to laugh at me when you find I've a fanciful imagination?"

"Would that bother you?"

"I s'pose not. Here's what I figure."

Welk leaned against the rock wall and winced.

"You know this boy; I'm not sure how, for he's a felid folk, no doubt in my mind. And you know it, too. So, you carry him away where none can see. So he can do his turning."

"Have you ever seen a turning?"

Here Krup let out a chortle and shook his head. "Mutterede, no. I ain't even sure it happens. You don't get any felid who live as folk, nowadays; they're turned right away."

"That much is true."

"I hear tell they slit their bellies before they can suckle once."

Welk shivered at the thought and nodded.

"Am I right, then?" Krup said.

"You are."

"But why are we in the cavern?"

"There is a rift in the rock, deep within, where the kell can be

176

seen. Long ago, I'm told, the felidae held their turning ceremonies there, where they could sense the kell most strongly."

"If the kell is there," Krup said, "why do they need the stone?"

"You know of the stone?"

"I do. Us folk out in the hills, we meet up with gnomes and brownies, sometimes a felid or two. We gots some of us come up from the coast what consort with mermaids and centaurs. Stories go around. And since you chased that boy out of the Ruud, the stories start making sense. You see?"

"Yes."

"So, why do they need the stone if the kell is here?"

"That I cannot tell you, for I do not know."

"Perhaps the boy here will know."

Welk looked at Lucas' face, his jaw held shut with a sling tied atop his head, drained of color.

"You thinking what I'm thinking, sir?" Krup said. "What if it don't work? What if he don't turn?"

Shaking his head, Welk groaned and lifted himself to standing. Krup leapt up to steady him. "I would not wish to consider that."

They made their way deeper into the cavern, Welk led by Krup with his cargo slung over his shoulder, holding the lantern high to guide the way, as Welk gave him directions from the memories of his youth when he and Elrundt lost themselves in the caves during their father's hunting tours.

Four times he thought he'd lost his way, but each time found a mark on the wall, his, Elrundt's, or some other adventurer's scrawl.

"Here," he said. "Hand me the lantern."

When Krup did so, Welk lifted the lid and blew out the candle. He heard a slight gasp from the folk, then another when the pale green glow of kell lit the path.

"There," Welk said.

They made their way down a set of natural steps into the chamber of slit rocks, green rays of light bursting from them, and Welk pointed to a flat rock against a far wall. Krup laid Lucas on the slab as gently as a mother putting her child to nap.

"Now we wait," Welk said.

"But..." Krup turned to him, worry in his eyes. "What if he turns a cat and...?"

Welk took a seat on a flattened boulder across the room and eyed Lucas' still body warily. "I've no more idea than you what to expect. You may return to the surface if you like, but I fear you will become lost on the path."

Krup nodded and found himself a rock. "I'll take my chances with the king."

They waited an eternity, it seemed. Until Krup said, "You sure we ain't s'posed to say some ceremonial words? A song or something?"

"I don't believe it to be a magical occurrence. I assumed it was natural."

They were silent again and Welk found himself concentrating on the rhythmic throb of his shoulder, the pain rising and falling, until he was aware of his head lolling, his eyes closing, his breath deepening. He startled awake when Krup let out a shout.

There in front of them were four felidae, the purring echoing so loudly in Welk's ears he could feel it in his chest.

"Voorspeld?" he said.

The cats shimmered, seemed to break apart. In the light of the kell, each tiny piece reflected the sharpest green and Welk put a hand to his eyes until the brightness dulled and they stood before him in folk form, svelte, lithe, wrapped in fur cloaks. Perhaps it was magic after all, he reasoned.

178

"I am," the old folk said.

"How did you know?"

"I should like to tell you we felidae are of one mind and sense the turning through some sort of ethereal connection. But as you were a friend of Belfen, I will not toy with you. The gnomes of the hills told the brownies of the Ruud, who in turn, brought the news into the forest. Lucas was killed by a folk of the Ruud and King Welk carries him north. And here we find you."

"Is he all right?" Welk said. "Will he turn?"

Voorspeld nodded. "But you must go. Your friendship with his parents is not enough to allow you to witness so personal an event."

Welk stood, wincing in pain. "Krup." He motioned for the man to join him.

"Thank you," Voorspeld said.

Welk turned back to the felid. He started to speak, but paused, gathering his words carefully. "I would wish a peace between our folk."

"Then build it," the cat said.

Chapter Twenty-nine

Iknow it's maddening," Leah said.

The children looked like rabbits caught in traps as they stood on the docks in Port Wonder. There was movement everywhere but the sky, bustling and noise. And the smells of fish, seaweed, and sweat fought against those of the pier stalls—the scented candles, bouquets of flowers, the cakes and pies and fried foods for sale. After the sweet, natural calm of the Ruud and the eastern continent, Leah couldn't imagine how the children and Rogget would fare here in Ruhm.

"And this isn't even the largest landing. But you'll get used to it."

"I've never seen so many folk in my life," Grayson said.

Sadie put her hands to her ears. "Is it this loud everywhere?"

"I'm afraid so."

She led them down the pier to the main road and into the little dockside town of Wonder, southwest of Rhum, where she found Fargel's Inn. A warm meal would do well for all of them, and Leah silently thanked her mother for ensuring she had plenty of spending money of her own on her trip east.

"One ought never find oneself beholden to others, if one can help it," she'd said, slipping the doars into Leah's bag.

She sat them all down at a table away from the window and ordered plates of roasted pig, hot salad, sliced tomato, and bread.

Rogget cleared his throat and said, "Begging your pardon, Miss Hallowsing, but, what's the plan, here?"

She smiled and laid a hand on his arm. "Dear Rogget. Please don't use my name here."

"Aye, I'm sorry about that."

She gave him a gentle pat and turned to the kids. "We'll get to the stationer's, to my home. I'm hoping my father is still safe there, or at least secreted away by now. If we can get to him, I think he'll tell us where to find Daken's journal."

"And if he's already left?"

"We'll search every nook and cranny and see what we can come up with. As a last resort, we'll have to follow where my father has gone."

Their meal finished, Leah led the children along the streets of Ruhm. She wished they could take a hired carriage to the city, but that would draw too much attention. A young woman of her new station—apprentice, at best—should not have enough money to pay for one. It was risky enough paying for a full meal at the inn. And a girl accompanied by a huntsman and three children would raise many a brow and quite a bit of interest, as it was. So they walked, daring not to run as that again was simply inappropriate for a folk of her age. Up the hard dirt streets of Wonder, through Truthspoke Park, where she'd been once on an excursion with the Hass school. Into the Community of Good, where the streets were wide and lined with witherwood trees and flowering shrubs: roses, lilies, and the aptly named Kirche's Pearl, a delicate, pale little flower with a powerful, too-sweet, conflicting smell, a mix of rose and peach. Finally she found Humble Lane; it would take her to Premier Road, cobbled and busy, and to the stationer's, and home. She kept her head down, pleading with Mutterede that she would not be recognized, but the street was strangely empty.

Approaching the building, her spirits rose in relief. *Home.* The stationer's office took up the first floor and its door faced the street, while a stair in the back led up to the second and third floors, where she and her parents had lived all her life. Ready to mount the steps to the door, Leah stopped—she breathed in and struggled to let it out again. There were three slats of wood nailed to the door. It was as she'd feared—they'd arrested her father already.

"What is it?" Sadie whispered.

"Too late," she muttered, and hurried around to the back of the shop with the others following.

The Hass must keep up the appearance of justice, she thought—hold him in jail for a short time before executing him. Mother would know what to do; she would know how to end this madness. She raced around to the back of the building and up the stairs, and gasped at the sight of the door to her home, also boarded. Her heart pounded in her chest and her gaze darted about the backyard as she tried to make sense of it. Her mother, too?

"What's happened?" Rogget asked, heaving up the stairs behind her.

"I don't know," she said. "I can understand the stationer's... but this is where I live."

Rogget crossed the small porch and pulled at the wood slats covering the door. He had them off in a matter of seconds and pushed the door open. He stepped aside, and Leah, frightened, walked past him into the house.

It was dark and still.

"Mother?" She called timidly, knowing her mother wouldn't answer. She turned to Rogget and the three children standing in the dim kitchen, the silence of her home shrouding them. "Would they have arrested her, too?" They couldn't answer, of course. "This way."

She led them through the kitchen to the little doorway at the steps, and down the stairs into the stationer's shop. It still smelled of ink and paper and oil and Leah forced the tears out of her eyes. She must keep herself in check, if she was to be of any help to her parents at all. Down into the cellar, they followed, through the tiny hall and into the canning room. She dragged the rugs from the floor and pulled open the trapdoor.

"The vegetable house," she said. "It's the only place I know where a book might be hidden. You'll find lanterns and candles in the front room, but be careful of making too much noise. No one must know you're in here."

"Where are you going?" Fenn asked her.

"I've got to find out what happened to them." She saw the desperation on the children's faces, like lost pups. "I'll be back soon," she assured them as best she could.

"Not to worry," Rogget said. "If we don't meet up here, we'll all be back at Olgut's landing on the morrow to take the boat back east."

That seemed to knock the air back into their lungs and Fenn nodded. "Good luck," he told her.

Trying to keep the panic at bay, Leah left by the back door and hurried across the street into the Community of Hope. Her first thought was Wilkins, her father's first apprentice. He lived only a quarter mile away; but, could she trust him? As she walked, she wrapped her arms around her waist and tried to think back to the few times she'd spoken with him; he was stern, to say the least. Always proper, never off his mark. She shook her head. No, she couldn't imagine Wilkins would not question her presence back in Ruhm without Kirche, her hair shorn, and asking questions about her father.

Quickly, Leah turned down another street and made her way south. She passed three servants, carrying laundry baskets to the nearest washing house, and nodded without meeting their eyes. Down another street and to her left, her heart racing, she forced herself not to hesitate. She had no other choice—no one else to turn to. She walked the path to the tidy little house and knocked on the door.

When Marigold pulled the door open, Leah held her breath. The young girl's face went pale; she glanced quickly at the street before pulling Leah into the front room.

"I'm so sorry," Leah whispered. "I do not wish to put you in this position."

Mari drew her farther into the house, to a small sitting room where she nearly pushed her into a soft chair. The house was silent like a roar and Leah felt as if she'd entered a tomb. The walls were frayed, natural wood adorned only with a framed drawing of a sailing ship. A basket in the corner held balls of yarn, two pairs of knitting needles pierced one of gray wool. On the floor beside her chair was a pillow, indented, as if the family cat spent much time there. And across from her, Mari sat in a hard-backed wood chair next to a table with a candle-lit lantern. Nothing was untoward, but still Leah considered it too picturesque —as if Marigold had laid it all out perfectly to appear normal.

"What are you doing here?" the girl said.

She'd lost her usual, submissive behavior and Leah was

reminded of how she'd long suspected Marigold only feigned respect. She no longer cared.

"I," Leah struggled to find the words, to explain. "Kirche is going to hang my father. I fled the east and came home to take him away. But the house and shop are boarded up. What happened? Do you know? Did they arrest my mother? I know it's madness—the idea that I could get them out of prison, but I have to find a way. Can you help me?" She put her face in her hands, exhausted from worry, realizing she'd come so far and still done nothing.

"Your mother sailed for the eastern continent two days ago," Marigold said. "She was difficult."

"What do you mean?"

"She didn't want to go. She believed it would be better if she shared your father's fate."

"Better?"

"Even those who are not allied with the wissenry would revolt at the thought of hanging her."

"The wissenry?"

Marigold drew her lids together and peered at Leah suspiciously. "Your father told me you knew nothing. But we'd hoped you were placed as a spy."

Leah blinked and leaned back in the chair, shaking her head, confused.

"Your father led an underground wissenry. They've been shipping the library of heresy out of Ruhm for years and secretly printing the truth about Hass, sending it out among the folk. After Kirche left, he was arrested. We believe it was Kirche's choice to remove himself from the act, so he could return and bring order, express his sorrow at what his stationer had done—the betrayal. If any evidence of your father's innocence could be presented, Kirche could absolve himself and lay the blame on his ministers."

"He planned to return with me as his wife," Leah said.

Marigold's eyes flew wide and her mouth fell open. Her gaze flitted about the room. "Yes." She nodded. "Even better. Is that why you fled?"

"No," Leah confessed. "I was prepared to marry him; he said he would torture and hang my father if I did not."

"And yet, here you are."

"Those who helped me escape said he planned to hang Father whether I wed him or not. On Founding Day."

"But Leah," Marigold whispered. The girl reached forward and put a hand on hers, surprising her. "It's too late."

"What do you mean?"

"He is on the gallows by now."

Chapter Thirty

Fenn couldn't say what irked him about their following him into the vegetable pantry, each with a lantern. He thought it was because he wanted to find Daken's journal on his own; he didn't want them touching it. But that seemed too silly an idea. Maybe, he reasoned, he wanted to be alone for a bit to think, to plan, away from their stares. Because they did stare. He found them watching him, wary, quite often and it was becoming frustrating, not because he blamed them for their distrust. No, it was precisely because he did *not* blame them. But he wouldn't add fuel to their belief, that he would become exactly what he claimed he would not, by telling them to let him find the book himself; so he let them follow.

They searched through all of the potato bins, looked on all of the shelves lined with canning goods, inside the cracker barrels, and stood staring into a murky barrel filled with pickles.

"Nope," Sadie said. "I'm not sticking my hand in there."

"It couldn't be in there," Grayson said. "It'd be ruined."

"We're going about this all wrong," Rogget said. "It can't be here."

"Why not?" Sadie said.

"It would stand out too much," Fenn said. "It's got to be in a library."

"But if the Hass knew about it, they'd look at every book the stationer owned."

"That's true enough," Rogget said. "But I'm saying we ought not be looking for the book itself here. We should look for a door."

"What sort of door?" Sadie said looking around, holding her lantern high above her head.

"A secret one," Fenn said. "Like the one in the cellar at the wissenry in Path. There." He pointed to the potato bins, and tried not to get his hopes up; it couldn't be that simple, could it? "Move them away from the wall."

When they pulled the bins from the wall, they found a small patch of hardwood against it, no more than two feet square. Fenn fell to his knees and pulled at it, but it didn't budge.

"I need something to wedge it away from the wall."

Rogget knelt beside him with his knife and dug at each side, twisting the wood until it popped off. Behind it was a gaping hole; it smelled of dirt and rotting grass, reminding Fenn of the tunnel Father Treacher had sent him into so many weeks before.

"I won't be fitting in there," Rogget said. "And I can't say I feel right about sending any of you in alone."

"It'll be all right," Fenn said. "If I get to where I can't hear you calling, I'll come back."

Rogget shook his head, but Fenn knew he wouldn't stop him. He set the lantern just inside the hole and, lying on the floor, pushed at it. He crawled after the lantern, pushing it farther and farther ahead of him, until he was fully surrounded by dank, damp kell, and slithering downward. The lantern dropped a few inches and fell to its side. Fenn grabbed it and pulled it back to standing before the candle went out. Inch by inch, the tunnel floor dropped and the ceiling lifted until he found himself in a rounded out hollow in the ground.

When he turned to look back, upward, he saw Rogget's head outlined in the lantern light behind him.

"I'm here," he said. "It's a room."

"I'm sending Grayson," Rogget said.

"And me," he heard Sadie protest.

Fenn could hear Grayson scooting through the tunnel as he looked around the room. Empty shelves stood against the walls, and three tables sat in the middle. A few pieces of parchment paper, some squares of wax paper, some ink wells, and pencils were strewn about.

When Sadie stood beside him, holding her lantern up, she marveled. "It looks like my dad's office, without the books."

"Exactly," Fenn said. "No books."

"But it was a hidden library."

They walked all around the room, shining light into the dark corners and cubbies, onto shelves and in bins. When he was sure there was nothing to be found, Fenn spied the corner of a book on the floor, tucked behind one of the shelves. He reached for it, daring not to hope, telling himself it was trash. As soon as his fingers touched the worn leather, he knew it was a journal. He pulled slightly on the shelf, forcing it to let go of the book, and held it up to his lantern.

"I found something," he said, carrying it to one of the tables.

Sadie and Grayson set their lanterns alongside his and they all three leaned over the table as he opened it. On the first page was a sketch of a tree, flames carved into its trunk.

"Herein lie all our reason, all our faith, all our sin," Fenn read aloud. He turned the page. "In the Year of Our Beloved Rett, 1045, I determine to set record of my journey to do his lord's bidding—a survey of the lands south and north."

"Is that it?" Grayson said.

Rogget called from the other end of the tunnel. "Did you find anything?"

Fenn continued to flip through the pages, looking for some sign of the kell stone, but it appeared to be a prayer manual more than anything, with drawings of the tree throughout.

"We won't know until we read it," Sadie said. "Let's take it upstairs."

Once through the tunnel and into the front room of stationer's where there was plenty of natural light, all but Rogget huddled over the book reading. Occasionally one of them would point out a passage and whisper.

"That's him," Fenn said. "His name is Daken; it must be the one."

So engrossed were they in reading that when the door in the back of the stationer's banged open, they jumped and the book flew across the table to the floor.

Chapter Thirty-one

Leah heard Marigold calling after her, telling her to wait, saying it was too late, no use, but she bolted from the house and darted through the streets, not caring if anyone saw her. She ran along Premier Road, past the shops and homes, seeing few other folk and finally realizing why—it was a hanging day. Once at the circle, at the base of Palace Mall, she staggered and paused, panting heavily for a solid breath, before forcing herself on, around the curves to the northern edge, where she raced along the street toward a large gathering of folk. Already they were shouting, but there was something different, something that frightened her more than the cheers that usually erupted on days such as these. Folk were not boisterous here, they were angry.

The crowd grew thicker, deeper, before she reached the Hall of Hass, where Kirche and Pren had their offices. When she could see the House of Premiers, she fought her way through, shoving folk aside. She raised her arms above her head, trying to make herself thinner, a wedge. It was unseemly, vulgar behavior but no one cared, no one noticed. They were tugging, pushing, fighting, yelling. Enraged. And then the smell of roses—sweet beauty—taking her back to the day she last saw Kettering with her flower cart on the mall—how joyous she'd been—and the day in the woods of the Ruud when Kirche murdered the brownie. The aroma filled the air around the mob, painting it bizarre.

Finally she could see the gallows. The rope. The hangman. And there he was—her father stood looking out at the folk, defiant, his chin high.

Leah screamed. But her cry was hidden in the shouts and protests of the folk around her.

"Father, no!"

She thought she heard a male folk calling her name but her father's lips did not move. She could see Kirche's Minister of Law standing at the front of the stage, reading from his scroll—no one could hear him. Suddenly, a folk was lifted onto the others' shoulders. Then another and another. They were carried toward the gallows stage on a wave but before they could climb onto it, the Hass guard marched up the steps and stood in front of her father, their firearms raised. Shots rang out and those folk fell into the crowd.

"No!" she screamed.

Undeterred, the folk surged and more shots pierced the noise. The hangman tried to put a hood over her father's head, but he shook it away. The brute looked to Kirche's minister, but the folk was cowering at the back of the stage. He shrugged and let the stationer's face remain visible.

Leah was near the foot of the stage now, looking up, screaming his name. If she could only get to him—climb onto the stage, take the noose off his neck, over his head, race with him down the steps behind, and into the crowd. Even as she saw it in her mind, she knew it was false, a dream, but even so, she struggled to the lip

194

of the gallows.

"Please, no!"

Even over the panic and chaos of the folk, the shots that only urged them on, and her name, called again and again from behind her, Leah heard the thump as the floor broke away beneath her father. She thought she caught his eye, just as he dropped. She was only aware of screaming when someone grabbed her from behind and pulled her back through the throng.

Prenalin had her tucked against his right side, one arm around her shoulders, the other grasping her arm. His face was hard, but when he glanced at her, his eyes were filled with terror. They moved along the Palace Mall with a crowd of folk, shots echoing behind them, while others ran against them into the fray carrying firearms, swords, sticks.

Leah was numb and let herself be carried away. Pren took her to the circle, and onto Premier Road. When she saw Marigold standing at the stationer's, wringing her hands, she shook her head, as if to let her know it was over. It was done.

"This way," Marigold whispered. "Hurry."

Pren led her around to the back of the shop, to the back door, and into her parents' empty kitchen.

Chapter Thirty-two

Leah's head throbbed but she felt no pain. In her ears, a river seemed to rush along into some dark distance. When its flow eased, she was suddenly aware of Prenalin, sitting next to her, his arm still wrapped around her shoulders.

"I only made port early this morning," he was telling Marigold. "I knew she'd try to help him; but he refused to be released."

Across the table, in her kitchen, sat Rogget and the children, quiet, watching, concern and confusion in their eyes.

"I could have told you he would," Marigold said. "He said this was the plan all along."

"No," Leah wrenched herself out of Prenalin's grasp.

"It's true," Prenalin said. "Your father would not flee Ruhm. He wanted to stand for something."

Leah turned to Marigold sitting on her other side. "Why do you trust him? He is a spy."

"Yes," Prenalin said, "for the wissenry resistance."

She shook her head, unbelieving. "You allowed Kirche to murder my father."

"Leah," Marigold nearly hissed. "Prenalin has been working

for the wissenry for seventeen years. Your father would hardly approve of you speaking to him in this manner."

"Did my father know?"

They both looked at her, but said nothing.

"Did he know Kirche's plan?" she asked Mari. "To marry me and force some bizarre peace between your revolutionaries and Ruhm?"

The girl shrugged. "I was not included in all of the plans."

"He did know," Prenalin said.

"I don't believe it." Leah scooted her chair away from the table, away from Prenalin, and stood to pace the floor.

"It wasn't to happen this way," he said. "Kirche planned to return engaged. He would call for a uniting of the old wissende class and the Hass, claim our differences resolved in the face of threats from the beast folk and the folk of the eastern continent. Edwin knew he would be called on to bless the union and he would refuse. Kirche believed your marriage to him, in the face of your father's death would be enough to keep the folk with Hass, turn them away from the resistance."

"Father would let me marry him?"

"No." Pren stood and took a step toward her but she backed away. "You were to flee with your mother before that could happen. As soon as I realized Kirche intended to marry you before returning to Ruhm, I knew I had to get you away from him. But...well, you managed it yourself."

"And still you let my father be hanged."

"I tried to get him out. But he would not leave. He believed if he ran, the cause would suffer; those who trusted in him, trusted he was telling them the truth about the Hass, would see him as nothing more than a coward. Don't you see? He had to die."

Leah surprised herself. Launching at him, she slapped him

hard in the face, and turned to the others, planning to lead them out the door.

"Wait," Marigold grabbed her and pulled her back.

"Leave me alone," she raged. "Why should I trust either of you? How could you let me be deceived this way?"

"We couldn't trust you," Marigold said, "if you want to know the truth of it."

"And so you allowed me to go along with Kirche, knowing all the while he intended to murder my father?"

"You seemed to enjoy it well enough," Prenalin said.

Leah lurched toward him again but Marigold put herself between them.

"I'll not have any lovers' quarrels right now," she said.

"How dare you?" Leah scowled at her.

"I dare plenty. You think you're the only one who's lost something? You think the Hass haven't already killed my parents? Pren's father and brother? You kept yourself pent up at the school well enough, didn't you?"

"That's enough, Mari," Pren said. "That was the plan."

"And I know all about it," Leah said. "Madam Always told me. I was nothing but a pawn for all of you—someone to smooth the path for your machinations. And now you expect me to believe you would not have forced me into a marriage to Kirche?"

"Are you certain you didn't want it?"

"I said there'd be none of that," Marigold scolded. "Come to the table. Your friends found the journal."

For a few seconds, Leah hesitated, eyeing them both. Marigold was sneering at her. Hadn't she always thought the girl was looking down on her in some way? And now she understood why. She was the snooty one as it turned out; Leah's cheeks flamed at the thought of it. All those years believing herself special, a student at the Hass school, and then appointed Aide to the High Preist. And all along her suspicions were correct, she was nothing at all as she pretended, while Marigold was the one true to her father.

Prenalin, unlike Mari, looked worried—as if he'd lost something and didn't know where to look for it. Perhaps that is the face of a spy being found out, she wondered.

At the table, Fenn pushed the worn leather journal to her.

"It was downstairs, in a hidden room," he said.

"A cache," Prenalin said.

"We got the manuscripts out of the archives in Ruhm," Marigold said. "Some from the school, others from the offices of the Inner Circle. We stored them here."

"You saw them?" she asked Fenn.

"They are gone," Marigold said. "Shipped east, most of them. To Madam Dania. All that's left is this." She lifted the book and pushed it at Leah as if she were angry with it. "Your father wanted you to have it."

"Daken's journal," Leah said. "Shouldn't this have been one of the first books secreted away?"

"He insisted it be saved for you," Pren said.

Leah let out a laugh, even with the tears spilling down her cheeks. "He wanted me to run away."

"We've looked through it," Fenn said. "We can't find anything about the kell stone."

"You'll have time to read it, today," Marigold said. "Tomorrow is Founding Day. The Hass will have the people subdued well enough, but they'll be on alert during the festivities. We'll continue with our plan and make north with the king."

"The king?" Leah eyed the girl as if she were insane.

"Aye. We're taking the king east to keep him out of harm's way."

Leah shook her head. "You're going to kidnap the king? A child?"

"Not the new king," Prenalin said. "The old king."

"How many kings do you have?" Sadie said.

"You would take him from his privilege of tranquility?" Leah said.

"Mari, you must leave us and continue the plan," Prenalin said. "I'll see Leah and her friends back east."

"I'm not going back home," Fenn said. "I'm here to find the kell stone."

"You can't search for the stone here in Ruhm; it's dangerous."

"I don't care."

"If you think denying the king his right to tranquility is going to help the cause," Leah said, "you're mad."

"It's not tranquility," Prenalin said. "It's murder."

"Murder?" Leah nearly laughed.

"What?" Sadie said.

"Sit down," Marigold told Leah.

Leah stared at the girl for several seconds, wishing she didn't feel so small and confused, but sat at the table again, and only shuddered when Prenalin took his seat beside her.

Marigold looked to Rogget and the children. "These are matters for adults, I'm afraid. But you're caught up now. I can't see setting you loose in Ruhm on a quest for the kell stone. You'll likely be caught and hanged. I'm sure Leah wouldn't approve of that." Here she turned to Leah with a glare.

"I don't care what's going on in Ruhm," Fenn said.

"But you very well should."

"You'll have to tell them," Prenalin said.

"That much is true," Leah said. "I would very much appreciate it if you two would stop treating me like an imbecile. My father has just been hanged by the Hass, my mother has fled Ruhm. I deserve to be brought into the plan."

Marigold turned back to the children. "Let me explain. In Ruhm a new king is crowned on a Founding Day every fourteen years. He's only four years old when he gets the crown and he wears it only until he is eighteen."

"Why would you want a kid to be king?" Sadie asked.

"They're easier to control," Grayson said.

"That's right," Mari said. "The new king is chosen by the High Priest of Hass. Every fourteen years, the priest meets all of the children who will be aged four on Founding Day and chooses the king's heir. When the day arrives, there is a great parade. All the priests of Hass are in it. All the posts in Hass, all those who serve the king, and our soldiers and sailors too. The old king is at the end with his menagerie."

"A zoo?" Grayson said.

"That's right. A collection of beast folk caught in the mountains north."

"They're sentient beings," Grayson said.

"Unfortunately, in Ruhm, they are not treated that way. After the parade, all the people of Ruhm cheer the old king. As everyone else circles, and marches back to the palace, the old king remains behind with his menagerie. Once back at the Hall of Hass, the High Priest lifts the new king onto his own parade carriage, and together they make their way to the palace, where only a select few are allowed to attend the crowning."

"And what happens to the old king?" Sadie said. "And the menagerie? Are they all murdered?"

"The people of Ruhm are told the old king is granted the

202

privilege of tranquility—that he ascends to the heavens to live eternally with Rett."

"And that is not true?" Leah said.

"Of course not."

Marigold glanced at Leah as if she were stupid, and Leah felt it. She wanted to protest, to tell Mari she'd doubted the tale herself, even as she recited phrases from *The Book of Rett* in school. She was not so dumb as she seemed, she wanted to say; but she dared not—unsure of herself.

"Some time ago," Mari was saying, "we learned that the old king is taken directly from the parade to the tomb of the kings—"

"We all knew that," Leah said. She turned to Sadie. "The old king worships at the tomb before he is taken—"

"He is not taken anywhere," Marigold said. "He's left there. Locked in the room with the bones of past kings. Left to starve to death."

"Easy, Mari," Prenalin said, nodding to the children.

Leah saw their eyes wide and their mouths open. "I hardly think," she murmured, "the Hass of Emorah, keepers of the morality of—" Leah stopped and turned to look at Prenalin. She shivered as the truth of it invaded her.

The kitchen was silent for several seconds. Mari seemed to be waiting, giving them all time to absorb the horror of it before she finally continued.

"It's all come to a point tomorrow. From what we can tell, Kirche was to be absent when your father was hanged so he can attempt to blame Edwin's death on infighting withing the wissende resistance movement. We assume he will attempt to link this with his preparations to overtake the Ruud."

"Overtake it?" Rogget blurted out.

"Indeed. He's been planning it for some time, hinting to the folk that the kings of the Ruud are aiding the resistence here. His ships are in port, ready to sail. We assume they will do so during the Founding Day celebrations."

"Can you stop them?" Grayson asked.

"Some of our folk are planning an attack. It will weaken the force, but not destroy it completely."

"And what of the king?" Leah said.

"I am to rescue him from the tomb and take him east. At some point, preferably once we've assumed control in Ruhm, we'll return him, put him before the folk. His presence will prove that the ascension is a lie. We will throw open the tomb. The folk will see the truth for themselves. Bones of past kings will convince them."

"I think," Prenalin said, his voice measured against Mari's passion, "you may find that folk without a sound education in logic and reasoning will hold tight to their faith, even in the face of irrefutable evidence."

Mari sighed. "Edwin was with me—"

"Edwin tolerated your enthusiasm."

"But," Sadie said, "there's an army going to the Ruud?"

"Yes, yes," Prenalin said. "This debate can wait." He offered Marigold a smile. "The Hass has long planned to retake the Ruud, and Kirche feels now is the best time. He hopes it will unite the folk, turn them from the resistance."

"We call it Kirche's folly," Marigold said.

"We call it home," Sadie said.

Leah leaned across the table, reaching her hand to Sadie's. "I do not think the wissendes would leave your folk under the rule of the Hass. If I knew my father, and I'm sure I did, he would not stop until all folk, beast and mortal, are free."

Chapter Thirty-three

Fenn thought if he didn't get to sit down in the next minute, he would keel over dead in the street. He was squeezed into the crowd like a fish in a barrel—he couldn't breathe, much less see anything of the festivities. There was a show, he was told. Sadie was perched atop Rogget's shoulders, her back pelted occasionally by a nut or a small rock, no doubt thrown by someone behind them who couldn't see past her. Grayson stood on his tiptoes for at least a half hour at a time watching, before bending down to yell something awful in Fenn's ear. Last time it was, "It's some kind of strange, hairy, folk-looking beast! It's playing a pop organ!" He'd laughed and crept back up on his toes to watch. Fenn could only look up at the sky at the fire displays, popping red and blue sparks, whistling and bursting over the noise of the crowd.

He grasped at his charm, clinking against the amber stone, under his tunic and closed his eyes. Where was she? Why had she deserted him? There had been, in the beginning, visions of a man as well. He once thought it must be his father. But now they were gone—his charm nothing more than a dead piece of gold. Brenna must have been right. It wasn't his mother's charm. It had no connection to him—only to the Ruud. The charm warmed him and sent him visions—only in the Ruud.

He was jostled from behind and tripped over his own feet, falling into Rogget. Rogget looked down at him and smiled, misunderstanding; he put a large arm around him and jostled him some more.

That morning, Marigold had given them money and sent them into the city, thronging with people. She, Prenalin, and Leah remained hidden and would meet them at the end of the parade route, when it turned back toward the palace. She told them to act as if they were enjoying themselves and so they wandered the booths of the market, eating all sorts of sweets and fruits and buying absurd trinkets—tiny kings made of sticks wearing crowns made of moss, and hand-carved wooden figures of various beasts, most of which they agreed had never existed and were stuff of legend. Fenn's favorite was a dragon, sculpted of hard clay, its wings pulled back as if it darted through the air. The woman who sold it to him—toothless and aged—claimed to have carved it from memory.

"Saw in on my early travels south, I did. Oh, but my days of traipsing about the kell are over. Told and done, they are."

Fenn only nodded politely. And now he found himself smothered while the others got to watch a show. Finally, the crowd began to disperse.

"What is it?" Fenn called out. "What's happening?"

Grayson lowered himself off his toes. "Speeches, I think. The old king and the new king are up on a stage. Can you see it?"

Fenn shook his head. The crowd quieted down somewhat, and Fenn thought he could hear a deep voice.

"He's got something like a trumpet," Grayson said. "And he's talking through it so we can hear him."

Fenn could hear little, but the crowd cheered occasionally. He heard war, and more war, and war again. And the crowd cheered. He heard about the east and evil. He heard about Rett and victory. And the crowd cheered. Grayson looked down slightly at him with a frown.

After a moment, though, he heard something else—something constant, underneath the cheering. It was a grumbling—a discontent. The folk were restless, unhappy, but not quite willing as yet to show it.

The crowd thinned more and more as the sun set. Music played behind them even before the speeches were finished. Dancing broke out spontaneously all around. Torches and lanterns were lit. They wandered the streets together, weaving around pockets of dancers, folk selling torches, and folk calling at them to buy their sweet breads. Fenn's feet ached and his ears thundered. He was sure he'd never heard so much noise in all his life. He'd never seen so many folk in one place. And he'd never walked on such hard ground for so long. He did not like the Great West at all, he decided. And he especially did not like Ruhm.

They spent the evening walking the cobblestone street of the Palace Mall, back and forth, eyeing the new foods, avoiding the sellers hawking their goods. Back and forth, until Fenn was sure his feet would fall off. He trudged for what seemed like days. His eyelids grew puffy and heavy and he scowled at everyone he saw.

Finally a great bell somewhere in the distance began to toll and the people let out a loud cheer. They pushed toward the outer edge of the street to await the parade.

"This is it," Rogget said. "Miss Marigold said we should find a place at the end of the road."

Fenn wanted to scream—more walking—but he grudgingly followed Rogget and the others. They made their way slowly through the packed crowd to the foot of the mall where the road became a large circle, nearly the size of Path itself, Fenn thought, and three roads branched off it—one east, one southeast, and one southwest. More torches were lit along the edges of the circle. He looked for Leah, but there was little chance he could recognize a face in the huge throng of folk.

"She said all the folk will amass here," Rogget said. "I don't know where they'll all fit."

And they did not fit. An enormous mass of folk crowded around them, filling out all the streets jutting off the circle. They were jostled and pushed, but Rogget held fast, leaving them at the edge where Fenn could see the first of the parade as it marched toward them. Dancers, flag bearers, jugglers, and musicians, all filed past, around the circle and back up toward the city. Then the menagerie carts rolled by. Fenn gazed, awestruck, at cages filled with trolls, brownies, even an eis. A glass cart was filled with fairies. And then about a dozen rather round folk wearing tall hats and purple robes walked solemnly by. And lastly, on an open cart, standing and waving, the King of Ruhm. His cart stopped and a silence fell over the mob. Fenn watched expectantly for him to say something, goodbye and good luck perhaps. But instead, he merely held his hands over his face and bowed low while the parade continued back up Palace Mall with the crowd of folk following.

Once the gathering was gone, their cheering and merry-making now echoing in the distance, the torches and lanterns carried away, the young king sat in his cart in the darkness.

208

"They just left him here," Sadie said.

Leah was suddenly behind him, her hand on his shoulder. Marigold and Prenalin were there, guiding them all quickly out of the circle, down the southwestern road ahead of the king's cart.

"Hurry, now," Marigold whispered.

They broke into a jog and left the road when it curved into a wood. They barreled into the trees, still making their way southwest, until they were hidden from the road. Only the moonlight told Fenn that Prenalin and Leah were ahead of him, and Rogget's grunts told him he followed.

"Far enough," Marigold said. They stood in a circle, panting, all of them looking at Mari in the darkness, waiting for her to lead them. "We walk from here." She turned and they all followed her through the woods.

At one point, they hid themselves behind trees at the edge of the road and carefully slipped across it, one by one, unseen, into more woods, thick with shrubs and vines. When they found themselves at the edge of the wood once again, Fenn saw they were at an empty mining camp. A hill on the right boasted a gaping hole with torches on either side of it. Beyond, the hill reached upward, curved, and sloped down again. In front of him, a field of tents, dark and cold, no fires burning.

"They're all in the city," Marigold told them. "Their work is now done. No one watches the king being locked away but Madam Sponhide."

"Madam who?"

"She owns the land, and the mine. For many years, we thought it was her devotion to the Hass that led her to go along with this ugly ritual of murder. But we've since learned—"

Marigold stopped and held up her hand. The cart was

approaching. Fenn peered through the trees and shrubs at the young king, still sitting in the front seat, his head in his hands.

"Welcome," a woman said on the other side of the cart.

Fenn struggled to see her, but the darkness hid her. She helped the king down from the cart and they disappeared into the mine. They all waited, silent, as if holding their breath, until the woman appeared again outside, no more than a shadow. He waited for her to leave, but instead, she walked toward the woods, straight at them. He felt every nerve twitch as he prepared to flee, but before he got the chance, Marigold stepped out from the bushes and greeted the dark figure.

"You can come out now," Mari called to them. She was still talking with the woman when Fenn approached.

The woman, he could see now, was tall, pale, and not fully folk. He was sure of it. She pulled a chain from around her neck and handed it to Marigold. Attached to it was a golden key that caught the moonlight. "They do not know I have this," she said. "I've left the torches burning. Follow them to the final door. You'll find him there."

The woman turned and glided away. Fenn looked to Marigold. "Do we go get him, then?"

She shook her head. "Not yet. Let's let him stew a bit."

"You were going to say something about Madam Sponhide. About why she lets the Hass lock the kings away in her mine."

"Indeed," Marigold said. She walked a few paces toward the door of the cave and sat on the ground. The rest of the group followed. "It turns out, she's an angel eis. We don't know much about them and she won't say much. But she's been living here in Ruhm for many generations, apparently. She's managed to fool the Hass into thinking she's always the next generation of Sponhides to own the mine."

"She can manipulate simple folk," Rogget said. "I've heard tell of it with the split eisen."

"That wouldn't explain why she'd let the Hass murder folk in her mine," Sadie said.

"Sure it does," Grayson said. "After what the Hass has done to the beast folk..."

"That's hardly an excuse to aid in murder."

Marigold shrugged. "Seems enough of an excuse for her."

They sat and whispered among themselves for what seemed hours, until Fenn wanted desperately to lie down and sleep. Finally, Marigold stood and stretched, and led them down into the mine, following the path of torches to a dead end where an enormous iron door stood in front of them.

She slid the key in a huge metal lock hanging from the latch and turned it. She pulled the lock off and stood back letting Rogget pull the heavy door open. Rogget took a torch from the wall behind them and held it forward into the doorway and Fenn peered from behind Mari as the shuffling of feet brought the dethroned king to the door, the confusion on his face aglow.

"Rett?" The king said.

Chapter Thirty-four

Y ou are Roren, are you not?" Marigold said to the young man with a smile.

"I am," he said.

He looked nothing like a king, Fenn thought. More like one of the children of the Ruud. Lanky, not quite grown into his bulk, as Father Treacher would say. He was fair and pale, like an eis, and had a look of innocence about him.

"Why are you here?" he asked, somewhat amused. "I was told only Rett would come for me."

"We've come to rescue you."

"I am to await Rett. He will take me to the hall of tranquility to live eternally with him."

"The only place you're going is on a shelf," Rogget said. He pushed his way past the king, into the room and lit the torches on the walls, illuminating rows and rows of shelves filled with bones.

Roren turned and watched as Rogget lifted a skull from its resting place. He walked to the first of the shelves and reached out to touch the velvet robes of one of the skeletons.

"Rett isn't coming?"

"Why would they need to lock you in a dark room to wait for him, anyway?" Fenn said.

The king shook his head and turned to Fenn. "Who are you? Why did you come?"

"I'm not Rett, if that's what you're thinking."

"And why rescue me?"

"Because it isn't right," Sadie said peeking into the room. "They're going to let you die in here."

The king seemed confused. "And so, you decided to free me?"

"Yes," Fenn said, wondering what was so difficult to understand.

Marigold held out her hand as if to guide him from the room. Prenalin and Leah walked out, followed by Sadie and Grayson.

"Wait," the king said. "I am to remain here and wait for Rett." Even while he said it, it seemed he was doubting it.

"It's all right," Marigold said to him, cooing. She took his arm and led him to the door. All the way through the cave, as Rogget doused the torches along the way in buckets of water below each one, Marigold explained to the king what she could about the Hass' manner of creating, and doing away with, its kings.

"And so I am now to be *your* puppet?" Roren said, his innocense seeming to disappear.

Fenn could see humor dancing in Marigold's eyes by the light of the last of the torches when she smiled at him.

"We will not force you to do anything. But we would at least like to give you the chance to live."

"We're going to bring you with us to the eastern continent," Fenn said.

He stood there, his face aglow in the torchlight, confused. "I don't understand."

"It's really very simple," Grayson said. "They want a new king every fourteen years. So they have to get rid of the old one."

The young king nodded. It was a more succinct way of saying it than Mari had offered, but Fenn winced at its abruptness.

"They told you Rett would come for you and take you off to...what?" Grayson continued. "Paradise or something? And you believed it. But they lied to you. They were just trying to get you out of the way."

The king nodded again.

"Do you understand now?" Sadie said.

"Yes," he said. "I think I do."

"Well, come on then," Grayson said.

Surprisingly, to Fenn, the king followed Grayson out of the mine.

In the darkness of night, the small group walked the long way, westward and northward, around the grand city of Ruhm. Rogget, Leah, and Marigold periodically looked behind them, or stopped and let them all pass before continuing on, taking turns at the back of the group. The young king walked along with them in silence and refused to answer any of their questions. At first Fenn thought he was just being kingly, and not speaking to those of inferior rank, but he caught his face occasionally in the moonlight and thought he was dazed and probably not hearing them.

They slept on the ground against a small wood on a plain north of the city.

"Would you like to use my blanket?" Fenn asked him.

The king stared at him.

"We're going to get some sleep now," Fenn said.

The king only nodded and lay down on the ground, closing his eyes.

Fenn shrugged.

In the morning, Fenn could see the marble buildings of the city far in the distance. He realized they'd walked most of the night and that only made him more groggy. Rogget dug a shallow fire pit and they all searched for kindling in the little wood. Northward, the landscape wasn't treeless, but their patches were few. Once Rogget got the kindling set, he stood over the pit and looked to Fenn.

"Go on then," he said. "Show them all what you can do."

Fenn cast a glance at the group, feeling small. "What if I can't?"

"I have every confidence you can."

Fenn squatted at the pit and held his hands over the kindling and fire sticks Rogget had tossed in. He sat still for several seconds, longer than was comfortable, and only when he thought he heard Marigold chuckle did he feel the fire burn through his fingers and catch the sticks. He wasn't sure how it had happened, why it had happened, or what it meant, but the gasps from all but Rogget told him it was unusual.

"He is beast folk?" Prenalin said.

"Split," Rogget said. "Born of an eisen and a folk, though we don't know who they were."

"But, how did you know?" Fenn said. "How does the wissenry know?"

Rogget shrugged. "Father Wold was there when you were born."

"And they thought it was okay to keep it from me?"

"It was for your protection. You know you wouldn't be trusted in the Ruud, nor in the beast forest."

216

"Don't bother with it now," Marigold said to him. She reached out and put a hand on his shoulder. "The world is changing. You'll see. The wissenry knows the truth—that beast and folk are the same. Soon, everyone will know and you'll be seen as no different from me."

Chapter Thirty-five

Leah was glad for a chance to rest and warm herself at the fire and Rogget's bitters were rustic, but welcome. They had a small breakfast of biscuits and roasted meats Marigold had packed for them. She was insistent they make their way quickly east to Lerringlass Port where she was to get Roren onto a boat. But she knew Fenn had other plans.

"If I may," she said, gathering the attention of the group. "I'd like to propose that we be open with one another. We're an odd lot, but I think our goals are, at the very least, similar. I am willing to share my secrets, if you are." She looked specifically at Fenn and he nodded.

Prenalin put a warning hand on her arm only once while she told them all about her father and Dakenruud and the kell stone. She did not shake him off, but put her hand over his. They were in deeply already, she reasoned. There could be no harm in revealing herself to the others, even to Roren. And so, in turn, Fenn told them of the wissenry and the prophecy, and his intention to find the kell stone and destroy it.

"You would do that to your own folk?" Marigold asked him.

The boy frowned. "The wissenry thinks it's best all around."

"And you think you know how to do it?" Prenalin said. "It was my understanding the Hass attempted it when they took it back from Michelruud, and failed."

"The wissenry in the Ruud has some ideas on how it could be done. I'm really just wanting to find it now. We can worry about destroying it later."

Leah nodded and glanced at Pren, wondering if he felt the same as she did. The boy was unsure, his opposing loyalties pulling at him. She took a look at Roren as she sipped her bitters. Odd that he seemed so ordinary now, when he was king just a few days ago. There was a pang of loss in her gut at the thought of her father; how wonderful it would have been had he fled, instead of allowing himself to be sacrificed. He could return to Ruhm with Roren as soon as the revolution started, triumphant, proven. Instead, he chose to leave Ruhm to its own devices. Leah cringed, realizing she was angry with him.

"Our man at Lerringlass will wait," Marigold said, "if you want us to stay together."

"I think that's best," Prenalin said.

"Was the location of the kell stone in Daken's journal, then?" Fenn asked her. "I couldn't make much of it.

"There were clues," she said, "but nothing definite."

"Marigold and I have read it also," Prenalin said. "We found nothing."

"When I read it," Leah said, "I kept hearing my father's voice as we sat together in his little office in the stationer's...just a day or so before I sailed east. I remember feeling as if he were playing a game, teasing me. But when I read Daken's journal, there were those same words, over and over again."

"And those were your clues?" Marigold said.

220

"Yes."

"Well," Prenalin said, "what were they?"

"First, both my father and Daken said he was to take the stone deep underground."

"That much is known to most," Marigold said. "It's believed that underground, it cannot aid the beast."

"But the repeated words—a good story. A story with a moral. It's all throughout the journal. My father said it referring to the story he was telling me—the story of Dakenruud. But Daken—he repeats it over and over as if in prayer; and he refers to the story of Rett."

"Yes," Marigold said. "He wrote poems about it, quoted *The Book of Rett*, discussed it at length. But we only assumed he was devout."

"Father knew," Leah said. "He knew it was a clue."

"But a clue to what?" Rogget said.

Leah looked at their faces, hopeful, agitated. "I may be wrong..."

"Naturally," Roren said.

She smiled at him. "I believe the kell stone is buried beneath the site of Rett's sacrifice."

They were all silent for several seconds, until Prenalin said, "Why?"

"It was something else my father told me. He said I was born of the wissende class. I was, therefore, prone to logic and reason. The truth would nag at me, he said, until it forced its way out. And I know the story of Rett's sacrifice is a lie."

Roren sputtered and laughed. "What?"

"The wissendes," Marigold told the young king, "long ago learned that much of the story is untenable."

"But a lie? How could you know such a thing?"

"I saw the flaming tree," Leah said. "There is one in the beast forest on the eastern continent. I *saw* it."

"You were mistaken," Roren said.

She shook her head. "No. I was brought up revering it just as you were. I know the shape and texture of its leaves; I know the unique nature of its bark, through the study of our art and history, through my study of *The Book of Rett*. And I saw it, I tell you—the tree still exists."

"Still, what makes you think the kell stone is there?" Fenn asked.

"I believe that's the moral my father meant—not Rett's sacrifice for our purity, not our shame in burning him to fulfill it. No. He meant skepticism. I am to be always skeptical, always seeking the truth. That's what he was telling me."

"And there are the drawings," Marigold said.

Pren nodded in agreement.

"Yes," Leah said. She opened the journal and flipped through the pages, showing the pictures to them as she found them. "Always the flaming tree of Hass."

"But," Prenalin said, "we have been to the sacrificial site many times. There is nothing there—certainly no pathway beneath the ground."

"Ah," Roren said, "but there is a pathway, nonetheless."

They all turned to the young folk, astonished.

"There is a cell in the palace dungeons where the walls are covered with maps and drawings—graffiti. They call it the lunatic's room. I spent many hours there, tracing the lines on the maps, imagining I could travel our world."

"What would the king of Ruhm be doing in the dungeons?" Marigold said.

Roren smiled. "I often sought solitude; and the dungeons

222

are ancient ruins now, uninhabited, except by the spirits of the dead. It was the one place my guards would not follow."

"And there were underground pathways on these maps?" Prenalin said.

Leah could almost feel Pren's doubt, and she shared it.

"Yes," Roren said. "There were drawings of the many mines in Ruhm, and some in the south I'd never heard of. Those who made the maps drew in the tunnels...from memory I liked to imagine. And in one small spot, I found a drawing of the place of Rett's sacrifice. Leading away from it, there is one long meandering line."

"Dakenruud," Marigold said.

"He was imprisoned in the palace," Prenalin said. "In the dungeons."

"How far is the underground entrance from the site?" Leah said.

"I could not say," Roren said. "It was only a drawing."

"How could we ever find it?" Fenn said.

"In the drawing it was marked by three fat toads."

"Rocks?" Grayson said.

"Don't all rocks look like toads?" Sadie said.

Roren turned to her with a smile. "I suppose we will have to see for ourselves."

"Are we prepared for an underground journey?" Prenalin said.

"Aye," Rogget said. "I've got two torches and a lantern from Sponhide's. Took the liberty. We've got enough food to get us to the north port, supposing this underground search don't take us too long."

"North port?" Marigold said.

"Aye. Begging your pardon Miss Marigold, but I wouldn't

think your eastern port is safe, what with Ruhm's army preparing to sail."

"We can argue that later," Leah said. "What do you say, Fenn?"

"It's worth a try. But if we don't find it there, is there any other place to look?"

Leah shook her head. "The mines of Galdred, I suppose; but I doubt it's there. I feared it may be in the southern lands, but I cannot find that Daken went there at all."

"But there is much time missing," Marigold said, "after he traveled north of Ruhm, as if he wished not to tell what happened. He could have gone south to hide the stone and left it out of the journal on purpose."

"But if he did not mean for his brother to find the stone, why did he not reveal its location to the Hass?" Prenalin said.

"Let us not puzzle about it now," Leah said. "If we find nothing, then we can start again."

Breakfast done and the fire doused, the group headed out across the plain toward a small village. Smoke rose from the chimneys of the small wood houses. Sheep and goats milled about in pens, kicking up dust, and several villagers tended plots of farmland.

"Good travel," a man called out to them. "Can I offer you any water, or a handful of carrots?"

Rogget accepted the man's generosity and thanked him with a promise to take a message to the next village. And so it went, from village to village, to encampment, to one lone woman living in a hut by a stream in a little wood. They were able to gather more food and a blanket for Roren. Roren made a trade for a knapsack, determined to carry his share of the load. As they neared the border of Ruhm, the land seemed to rise and rise

224

until they were above the world and looking back, Leah paused to view the plain sloping downward gently to the city and the sea beyond. Eastward, she could see tiny white specks where the land ended and the blue ocean began—Ruhm's ships, readying for an attack on the Ruud.

When they came upon the site of Rett's sacrifice, just inside the province of Galdred, they stood quiet for a time. There was nothing there; Fenn looked disappointed.

"Not what you were expecting?" she teased him.

He shook his head.

Just east of the village of Sacrifice, the site was no more than a ring of stone markers around an empty piece of ground.

"It doesn't look as if anything remarkable happened here. How do you know it's the right spot?"

"If the sacrifice happened at all—"

Roren's gasp interrupted Marigold; he sputtered.

"If it happened at all," she said looking at the young king, "which we doubt, it was probably not here."

"The people of Sacrifice," Pren said, "claimed the site when they founded their village; they set up the markers and enjoyed the increase in travel from the pilgrims of Ruhm. At least, so far as our research can tell."

Roren stared at them all as if they'd gone insane. He shook his head and turned away. "North then," he said.

The landscape was still brown and dry, but suddenly, as if by magic, gray mountaintops, far in the distance, decorated the horizon. And their trek was now spotted by small bits of wood.

"They say this was all forest once," Leah told them.

"What became of the trees?" Sadie asked her.

"Taken down. Some used in the building of Ruhm. Some shipped off to the southern and eastern lands."

"I prefer the forests," Sadie said.

"I do, as well."

"There." Roren led the way toward a rocky hill in the distance. "Those are toads if ever I saw one."

Sadie shook her head. "Looks like a pile of rocks."

"Use your imagination," Roren said.

"Yes," Leah said. "And just think, underneath them is a secret passage."

"Aye," Rogget said. "The tunnel could be right under our feet."

Sadie stepped back and looked to the ground, lifting up one foot and then the other as if she might be stepping on someone. Leah laughed and took the girl's hand.

"You say it was one, long meander?" Rogget asked.

"On the drawing, yes."

"You're concerned," Leah said.

"Aye. The mine passages I am familiar with go on for miles, twists and turns, cliffs and drops, pathways to nowhere. Very dangerous."

Leah shuddered—well she knew. It only then occurred to her their plan was to go underground. When they came to the boulders, they walked around and around them, looking for an entrance, but there was nothing.

"Of course," Marigold said. "He wouldn't have left it open."

Rogget and Prenalin gripped the bottom edge of one of the rocks—the head of a toad—and lifted, but there was only dirt beneath it. In groups, they worked to lift the heads and feet of the toads, and Leah let out a yell.

"Here," she said, laughing, trying to regain her breath. "It's here. I can't believe it. It's true."

Beneath the larger of one of the toad's feet, lifted and rolled

226

by her and Rogget, was a hole, wide enough for one small person to drop into. Smiling, Fenn looked to the dark crevice in the ground and then to Leah. She knew her excitement had vanished; she could see that her appearance frightened the boy. Still, she couldn't manage to stop herself from trembling as she felt the blood drain from her face.

Chapter Thirty-six

Are you all right?" Fenn asked Leah. She looked as if she were wound tight, ready to bolt.

Prenalin moved to stand beside her and she shivered. "You don't have to go," he said. "I'll stay here with you, above ground."

Relief seemed to wash over her.

"Aye," Rogget said. "We'll need someone to shout them out, help them find the opening again, in case there are many paths. Maybe someone just inside as well with the torch."

"Well, I'm going," Fenn said. He found the lantern among their bags.

Leah turned to him, frowning. "It's dangerous," she said. "Rogget should go; he's the one of us with the best tracking skills, I'd bet."

"I can't fit into that hole," Rogget said.

"I want to go," Sadie said.

"I'd rather you didn't," Leah said.

"But why not?"

"I was lost," she said, "for days, in the mines in the east. I would have died if it hadn't been for Fenn's friend, Lucas. If you were to go, I...well, my heart would break every moment you were gone."

"She's right," Rogget said. "We can't have you going just because you want an adventure."

"I'm going," Fenn said.

They stared at him for a moment. Leah nodded.

"Why is it all right for Fenn to go, and not me?" Sadie said.

"This is Fenn's challenge," Leah said, "not ours."

"But your father left the journal for you," Marigold said. "He wanted *you* to find the stone."

"I don't believe he did."

"But the journal—"

"My father wanted me to know the truth—about Rett, about Dakenruud, about the wissendes. I can't imagine he expected I would find the stone. No, I think he meant for the journal to be taken from Ruhm with the other texts...used against the Hass, if possible."

"You aren't going, then?"

"No. But only because I'm frightened. If I never go underground again, I'll be happy."

"I'm not sure any of us can fit through that hole but the children," Rogget said.

"I'd rather not," Grayson said.

"I don't care if I have to go alone," Fenn said.

"No," Leah said.

"She's right," Rogget said. "It's not a good idea."

"I'll go," Marigold said. "I think I can fit."

Rogget eyed the girl, sizing her up, admiration in his smile. "Take this, then," he said, giving her the knife and sheath he wore around his calf.

230

Mari wrapped it three times around her left wrist and let Rogget buckle it. "Perfect," she said.

"What do you think we're going to find down there?" Fenn asked.

"You never can tell," Marigold said.

"Take my bag," Roren said. "It's small and won't be in your way. You'll need something in which to carry the stone...if you find it."

Fenn slid a matchstick against one of the rock toads and lit the lantern. Rogget lowered a sturdy rope into the hole and wrapped the other end around one of the bigger rocks. "Hang on, in case there's a drop," he said. "And stick with the main path."

Fenn lowered himself into the ground, the lantern held above his head. It was a small space, but he was able to scoot himself downward until he felt the ground open against his back just as his feet hit the bottom. From there he crawled backward until the space was wide enough for him to stand. He watched as Marigold's feet came into view, her skirt twisted up in her legs.

When she stood and turned to him, she was smiling. "I'm going to be a right mess after this, aren't I?"

They walked along a large, main tunnel with smaller paths leading off into darkness.

"Those don't look big enough to have been made by miners," Marigold said.

"No. But how do you suppose this big tunnel was made?"

"I've no idea."

"Do you think it has anything to do with the story of Rett?"

"I don't see how."

"Don't you wonder how this Daken fellow found it?"

"I do now, yes. How far were we from the site?"

"A quarter mile at most."

A rustling echoed in the darkness around them.

"What was that?" Marigold said. She grabbed at the lantern and jerked Fenn's hand this way and that.

"It's probably just burrowing rats."

"Too big."

Fenn agreed with her, but didn't want to let her know that. It didn't matter; he wasn't going to let anything stop him. As soon as he'd stood in the tunnel and turned south toward the spot where Rett had supposedly been hanged and burned, he'd felt it. Something drew him along, promising him the answer to every question he had.

Scurrying and pattering of feet continued around them, just beyond the reach of the lantern's light.

"Do you have gnomes in the east?" Marigold said.

"Yes, lots."

"Are they...deadly?"

"Not at all. Mischievous, maybe. But it can't be gnomes; there aren't any mounds on the landscape."

"Perhaps some gnomes do not build mounds."

"I've never heard of such a thing; aren't the mounds created from the dirt they dig out?"

"Well, I've never heard of anything bigger than gnomes burrowing underground."

He looked behind him, to be sure Marigold wasn't frightened. She smiled at him pleasantly enough. When he turned toward their destination, he thought he saw light, but when he lifted the lantern it was gone.

"Take this," he said, giving the lantern to Marigold. "Put it behind your back."

When she did so, he was sure there was a faint green glow

ahead.

"Go back twenty or so paces and hide it behind you again."

"And leave you here in the dark?"

"I'll be right here."

As she walked away, he saw it—a distinct green light.

"It's there," he said. "I see it. Come on."

He moved ahead, into the darkness, the light guiding him like a beacon. Marigold called to him to wait, but he kept on. A booming silence pulsed in his ears, louder and louder until Marigold's words were muffled and distant.

"Hurry," he said.

He hadn't realized he'd broken into a run until he could see it—a deep green sphere, giving off a brilliant light. The closer he got to it, the faster it seemed to pulse in his ears and in his chest. As soon as he was on it, he was certain it was part of him and the pulsing was his own heart beating. It sat atop a stone pillar in the middle of the path and Fenn reached out, put his hands on either side of it, and everything stopped—the pulsing gone, silenced, the light extinguished. Only Marigold's screams echoed in the tunnel behind him.

"Mari," he called.

Fenn grabbed the stone and turned toward the lantern, only to find it sitting alone on the path; he ran and grabbed it as he passed.

"Mari?"

He could hear her up ahead in the darkness—her screams had become guttural, angry, courageous, and when he finally came upon her, the lantern light dancing all around, she was battling shadows, a bloodied knife in her right hand.

Fenn darted forward, dropping the kell stone and the lantern to the floor of the tunnel. He grabbed at the shadows, flinging them off Marigold and against the walls where they hit and squealed, only to come at him again, growling, biting. Instinctively, he threw his hands at them and away, forcing them, as if with wind, against the walls, several at a time and Marigold with them. Finally, they scurried off into the darkness and Fenn turned to see the green glow of the stone bouncing along the tunnel—they'd taken it.

"Take the lantern," he said. "Get to the entrance."

"I'm not leaving you."

Fenn heard her running behind him and was grateful for the light of the lantern, aiding him in stepping over the uneven floor. He no longer needed to see the stone; he could feel it drawing him forward. When they caught up to the shadows, he dove into them, grasping for the stone and as soon as he'd got his hands on it, a wave of powerful wind exploded from it, forcing the creatures into the darkness once again.

He found Marigold sitting on the ground, her hands behind her, propping herself up.

"What was that?" she said.

Fenn struggled to catch his breath, looking to the stone in his hands. Its light, no longer cast outward, instead seeped into his hands and up his wrists.

"It was the kell stone," he said.

Chapter Thirty-seven

I think you were right," Fenn told Marigold, putting the stone in Roren's knapsack, as they made their way to the entrance where thin rays of sunlight beckoned. "They were gnomes. Changed into something different here underground."

"What's that, you say?" Rogget said as he grabbed Fenn's hand and pulled him from the hole after Mari.

As soon as Fenn was above ground, he was knocked to his knees as if someone had punched him. He watched as the others sank to the dirt around him, and he smiled. The pulse of the stone slowed and after a few seconds, Fenn felt as if he could breathe again and his ears popped open. Every noise—the chirp of a bird a mile west and Leah Hallowsing's gasp—was crisp, potent, and imbued with meaning somehow, as if the stone could portend which was most important, which would bring him more joy; it pulled those sounds closer to him, let them resonate within him.

"What happened?" Sadie said.

They all found their feet; Rogget pulled Fenn to standing.

"It's the stone," Rogget said. "You found it."

Fenn could see, as if for the first time. The largest towers of Ruhm in the distance, open windows, paintings on the walls inside. The mountains in the north, frozen, snow-capped—deer and hare loping in a clearing.

"Fenn," Rogget said, "what is it?"

"Nothing," he said.

"Do you have the kell stone?" Leah said. "Could it truly have been that simple?"

Fenn turned to Marigold; she was cut and bloodied. Her hair had escaped its binding and played wild about her head and shoulders. A jagged tear in her skirt cut from the middle to its hem. But she was smiling, her eyes dancing as if she'd had a great adventure.

"What's happened to you?" Leah said.

"Gnomes," she said. "Turned into vicious shadowy creatures. They attacked us."

"They were probably protecting the stone," Prenalin said.

"Indeed," Mari said. "When Fenn came to my aid with the beasts, they took it and ran. But he took it back and—" She looked to Fenn, her eyes wide, mouth open, without words.

"It was the kell stone," he said. "It just...knocked them all away."

"Not the stone," Rogget said. "It was you, yourself."

Fenn shook his head. He pulled Roren's pack from his shoulder and dug the stone out of it, holding it in one hand while they all stared at it.

"It's beautiful," Leah said.

"Perfectly," Marigold agreed.

"Don't you see, Fenn?" Rogget said. "You're part eis; having the stone above ground is enough to make you stronger. But you're *holding* it."

236

"What do you mean?" Sadie said.

"The beast folk get their power, their strength, from the stone," Grayson said.

"My guess is," Rogget said, "Fenn commands wind and fire. I've heard tell of many an eis who could do it; but it's strongest, they say, in the split folk."

"But he's already done that," Sadie said. "With the angels, remember? And you had him light the fire."

"That's so," Rogget said. "Imagine what he'll be able to do now."

"There's more," Leah said to Rogget. "With the angels. When they were taking you. He commanded the angel to drop you, and it did."

"Did I?"

She nodded at him. They were all watching him; their gazes vacillating from his face to the stone; they were afraid. But Fenn only cared about the kell in his hand. Energy emanated from it, traveled through him, through his chest, through his brain—he felt as if he were breaking apart, as if he might fade into nothing. No, not nothing—the stone itself.

Rogget stepped forward and put a hand on the kell stone. "Fenn," he said. "Fenn."

Finally, Fenn took his gaze from the sphere and looked to Rogget. "I think it be best to put the stone into your knapsack. For safekeeping, eh?"

Fenn nodded. He let Rogget take the stone and watched him, ready to pull the stone back, as he put it in Fenn's pack and handed the bag to him. And without thinking, without being truly certain, he blurted out, "I'm going to take it back to the Ruud and give it to the beast lord."

His words stunned Sadie and Grayson, he could tell. Leah,

Prenalin, and Marigold considered them, and said nothing. Rogget nodded slightly; and Roren smiled.

"It does seem an awful thing to destroy," the young king said.

"But—" Sadie's face twisted with concern—"you'll give power back to the beast folk. They'll take the Ruud."

"They'll take back what was theirs," Grayson said.

"You can't mean that."

"I didn't say I agree with Fenn. But the kell stone was never ours. We stole it from them."

"Maybe for good reason."

Fenn turned to Leah. "What do you think?"

She opened her mouth to speak, shook her head, and closed it again.

"I believe," Prenalin said, "the wissenry originally intended to return the stone to the beast folk."

"Yes," Leah said. "My father would have us do what is right. The kell stone belongs to the beast folk. It always has."

"This is exactly what the prophecy foretold," Sadie said. "You're doing exactly what it said."

"I am not. I'm not wielding the stone and destroying the Ruud. I'm not going to kill a king."

"Returning the stone to the Ruud is what will destroy it."

"How do you know that?"

"Because that's what Dag Anfang said. That was his prophecy. And King Welk is likely already dead."

"But I didn't kill him."

"Didn't you?"

"Sadie," Grayson reached a hand to grasp her elbow and she shook him away.

"Would he have been in the ice realm if not for you?"

238

"We don't know that," Rogget said.

"I *knew* it," Sadie said. "I knew it all along. You are the bairn. You're fulfilling the prophecy."

"I am not."

"You are. Rogget, you can't let him do it. Even Father Britt wouldn't want him to. He told us it had to be destroyed."

Rogget looked to the ground and shook his head. "I don't know what the right thing is, Sadie. But I have to agree with Fenn. The stone does not belong to us. It belongs to the beast."

"Well, I'm not going to let you take it to the Ruud."

Sadie stepped toward him and grabbed for his knapsack. Before she could get her hands on it, she flew backward against Rogget and fell to the ground.

"I didn't do that," Fenn said. "I swear I didn't."

"Of course you did," Rogget said.

Sadie climbed to her feet and rushed at him. "I'm taking it," she growled.

"You are not." Fenn let her grab at his pack and pull it, but he wouldn't let her have it. He concentrated on not pushing her away, but as soon as he wrenched the strap from her grasp, she flew off her feet again landing hard on her backside.

"That's enough," Leah said, kneeling beside her. She looked up at Fenn, anger in her eyes.

"We're supposed to destroy it," Sadie yelled. "You promised us you would."

"I never promised."

"Why don't you let us have it," Grayson said. "It's best for everybody if it's destroyed."

"I thought you'd be on the beast folk's side," Fenn said.

"We won't destroy it; we'll take it to Father Britt. We'll let the wissenry decide."

"No one will be taking the stone from Fenn," Rogget said. "I'm not letting you do that."

"Nor I," Roren said in a smooth, calm voice.

There was a brief silence as Fenn watched a light breeze lift Sadie's hair.

"Then I'm leaving." Sadie rummaged around the site stuffing her belongings into her knapsack. "I'm going back to the Ruud to warn them about you. I can't believe I let you drag me all over two continents and you turn out to be the bairn of prophecy. I can't believe it."

"There is no bairn," Fenn said. "There wasn't even a prophecy."

"You knew all along you weren't going to destroy it. Didn't you?" She walked up to him, her face only a few inches from his, close enough to make Rogget step forward. "Didn't you?"

"Not at first," he said.

"Fenn Foster, you are a liar. You've done nothing but keep secrets from us—from the beginning—and we trusted you. Our parents are going to be hanged because of you."

"Now, Sadie," Rogget said.

Sadie stomped away from the group.

"She can't go by herself," Leah said.

"We need to stay together," Rogget said.

"You can't leave," Grayson said.

She turned back to glare at them. "I can and I will. There is no way I'm traveling to the Ruud with him and that stone, just be hanged as a traitor because of him."

"I'm going, too," Grayson said quietly and began packing his things.

"You don't have to go with her," Fenn said. "She'll be fine."

"I don't need looking after," Sadie said.

Grayson set a hard, angry face on Fenn. "I'm not going with

240

her to take care of her. I'm going because I agree with her."

"Fine, then."

"It's not fine," Rogget said. "I can't let you two travel here in the west alone. You'll stay with us if I have to hogtie you and drag you along."

"I dare you," Grayson said walking toward Rogget. "Go on. I dare you."

"Sadie," Leah said, "listen to reason."

"Reason? I'm listening to what I should have been listening to all along—my gut. And my gut tells me this whole thing stinks. As soon as I saw the mark on his arm I should have turned him in."

"That's enough," Grayson said. "Let's just go."

"I can't let you go," Rogget protested.

"You don't have any choice."

"We'll go with them," Leah said. "It'll be all right." She gathered her knapsack and, as if waking from a sleep, Prenalin and Marigold did the same. "We'll get them home." She put a hand on Rogget's arm. "No harm will come to them."

Rogget frowned, but nodded. "Aye. The eastern port?"

"Lerringlass. You can follow at a distance if you like and find a boat as well."

"Not with the stone," he said. "We'll go on north and take an ice cutter."

"Roren," Marigold said, "come along."

"No," the young king said. "I will stay with Fenn."

"But, we were to take you east."

"I am no longer slave to the plots and fancies of others. I travel east with Rogget and Fenn. If I decide to return to Ruhm to aid you in your plans, I will let you know."

Leah, Prenalin, and Marigold stood looking at one another for several seconds until Marigold shrugged, helpless.

"My father would not have us force anyone," Leah said.

Mari nodded and they all said their goodbyes. As he, Fenn, and Roren watched them follow Sadie and Grayson, Rogget put his hands on his head and let out something of a sob.

"You cannot protect everyone," Roren said.

Rogget walked forward, toward Sadie and Grayson and the others, watching them trudge off across the plains toward Ruhm. Fenn's breathing quickened and his face burned hot. He paced back and forth as anger boiled inside him. He should have known. He should never have allowed himself to trust them. He should have been more careful from the beginning. Suddenly he walked to the fire and swung his arms wildly toward it and then up to sky.

"Watch it," Rogget yelled shoving Roren aside. "Don't be flinging fire at random. You've got to learn to control that."

"What difference does it make?" Fenn said. "There's nothing here to burn."

"There is your honor," Roren said.

"What's that supposed to mean?"

"To have power and use it recklessly is to live without honor."

Fenn sucked in a deep breath and struggled to let go of his anger. He nodded.

Chapter Thirty-eight

Seize them."

Rogget and Roren both put their hands out to stop Fenn when they realized they'd come upon a small encampment of beast folk—eis, trolls, and strange creatures that reminded Fenn of death itself.

They'd hiked north for two days—the stone's effect on Fenn had eased over that time. He found his sight and hearing had settled back to normal, with occasional bursts of intensity when he least expected them. This would be a part of him he would have to explore and learn, he realized. But he didn't fear it.

Rogget told him they were almost to the tiny port where they could take an ice-cutter ferry across the slushy sea to the eastern continent. They'd be north of the wasteland, he told them; they could make their way into the beast forest unseen, through the woods along the west coast of the Ruud.

Now they stood wary, as an eis, pale and blond, with eyes like a clear sky, approached them; behind him, two others readied their bows. The eis called out and two trolls lumbered forward.

Fenn startled and Rogget took a step forward.

"Hold," he whispered. "No need to let on who you are."

Relaxing, Fenn allowed the trolls to yank off their knapsacks and push them along to a stand of trees. The ghostly beast folk, a sort he'd never seen the like of before—tall and gangly, gray like the dead—joined the bulbous, ruddy trolls and helped lash them to the large pines.

"What is this about?" Rogget said. "We're folk of the Ruud, making our way back home. We mean no harm."

"Find it," the eis ordered and the trolls rummaged through their sacks until one of them roared in delight and held up the stone.

The eis looked at Fenn with relief. "If you had destroyed it, I would have killed you."

"How did you know?" Fenn said.

"I felt the stone when you were in the small valley of wither-wood some miles away," he said. "And I heard you discussing your quarrel over it as you approached."

"Then you know we weren't going to destroy it," Fenn said.

"It doesn't matter. I have it now and will keep it safe."

"Who are you?" Rogget asked.

The eis peered at him suspiciously. "I am Quiren of the eis. News is already spreading that the stone is with us again." He nodded at Fenn. "I thank you for your part."

"You have to give it back to the boy."

"I need do nothing of the sort."

"He's the fulfillment of the prophecy."

Stunned, Fenn looked at Rogget. "I am not."

Quiren frowned at Rogget. "Which prophecy?"

"I'm not part of any prophecy."

"You know very well which one."

"It's not true," Fenn protested.

Rogget gave him a stern look.

"The boy says it isn't true," Quiren said slyly.

"He's born of a king of the Ruud, orphaned to the wastelands, and now here he is with the stone."

Fenn struggled to listen, but thoughts raced wildly in his head. What sort of game was Rogget playing? Quiren didn't say he planned to harm them; he only said he would have, if Fenn had destroyed the stone. Still, they *were* tied to trees. But what difference would it make if Quiren returned the stone to the east instead of him? Fenn shook his head and looked up at the eis.

"Is it true, boy?"

"I was born in the wasteland and I am an orphan. That's all I know."

"It's true," Rogget insisted. "Dag Voorspeld named him and gave me the task of helping him along."

Now Fenn was sure Rogget was lying.

"If that is true, then you know what the prophecy stated."

"I do," Rogget said.

Fenn looked quickly again at Rogget. Did he know it? Fenn tried hard to remember if he, Grayson, or Sadie had repeated it to him, but he was sure they hadn't.

"Then speak it," Quiren demanded.

"A new bairn. Born of a king, cast into the wasteland. Raised an orphan. He will rise up against you, King of Michelruud. Dead you are; dead you will be."

Fenn breathed a sigh of relief. He was sure that was correct. It was, at least, close enough. After all, how would Quiren know exactly what Anfang had said?

Quiren stared at them for a moment and turned to Roren.

"And who is this?"

"I am Roren."

"We stole him," Rogget said, "from the Hass."

"Stole him?"

"He was their king. Revolution is brewing, resistance. The wissenry plans to—"

"Enough," Quiren said. He returned to the fire where the other beasts had gathered and together they spoke in whispers for some time. Fenn struggled to hear, but their words bounced about as if in a bubble, and he couldn't make them out. Somehow, he realized, eis must have the ability to keep their words from being heard by others; but he had no time, just then, for figuring that out. Finally Quiren returned and approached Fenn.

"And you say you plan to return the stone to the beast lord, Voorspeld?"

"Yes."

"But you do not claim to be the new bairn?"

Fenn shook his head. "I'm not the son of a king. I'm just another orphan from the wasteland. There's tons of them."

"Then why do you plan to return the stone?"

Fenn shrugged against the ropes that bound him and the stiff bark of the tree scratched against his back. "It belongs to the beasts."

"Then why don't you give it to me and let me take it to Voorspeld?"

"You know it has to be him," Rogget said.

Quiren stared silently at Rogget for a moment. He nodded slowly. "Very well; release them."

The strange beast folk came to them and untied them from the trees. Quiren led them to their encampment and they sat gratefully by the fire and accepted mugs of warm honey mead offered them.

"I will take you aboard the cutter and transport you to the east myself. I will ensure you do as you have promised. Will that be acceptable?"

"Aye," Rogget said. "That'll do."

The trolls were set to guard them while the eis walked away in their small group and the gray folk hovered at a distance.

"Rogget," Fenn whispered. "What are those strange creatures?"

"Anthropophagi."

"What?"

"Ann-throw-poff-uh-guy," he said. "Eaters of flesh."

"What does that mean?"

"Cannibals?" Roren said, looking startled.

Rogget nodded. "I have only seen them deep in the great mountains of the north. I didn't know they ventured this far out."

"What do you mean, cannibals?" Fenn said.

"They eat folk," Roren said, disgusted.

Fenn's eyes popped wide and he gawked at the creatures watching them. They were taller than Rogget, slender and willowy. Their gray skin almost glowed. But they stood quietly, hands clasped at their fronts or behind their backs, their faces placid. Still, his heart raced. The eis wouldn't let them be eaten, would they?

"They eat only dead flesh," Rogget said. "Long dead. Scavengers. Much too weak, or lazy, to kill you for food."

"That's helpful," Fenn muttered. But there were six cannibals and only three of them. "I hope they're not coming with us to the east."

Rogget shook his head. "I don't think they can stay long out of the mountains. I've been told they melt in the higher temperatures."

Fenn decided he'd try to throw fire at them, if it came to it. "When were you over here in the west?"

"Long time ago. When I first ran from the guard."

Finally the eis returned with baskets of breads, aged sharp cheeses, and fruit. They ate and Fenn filled himself so full he needed to lie down. He slept fitfully, jumping up and throwing off his blanket several times prepared to flee the cannibals in his dreams. But they remained standing about them in a circle, their hands clasped neatly, their white hair and dead skin lit dully in the moonlight.

The next morning they were awakened, fed, and led across the land all day until night fell again, where they camped and once more Fenn's sleep was tortured by anthropophagi and grub demons and Lucas rising from the dead only to be eaten up again by the cannibals. Exhausted, he hiked all the next morning to the edge of the western continent and a rocky wet shore, looking out across a blue sea dotted white with ice floes. The eis ship was anchored far off shore and they called out for a boat. It was not as large as Captain Olgut's and Fenn was glad. Even if the cannibals wanted to come, there would not be enough room.

The small rowboat was pulled up to the shore and Fenn waded into the frozen water to grasp it. He pulled himself over the rim and as soon as he landed in the boat, he felt a warmth that began in his chest and spread slowly out across his body. He reached to his neck and felt his mother's charm; it was hot against his skin. It knows, he thought. And then something occurred to him. He pulled his sack off his back as a few of the eis remaining on shore pushed them off and two other eis rowed them toward the ship. He dug inside to the bottom and pulled the kell stone up into his hand, without removing it from the bag. It was warm. It glowed and shimmered. Home, Fenn thought. We're all going

248

home.

One night, several days into their journey, Fenn couldn't sleep. He wrapped himself in a blanket and found Rogget on deck, in the frigid night air.

"Here," Rogget said, wrapping another blanket around Fenn's shoulders. "Can't you sleep?"

Fenn shook his head and his teeth chattered.

"We'll be home soon," Rogget said. "Like as I can tell from the eis maps, the continents aren't so far apart up here in the icy parts. But the trip's tougher on the boat."

"Rogget," Fenn said quietly. "When you told the eis about the prophecy, you were tricking them, weren't you?"

Rogget looked out into the darkness.

"You didn't really tell Dag Voorspeld you would help me fulfill the prophecy, did you?"

"Does it matter?"

Fenn didn't want to answer. He looked to the deck at his feet, kicked at the wood a bit with the tip of his long boot and shrugged.

"I suppose not," he said. But it did matter. "I just wondered, that's all. I mean, I wondered how you could have got into the beast forest when you said you couldn't go."

"Aye, I couldn't go in, not without the stone. It is my penance for killing the centaur. It was given me when I threw myself on his lord's mercy not days after it happened. I'm not allowed to enter the forest again until you and the stone are with me."

Fenn continued looking down. Tears stung at his eyelids. "So that's why you went west afterwards? You were trying to find out about the stone and all?"

"Aye."

"Okay, I was just wondering. Thanks." Fenn walked back

toward the stairs to the sleeping deck below.

"Are you all right, Fenn?" Rogget said behind him.

He nodded, but didn't turn around. "I'm fine," he mumbled.

But he was not fine. He was alone and he realized it with a stabbing pain in his chest and a wave of nausea in his stomach. There was no one left. Father Treacher and Father Britt were useless fools. Lucas was dead. Sadie and Grayson had deserted him and their pact. And now Rogget betrayed him. He fumbled with his blankets on the straw bed and lay in the dark in the rocking ship as it plunged through the ice toward home. All he had now, he supposed, was the Ruud itself. But even that was gone. He could never go home and be a kid again, even if he was just a wissenry orphan.

Fenn sucked in a big breath and closed his eyes tight. Even though it was put on him, and he didn't choose it himself, he loved his life before the tunnel, before Sadie and Grayson and Rogget. He'd give anything to have it back. He let out a long breath. That wasn't true, he admitted. That wasn't really true.

Fenn tossed on his mat, just as the boat rocked him. In his sleep, the turning of his stomach sent waves of disjointed visions through his mind. The woman's hand was cut and bleeding. Lucas laughing. Father Britt's voice saying over and over, "you must escape north, you must escape north." Clutch of The Wretched smirking, Fenn's gold charm dangling from his dirty neck.

Fenn bolted upright, knocking his head on the curved wooden hull, breathing heavily. He darted from his mat and up the steps to the top deck, ran across the ship and fell forward against the the side, vomiting. Again and again he purged until he was gasping for breath and sobbing. Wiping his mouth on the sleeve of his tunic, he stared below him at the black waters, dotted with pale gray ice floes.

"You are unwell?"

Quiren leaned along the rail beside him, but Fenn didn't speak. He swatted the tears off his face with his hands, still trembling.

"We will arrive soon, young Fenn, and you will feel better. There is much to be done in the eastern realm. Much there I love and would fight for. Much for you to save."

They were both silent for some time until Quiren spoke again. "The hero's path is lonely, with no one to trust but himself."

Fenn finally turned to Quiren and smirked. "I'm no hero."

"Heros usually say such things."

Chapter Thirty-nine

1268 Autumn

Aliara grabbed for the midwife's hand and tried to scream, but still she could not make a sound. Her life had already left her, she knew, and her soul only remained to push her child into the world. The midwife and her folk had to help; they lifted her legs, pulled her knees to her sides. One sat behind her, propping her up.

"That's it, love," Clara cooed. "Try to push."

Panting, she did her best to pretend she felt something more than pain, but all that made her who she was, had fled. Elrundt, dead. Her sister Rue-Anna and her betrothed, murdered. Her home—for they were the only home she had after fleeing the ice—gone.

"I'm sorry," she managed to whisper to him when he was swaddled and put in her arms. If she hadn't been attacked by the guard, perhaps...she thought, she could have lived for him. But it was too late. "I'm sorry."

She woke to find she was nursing the infant and she felt a

smile at her lips. A wetnurse had been sent for, Clara told her. In the meantime, the wissende, Father Wold, had arrived.

"He's here," Clara whispered. "Right here."

"Name?" the wissende said.

Aliara shook her head, knowing it was barely perceptible, but still it took all the energy she could muster. She dug deep, forcing herself to lift her eyelids, and turned to him.

"One of the ancient kings," she said, as a long breath escaped her. "One of Elurundt's..."

The wissende nodded and she let her eyes close again. She waited.

"I think," the wise old folk said after a moment, "there has not been a Fenn in the line, since the last one, oh, more than one hundred years ago. Way back to near the beginning. He was a son of Alfred, who was son of Roarn. Roarn being the son of Michelruud. Not *the* Michelruud, no, but Michelruud's son. Michelruud, our founder, had three sons."

And so the wissende spun the tale of the Ruud for her little Fenn. Aliara let her hand rest on his arm as he spoke, silently she asked him to take care of the orphan. With the last of her strength she bound the old man to him as best she could. And when the time came, Aliara could not tell if Fenn was being lifted from her arms, or if she was falling away from him. But the pain of the separation took her last breath.

1280 Autumn

It was not yet dawn when Leah heard the shout. She was used to the voices of the sailors, but this was different—fearful. The steps on deck above her cabin were not the soft, bare feet of the crew, but boots. They'd made port, she realized. And something was wrong.

Prenalin met her on the steps and gave her a warning look, before he bound her hands behind her back.

"This is necessary," he whispered, barely audible, before pushing her ahead of him upward and onto the main deck.

Kirche stood there, his feet apart, one hand on the hilt of his long sword, his cream colored cape glowing in the pale lights of the morning at Cold Sea Port. She heard another muffled cry and realized Sadie and Grayson were bundled up and gagged, being dragged down the gangplank into the city.

"Prenalin," Kirche said. "I can't tell you how relieved I am to see you've returned successful."

Leah's chest lifted with a ragged breath and she forced herself not to cry out. Was it true? Was he with Kirche all along? She cast her glance about the deck looking for Marigold, but the girl was nowhere to be seen.

"But...what's this?" Kirche walked forward, squinting in the dim morning light. He reached out and grabbed at her shorn locks, jerking her head toward him. "What have you done?"

"It was her attempt at disguise," Prenalin said.

Leah recognized the cold, impersonal tone of his voice and wondered how she could have been fooled by him. Was she fooled? Again she had to force herself not to let out a sob, instead, drawing a deep breath.

"It worked," Pren said. "Though she did witness the hanging."

Kirche's head tilted and his brow creased. He made a tsking sound with his lips pursed together. "I so wanted to shield you from that horror, my love. But I suppose it is in a daughter's nature to want to be at her father's side when he pays for his crimes. That is the story we shall tell." He motioned for them to follow.

Prenalin took her by the arm but she pulled away from him.

"I can walk on my own," she seethed.

"Concerned, of course," Kirche was purring, "and riddled with guilt over your father's abuses of his station, you ran dutifully to his side to witness his execution." He walked the gangway, his hand in the air, gesturing as he spoke. "And of course, you were unprepared for such an awful sight and out of shock, cut your hair. Yes, that's right." He held out his hand to help her step onto the pier. She refused him. "Such a sight would make a woman of Hass wish to rid herself of her past. To start over."

"Excellent, Lord Kirche," Prenalin said.

Finally a sob escaped her. Leah glanced behind her at the ship and caught a glimpse of a horrified Marigold before she was forced to follow Kirche into the bustling early morning of Cold Sea Port.

Chapter Forty

When Fenn, Rogget, and Roren followed Quiren off the ship at the rocky cliff shores of Imlich, gray clouds puffed up the sky like dirty cotton in a bowl. Fenn wrapped his arms around his waist against the cold. Imlich. He'd heard stories of this village from Father Treacher on occasion. Beasts of the Ruud were driven either into the ancient pine forest just southwest of Michelruud, or northwest, beyond the wasteland, into the lands of ice. There, they traveled back and forth along the base of snow-capped mountains, between the frozen sea and the ice realm. That was their only territory. Too far north, and they would interfere with the angels. Too far south and the folk of the wasteland and hill country would herd them off. Imlich—where folk dare not tread. Village of the beast, they called it.

Fenn had seen, in these last months, that there were beast folk living all over the land. Fairies still inhabited the faire glade in the Ruud. Gnomes buried themselves under the ground in the hill country. Brownies occasioned the forests. Trolls roamed, though rarely, through Michelruud. But here, in Imlich, *he* was the rarity.

At the shore, Fenn looked up to the rocky ledge he must climb to reach the mainland and saw a large herd of rhinobears and eleshags lumbering across the path at the cliff's edge. And once they passed, a committee of gnomes, trolls, and what looked like elves the size of brownies appeared, frowning down at him. They wore rabbit fur coats and hats and most had pipes, smoke twirling about their heads in the cold morning.

"We were not expecting travelers today," a large, fat troll said.

"We did not expect to arrive today," Quiren said carelessly, and began the trek along a path upward through the rocks.

"We have enough of their kind already." The troll pointed a thick finger at Fenn and the others.

Quiren glanced back at Fenn briefly and continued his hike. "They only return home."

"They belong south, in the Ruud."

"And that is where they go."

"Hmph." The troll stomped a fat foot on the dirt. "That's what the others say."

Fenn was out of breath once he reached the summit. Across from the wide herd path, a village, spotted with huts and fires, filled the plain between two forests, south and north. The forests were populated mostly with pines, bright green against the dull gray sky; but other trees stood bare of leaves, like dead hands reaching for water from the clouds above.

"We need food and drink," Quiren told the committee.

"Take them to the holding place," the troll said. "They may eat with their own kind."

Quiren turned to Rogget as they headed in the direction the troll advised and said, "I have no idea what he's going on about. I've not seen folk this far north in all my years of travel for the eis."

But as they walked the outer edge of the village, along the tree line, they saw, beyond the easternmost point of the village, settled on a widened plain, an unorganized encampment of folk, cordoned off with thick heavy rope tied to stakes dug deep into the ground. Inside the large circle were tents, fires, and folk milling about.

"He's not welcome here." One folk stood and approached them, pointing at Quiren. "You folk come on over the ropes. No beasts allowed."

"He's not a beast," Fenn said. "He's an immortal."

"What's the difference?"

Quite a lot, actually, Fenn thought. *Grayson would give him an earful.* Fenn frowned at the thought. He hoped at least that Sadie and Grayson had made port by now; but anger still bubbled up within him when he let himself rest on the subject of his former friends.

"I will make camp in the village and find out what news explains this," Quiren said.

Fenn looked at Rogget and shrugged. The three of them stepped high over the ropes into the encampment.

"Where do you come from?" the old folk said. "Michelruud? Damon Wall?"

"Michelruud," Rogget said. "But we've been away to the west."

"Why would you be away from the Ruud?"

"It's a long story, and we're tired."

"Of course. Come to my tent. I am Hargodt of Aaronland."

"I'll be Rogget. This is my charge Fenn, and our friend, Roren."

They followed Hargodt around and between campsites to a

large tent where a thin and haggard woman stoked a pot hanging on the spit over the fire and three children sat on the ground wrapped in blankets with wooden bowls in their hands.

"Agatha, my wife," Hargodt said with a wave of his hand. Agatha bounced up and down several times in greeting.

They all fell easily to the cold ground on one side of the fire and were grateful to receive large, round loaves of bread. Fenn showed Roren how to pull out the center and eat it, forming a bowl for soup. Agatha ladled soup for each of them with a slight smile and then handed them wooden spoons.

Over dinner Hargodt told them of the troubles in the Ruud.

"They came over in boats, I hear. Brought horses and firearms. Went into Michelruud and took over the castle first thing."

"No sign of King Welk?" Rogget asked.

"None for weeks, nigh on two months."

"And you left the Ruud?" Fenn said.

"Had to. They was slappin' bands around everyone's arms and tellin' 'em what to do and what to say...even what to think."

"What do you mean?"

"We was told the Ruud is dead and gone. Michelruud failed us. The Hass will free us. We got to smile all the time and be pleasant. We got to say thanks to Kett, or Bett, or some such folk, for nearly everything all day. And no arguin' even over money owed you. If you didn't obey, you got put in what they call stocks. Awful things."

"So the Hass has taken the Ruud," Rogget said.

Fenn could only think of Sadie and Grayson. And Miss Hallowsing. What must have happened when they sailed into port? Were they hidden? Were they all right?

A flurry of activity erupted eastward—people shouting. But it was a moment before Fenn could understand them.

260

"It's the king," someone said.

Rogget looked quickly at Fenn and Fenn's heart began to patter rapidly in his chest. Not King Welk, surely. But did it matter? Any of the kings of the Ruud would be after him.

"My boy here is not feeling well," Rogget said quickly to Hargodt. "Might he lie in the tent?"

"Of course," Hargodt nodded and his wife smiled and patted Fenn's shoulder as she led him into the tent. She busied herself punching down a mattress for him to lie on. Fenn huddled by the open flap and watched Rogget and Roren stand. A small crowd of folk gathered in front of Hargodt's tent chattering.

"Where have you been?" someone called out. "They've taken the Ruud."

"Good folk."

Fenn startled at the deep, scratchy whisper; in it he remembered the strong voice of King Welk.

"Give him some time to rest," another folk said. "He needs food and drink."

A member of the guard in a tattered, faded, red uniform pushed through the crowd toward Hargodt. Without a word, Hargodt waved him and the king to his fire pit where they lowered themselves, weary and worn, to the ground. Hargodt's wife silently pushed past Fenn with a blanket and left him alone in the tent to peer cautiously around the flap. He watched as Rogget and Roren sat to the left of the fire, giving him clear view of the king and his guardsman over the embers. Fenn pondered Welk's face, drawn into a exhausted frown. He took a mug of bitters from Hargodt, and shivered. Folk gathered around, squeezing in, jostling one another for a better spot to hear Welk speak.

"The king has been chased and accosted by the angels these

last weeks," one of Welk's folk said.

Fenn suddenly recognized him as one of Clutch's men. He couldn't fathom how it happened that he would be with Welk.

"Our sire was near home when he received word that the Hass had taken over Michelruud," one of the guards said. "Nay, the entire Ruud. We were told to come here, that a gathering of refugees could be found and we are heartily glad to see Ruud folk once again."

"Can the king not speak?" A lanky, blond folk with a bushy beard peered at Welk, quivering in front of the fire.

"I can," Welk said. His voice was dry and quiet, "but I am severely injured."

A sigh floated around the crowd.

"Can I help, Sire?" A woman came forward, her hair tied tightly back from her face. She wore an apron and wiped her hands nervously on it. "I've tended many a soldier of the Ruud."

"Dear Madam," Welk said with a slight smile on his thin lips, "I am afraid it is angel magic that haunts my wound."

She gasped and whispers fluttered through the crowd. "Too true, that I am not versed in the evil arts of angels," she said. "But I will make you a place near our camp, just over there. We have a thick mattress stuffed with goose down. The softest in the Ruud. You can lie there and I'll feed you chicken soup."

Hargodt's wife stepped to the side, blocking Fenn's view. She put her hands on her hips, but she said nothing that Fenn could hear. By the time she'd moved out of the way, Fenn saw King Welk leaning against Clutch's man, hobbling across the encampment.

Fenn let out a deep breath and realized he'd been holding it for nearly two minutes. He breathed in and out for a time, calming his nervous hands.

262

"Now, now, dear," Hargodt soothed his wife. "It was for the best. We have three children, and travelers to care for. Liberna did you a favor by taking on the king."

When she returned to the tent, Agatha's cheeks glistened with tears. But she smiled at Fenn and patted his shoulder again.

"Thank you," Fenn said, "for taking us in, but we have to leave soon."

She nodded.

Fenn poked his head out of the tent. "Rogget, we have to get out of here."

Rogget smiled at Hargodt and then turned to Fenn. "Aye, we'll leave as soon as we can."

"But why?" Hargodt said. "There's nowhere to go."

Rogget smiled and nodded. "We'll see."

Fenn remained inside Hargodt's tent despite the old man's pleadings, and those of his three little girls, to come out and sit by the fire. King Welk was only two tents away, resting on a mat under a tarp strung to three trees. Fenn wished Rogget would join him inside the tent in hiding; but that would be suspicious. Rogget sat uncomfortably on the ground with his back to Welk and his guardsman all afternoon while Hargodt left and returned to his camp several times. Roren disappeared for long stretches at a time, exploring the camp.

Just as the sun was setting, the king rose from his mat and sat by Liberna's fire. Fenn watched his movement carefully from the door of the tent. Finally, darkness fell and only Welk's shadowy silhouette could be seen against the flames. When Roren returned, Fenn left the tent and grabbed his knapsack.

"Thank you for your hospitality," Rogget whispered to Hargodt and his wife.

Hargodt nodded weakly, the firelight below them casting

strange shadows on his face.

The three of them walked behind Hargodt's tent and through the encampment eastward, crossed over the rope and picked up their pace as they headed across the small plain to the forest of pines. It occurred to Fenn that he should have left Rogget in the encampment and snuck off with Roren, or just on his own. It would serve Rogget right if he escaped him and returned the kell stone to the beast lord without him. He'd tell Dag Voorspeld that Rogget was a lying fink and not to be trusted. But Fenn's heart sank at the thought of it. He knew he'd never actually say such a thing. Suddenly, Fenn's eye caught movement ahead. Shadowy figures in the pale moonlight emerged from the trees up ahead and approached. Guards.

Chapter Forty-one

"Halt," the guard up front said, pointing a firearm at them. They were surrounded before they stopped walking. Rogget, as if sensing Fenn's fear, reached out to stay him, just as he'd done when they'd been accosted by Quiren's group of beasts. A warning.

"We're just travelin' through," Rogget said. "Wanderers, is all."

"Wandering where?" A familiar voice cut the night and Fenn turned, startled.

King Welk walked forward and peered at him in the darkness. "Fenn Foster," he said, drawing out the name as if he didn't know it so well. "We meet again. I trust the felidae will not divert our attention this time; nor will your friends ride up on horseback and whisk you away."

It occurred to Fenn, despite Rogget's hand on his arm, that he could simply push them all away; at least, he *thought* he could do it. Each time he'd managed this repelling, if that was what it was, he hadn't thought about it, hadn't done it on purpose. It came more from anger or fear. He lit the fire for Rogget without emotion, but could he do the same in shoving folk off? And should he? Rogget's grasp tightened and Fenn accepted his caution. He had to admit that King Welk should not know the truth about him; at least, not yet.

Welk motioned to his guard and they were all led back across the brief plain to an encampment separate from the refugees, about a quarter mile distant. A great tent was set up at one end with a fire pit burning orange and yellow. Two rows of smaller tents were pitched on each side of the king's tent. Another fire pit sat in the middle of these, to be shared by the guards.

Fenn was taken to one of the tents next to the king's, shoved inside and left there alone. A guard stood just outside the door and he heard the footsteps of others moving into position all around outside. Removing his knapsack, he felt inside for the kell stone, just to be sure it was safe. He sat quietly for a while, wondering what he should do next. Welk was right. Who would save him this time?

Roren's words returned to him and he frowned. He could force them all away and run; he was sure he could manage it. He could cast fire all about, burn the camp, and escape in the chaos. But should he? What was honor, really, anyway? It wasn't in running away, he was sure of that. A sense of calm come over him, a realization that he had choices. He could wait and see what might happen; he didn't have to use force against anyone...yet. And anyway, he doubted he could repel a bullet. More worrying, however...he knew that once he revealed himself, he would only convince folk that he *was* the bairn of prophecy; that would only make his situation worse.

Suddenly a guard peered into the tent and beckoned him. He followed and knew all the guards' eyes were on him as he was taken into the king's tent. Welk sat inside on a stuffed mat;

266

lanterns hung all around casting shadows on the heavy fabric walls. Toward the back, silken sheets hung from ropes tied across the top of the tent and were pulled taut to hide the king's bed.

"Sit," Welk ordered and gestured to a mat nearby.

Fenn stepped gingerly through the tent and sat in front of the king. The charm against his neck warmed quickly, startling him. He had to force himself not to reach up and touch it—a gold charm of great worth was none of Welk's business.

"Are you hungry?"

Fenn shook his head.

"Thirsty?"

He shook again.

"No? What about honey mead?"

Fenn stared at Welk, his eyes felt wide open and he tried to close them up again and look normal.

"Honey mead," the king called out and suddenly Fenn realized a servant had been in the corner.

"Are you frightened?"

Fenn said nothing.

"You weren't frightened the last time we met."

"Yes I was," Fenn said, before he could stop himself.

The king smiled at him and his charm throbbed with heat.

"I'm glad I arrived ahead of my guardsmen and took brief respite in the refugee encampment. If I had not, I would not have heard that you were there in hiding."

Fenn's cheeks burned hot with betrayal. Who had given him away? Maybe he was recognized by one of the folk. Could it have been Roren? Or maybe it was Rogget. What if he wanted to take the stone back to the beast lord himself? No, no, Fenn told himself. He must stop all this nonsensical thinking; it only led to confusion.

The servant pushed through the tent flap carrying two mugs. He stood before Welk and sipped one mug before handing it to the king. He handed the second mug to Fenn.

"Richard." The king pointed to Fenn's mug.

Richard took it from Fenn and sipped it also, then handed it back.

Fenn stared at Welk and blinked several times. No matter what he did he could not get his eyes to soften, and his charm burned hotter, searing against his skin. Strangely, the amber stone that hung with it cooled, as if to counter the heat. His hands warmed quickly with the warm mug between them and he relaxed, if only a little.

"You never can tell," Welk said.

"Huh?" Fenn took his eyes off Welk and cast them down. That was a stupid thing to say to a king.

"Poison," Welk said. These days, Richard always tastes my drink and food. But I would not have anyone poison you, either."

"Why would anyone poison me?" Finally, Fenn's eyes felt normal again and he looked on the tired king. He brought his focus quickly to his mug, remembering too late that folk were not supposed to look into the eyes of the king. Why had Welk not scolded him before for staring? Fenn shuddered slightly and his hands shook.

"Look up, boy."

Fenn looked up, first by raising his head slightly, then his face, then his eyes to the king.

"That's better. Can you imagine going around talking to folk and having them not look at you?"

Fenn nodded. "Why would anyone poison me?"

Welk smiled at him. "Don't you know?"

268

Fenn shook his head.

"You're the evil bairn, of course. Come to destroy the Ruud."

"I am not." His voice surprised himself. He sounded old, and tired, but resigned as well.

"Perhaps not."

"You think maybe I'm not?"

Welk nodded. "I think it's possible there has been a big misunderstanding."

Fenn sighed with some relief. Finally a grown-up who sounded like he knew things.

"But you do have the mark," Welk said.

"It doesn't mean anything."

"I think it does. I have seen its like before."

Fenn frowned at him. "What will you do with me?"

Welk peered at him and put his hand to his mouth and rubbed his chin. "I don't know."

"Can't you just let me go?" Fenn desperately wanted to tell the king about the stone. Maybe he would understand and let him return it to the beast. But his reason told him the king would not agree to it. It was too risky. Neither of them knew what the stone's effect on the beast might be.

The king shook his head and sighed. "It's not safe for you now. The Ruud is overtaken by the Hass. They would use you, I'm afraid, in a most despicable manner. In the hill country and the wasteland, the Wretched are arming and organizing. That is no place for a boy, either."

"What are they organizing for?"

"For battle. We will take back the Ruud. I think your place is here, in this northern land. When the battle is done, we will try to find a way for you to live in the Ruud. If the people will believe you are not a child of prophecy, nor plan to harm anyone. Do you want to go home?"

Fenn paused and said, "I don't know if it is my home."

"You lived in the Ruud all your life."

Fenn shrugged. "There's no one left there for me." His charm seemed to breathe hot air on his chest and he desperately wanted to pull it away from his skin. He thought of the amber stone, called for it to cool him...and it did.

"What of the wissendes who cared for you as a child? They would be much like parents, would they not?"

Fenn shook his head only slightly. "They kept sending me away. I think even they believe I'm the evil bairn."

"Your friends, then. The ones who so gallantly saved you from my grasp."

Welk was smiling at him now, teasing him. Fenn frowned deeper.

"They're not my friends, anymore."

The king nodded. "I see. What of the huntsman, Rogget?"

Fenn shook his head and let his eyes fall to his fingers wrapped tightly around his mug of mead. "He's only doing a favor for the beast lord in taking me back to the forest." He squared his shoulders and raised his head.

"Why do the beast folk want you?"

Fenn shrugged. "Maybe they believe Dag Anfang's prophecy."

Welk tilted his head and peered oddly at him for a second. "You know of Anfang?"

"I went into the beast forest, to the lord's lair; I heard Anfang speak the prophecy."

Welk smiled and rubbed his chin again. "You are an adventurous sort, aren't you. Ah, well. The land of the Ruud is in your blood; it will beckon you back. I'm afraid for now you'll have to remain here under guard. But why don't we set you a mat here in my tent. It's warmer here, and there are books and trinkets to amuse you."

Fenn nodded in agreement; but he knew the king just wanted to keep an eye on him.

"What about Richard?" Fenn asked.

The king chuckled. "What about him?"

"I don't think he wants to get poisoned, either?"

"Then he'd better keep a sharp eye on the cook, hadn't he?" Welk laughed. "It's a nasty business, this kingship nonsense. I recommend highly against it."

Chapter Forty-two

There was such a flurry of activity that Fenn felt it, even tucked away inside the king's tent reading a book of fables about knights, ladies, and dragons. At one point, he heard someone shout something that sounded like "rebels" and he could stand it no more. He put the book down, cast off his blanket, and went to the door of the tent. He stood just inside with the flap raised and looked out at the folk gathered in the king's encampment.

"What's going on?" he asked the guard standing just outside the entrance.

"Meeting," he said. "The Wretched have arrived."

"Can I go?"

The guard, his hair gray and his face lined with age, smiled at him. "I am to bring you once the fire is full aflame and the stumps and logs are set."

Fenn waited, watching the commotion of folk until another guard approached and whistled at them.

"Let's go, then," the older folk said.

Fenn followed the guard through the crowd, thinking he

should have brought his knapsack in case he saw an opportunity to flee. Gray clouds hovered low in the sky and a wind whipped at his overcoat, a gift from the king—one he said he'd bartered for among the refugees. They came to a large opening in the throng where logs and stumps had been placed in an imperfect circle with a fire pit in the middle. He was surprised to see Rogget with Hargodt and other folk from the refugee camp. He raised his hand briefly in greeting and Rogget smiled and winked, as if to reassure him all was well.

King Welk sat on a chair lined in rabbit fur; he was covered in a thick, worn quilt. Fenn was led to his left and sat on a folded blanket beside him. Despite the wool beneath him, he could feel the cold of the ground seeping into his body.

Welk raised his left hand and the crowd quieted.

"Let us hear from the Wretched of the hill country," he said. Though his voice was dry and laden with pain, it was deep and commanding, carried to all present.

When Clutch stood from his seat on the other side of the king, Fenn was startled, though he scolded himself for not expecting it. Somehow, the king and the thief were known to each other and shared a casual friendship—a fact Fenn had difficulty understanding, even more so now, after finding Welk kind and compassionate, nothing like the leader of The Wretched. Clutch sauntered toward the fire pit in the middle of the circle of folk—his face twisted in a sarcastic smile as he bowed ridiculously low. Fenn was certain he meant to mock Welk, but the king did nothing. And as Clutch bowed, Fenn caught sight of the stone charm, made for him by the children of Path, tied onto a hemp rope, dangling from the thief's dirty neck. Fenn caught Clutch's glance and frowned hard at him; he nearly forced the man off his feet, but remembered, once again, Roren's words. Honor. He

274

must learn to use his skills with honor and respect. Still, he felt certain he could force the charm from Clutch's neck and into his own hand if he had the nerve. But he must not reveal himself.

"Word has spread quickly through the wasteland and the hill country," Clutch said. "We have heard from emissaries all about, willing to go to battle against the Hass to free the Ruud."

"And the eis?" Welk said.

A low hiss, like a sigh, rustled through the crowd.

"We don't need their kind to help us," someone called out.

"Rogget," the king called and Rogget stood with a nod.

Welk surprised Fenn, once again, with the friendly way he greeted the wayonder—as if they were equals.

"You have recently returned from the west. What can you tell us of their strength?"

Rogget fidgeted as he stood encircled by the crowd of folk, clearly unaccustomed to public speaking. "Aye. They've...well, they're...," he stammered. "I saw an army of ships, a dozen at least, ready to sail when we left a week or more ago."

"More ships?" someone in the crowd said.

"Aye. And their folk have got more firearms than we do. But I was told there was to be an uprising of the folk over there. They planned to burn as many ships at port as they could. I don't know if they managed it, though. So, I say we need all the help we can get."

"There's more," Clutch said, scanning the crowd. "The angels will fight with the Hass."

Confusion broke out for a moment while everyone talked and a few shouted to be heard over the grumbling. Finally, Welk held up his hand again.

"It's true," Clutch said. "The angels have agreed to help Hass take the Ruud in exchange for the ice realm. The eis are to be removed or killed. And all folk are to be contained within the boundaries of the Ruud. While that is their agreement, I think we can assume the folk will be slaughtered as soon as the angels get the chance."

There was less muttering this time and silence fell naturally after only a few seconds.

"It is agreed then" Welk said. "We need the eis as much as they need us. We will fight together to defeat the Hass. And if the beast will aid us, we will fight alongside them as well."

Welk allowed the crowd to mumble their complaints, but it was clear to Fenn they were fast resigning themselves to their situation.

"We need someone to return to the Ruud and spread the word of battle secretly. We have a network of spies set up already in Michelruud, and no doubt Damon Wall and Aaronland do as well. We will utilize these spies to our advantage. But we need someone to send messages between here and Michelruud. Who volunteers?"

"I'll go," Fenn said. Many folk squirmed and leaned to see him sitting on the ground beside the king, as if they only now noticed his presence.

Welk shook his head. "We will not send a boy to do a man's job," he said quietly. "No. We need an ordinary folk, used to traveling across the boundaries of the Ruud."

"I'll do it," Hargodt said, raising his hand. "I am a merchant and travel all the Ruud, trading tobacco and wheat."

"Very well," Welk said. "You will meet with us later to discuss the plan before you go."

Rogget stood again. "We need someone to travel to the beast forest and alert them, ask them for help."

Welk nodded. "And you volunteer?"

"Aye, but the boy will have to come with me."

Welk looked down at Fenn and then back to Rogget. "The boy must stay here under guard."

Rogget nodded, but said, "I am not allowed to enter the beast forest without him. And I'm likely the only folk willing to enter at all." He looked around at the faces in the crowd.

Welk shook his head. "Then we'll have to come up with another plan for the beast. The boy remains here."

Fenn found Hargodt's questioning eyes on him and returned his gaze.

"Who is the boy?" someone in the crowd said.

"Our meeting is ended," Welk said. "I ask that you disperse so that I may rest. The guard will keep you posted of our plans for battle."

Grudgingly, the folk muttered and meandered away, left with questions and a growing unease.

Two days later, while Fenn was alone in the king's tent looking through a book on planting seasons, he heard Hargodt talking to the guard outside.

"But I must accompany her," the old man was saying. "She cannot speak and only I can interpret for her."

"Why not the boy?" the guard said.

"A man understands his wife much better than her son."

As Fenn approached the tent flap, in walked Hargodt, his wife Agatha, beaming with a bright smile, and a thin boy about Fenn's size, with pale blond hair. Agatha carried a plate covered with a napkin. She bowed and rose several times, still smiling.

"Hello," Fenn said, happy for the company.

"Come, young Fenn," Hargodt said rather loudly. "Sit and enjoy Madam's sweet potato pie."

Hargodt nodded his head and winked.

"Thank you," Fenn said.

Agatha pulled the cover from her pie plate, but there was no pie. Fenn looked at the strange pile of blond hair on the plate and then to Hargodt, who put his finger to his lips. Hargodt pulled the hair off the plate and showed it to Fenn. It was sewn neatly onto a thin piece of cow hide. Hargodt plopped it on Fenn's head. Madam got a comb from her pocket and set about combing it. When she'd finished, she stepped back and clasped her hands to her chest.

"Oh, it is good," Hargodt said. "Madam is so happy you like it."

Fenn giggled a bit; he hadn't realized before that the Hargodts were insane. But as Hargodt took the blond boy by the shoulder and led him to the mat Fenn had been sleeping on, the whole plan began to put itself together in Fenn's head.

"Tired? Well of course you are," Hargodt called toward the front of the tent. "Yes, yes, you rest now. We'll bring more pie tomorrow."

Fenn stared at Hargodt, wide-eyed, and shook his head. This would never work. How stupid did he think the guards were? They'd never buy it. But Madam smiled at him and put her skinny arm around his shoulders and all three of them walked out of the tent and across the encampment as if they were heading back to the refugee camp.

"Are they following?" Fenn whispered.

"Don't look back. And don't worry. Benjamin will lie in your bed until the next check. We've been watching. They check on you only every two hours while the king is out of the tent. Once they make the next one, Ben will climb out the back as the sun sets. If a guard sees him outside the tent, he'll run. But you'll be far away by the time they figure out he's not you."

As they neared the refugee camp, Rogget and Roren joined them and they all smiled and nodded and pretended to take a walk about. Once they neared the trees of the forest, Hargodt and his wife turned and faced the camp.

"I see no one watching. Take care my friends. And good luck with your mission."

The three of them darted quickly into the trees and didn't stop running until they were three miles in.

Chapter Forty-three

Fenn decided it was better to be on his way to the beast lord and out of Welk's tent, even though he had to be in Rogget's charge again. And it wasn't as if Rogget had become mean or cruel. He was still Rogget. But Fenn couldn't help remembering his betrayal, every time he caught him looking at him with his worried face. Let him worry. He had lied, after all. He shouldn't be trusted again. Fenn refused to smile at Rogget and kept his glare firm and his mouth rigid, long after his jaw ached to be relaxed.

They walked for miles and miles in the forest seeing no one, folk or beast.

"This will lead into the deepest part of the western wood next to Steingefan." Rogget said after they'd all been silent for several hours.

Fenn shivered. "We've got to find shelter for the night. It's freezing."

"Aye."

They walked on for another hour and came to three huge boulders jutting from the ground among a dozen large rocks.

There, Rogget dug a pit and lit a roaring fire without asking Fenn for help, and the three of them huddled around it, shivering. Finally, Fenn began to warm; he looked at Roren, who hadn't spoken in so long Fenn worried he could no longer do so. His cheeks were flushed pink and he stared into the flames, despair etched on his face.

"Are you all right?" Fenn whispered to him.

Roren stared at him for a moment before nodding.

"Can you talk, anymore?"

"Why do you ask?"

Fenn sighed with relief. "I don't know when the last time was you said anything."

Roren looked back into the flames. "There is nothing to say. I was king to my folk, servant of Rett; and yet, I had no power. I was discarded by them both so easily, and sent into a dungeon to starve to death. Rescued by strangers who cared for my life more than my own folk. And now I travel with you, a burden. I am adrift in this wood; adrift in the world."

"Sounds like there's a lot to say," Fenn said with a smile. But Roren didn't respond.

Rogget set up his spit over the fire and walked deep into the wood, without a word.

"A rift has formed between you and your guardian," Roren said.

Fenn only nodded.

"Despite his reasons for protecting you, it's clear he cares for you, much like a father for his son."

"Maybe." Fenn found a stick and poked at the fire with it.

"And you miss your friends."

Fenn tossed the stick into the flames, angry. "I don't miss them."

"No?"

He sighed. "I guess I do. I miss feeling like I had friends. But when I remember what they said, I think it was all a lie. I get so—" Fenn pushed at the fire with both hands and flames flew at the trees, licking the evergreen needles. He sat fuming for a moment before turning to look at Roren. "I keep thinking about what you said when they left, about how I had to act with honor."

"It is clear you are honorable; but you are young."

"It scares me. The way I knocked Sadie down without thinking at all—I didn't mean to do it. And when the guards took me to Welk, I did nothing. But, they had guns. I don't think I can repel a bullet."

"It is good to learn control."

"Is it? I mean...can I hurt someone if I'm not upset? It would seem...cold. Calculating. I don't think I want to be that way. It doesn't seem honorable."

Rogget returned with water in a leather pouch. They boiled potatoes, onions, and carrots given them by Agatha. They warmed honey mead in another pot and poured it into their mugs.

"What will you do," Fenn said to Roren, "now that you're free?"

"Free?" Roren shook his head and sipped his mead.

"You can stay with me."

"But where will *you* go?"

Fenn laughed. "I see what you mean. I suppose we'll have to be wayonders together, like Rogget."

"There's something I need to tell you, Fenn," Rogget said. "About this prophecy thing."

"You mean about how you made a deal with the beast lord

to make sure I got the kell stone?"

"Aye. About that."

"What more is there to say? You lied to me."

"Not exactly."

"You let me think—wait, you let the wissenry think you were working for them to protect me. But—"

"I *was* protecting you."

"You were protecting yourself."

"I don't see the harm done," Roren said. "If he was also making sure you got the stone, he was still your guide and protector. What difference does it make?"

"We made a pact," Fenn said. "We all four swore to not lie to one another anymore and to stick together. And I'm the only one who stuck to the pact. Sadie and Grayson ran off, and now Rogget turns out to be a traitor."

"That's a rather harsh description," Roren said.

"It's the truth."

"How so? What did he do to betray you? He did not tell you the whole truth. We are all guilty of that, at some time in our lives."

Fenn knew Roren was right, of course. He hadn't been honest with Sadie and Grayson about himself; not at first. And the truth was that he still hadn't told Sadie, Grayson, or Rogget everything. He hadn't told them about his visions. But that was different, he reasoned. His visions had nothing to do with them—they were personal. And Rogget working for Dag Voorspeld to bring Fenn to the beast forest had everything to do with Fenn.

"Why didn't you just tell me?" Fenn heard the disappointment in his own voice and struggled to not allow tears in his eyes.

Rogget shook his head, despondent. "How could I? You didn't believe you were the child of prophecy—for all I know you're not and this whole thing is nonsense. I was afraid it would scare you, thinking that Voorspeld was after you, on top of the kings of the Ruud. And then, you were determined to destroy the stone."

"What would you have done if he tried to destroy it?" Roren said.

"I would have let him—not that I think it can be done."

"You would?" Fenn said.

"Aye. I don't have to make peace with the beasts. I want forgiveness, but I can live without it. I was happy to help you and Sadie and Grayson—happy to protect you and guide you. There are so many secrets I've had to keep."

"There are more?"

Rogget nodded. "Aye. Father Britt would not allow me to tell you about your being a split folk and the powers you're likely to have."

"How did Father Britt know?"

"It was the mark, of course. It's the mark of split folk."

"No."

They all jumped as the darkness seemed to move. Quiren walked forward from behind one of the large boulders, smirking at them.

"It is not the mark of split folk."

"How did you find us?" Fenn said.

Quiren laughed.

"He's an eis," Rogget said. "He could probably hear our footsteps a thousand feet away."

"I mean you no harm." Quiren joined them on the ground around the fire. "Unless you do not fulfill your promise."

"We're taking the stone to the beast lord," Rogget said. "You have my word."

"Like that means anything," Fenn said.

"Hear now," Rogget said. "I'm sorry I didn't tell you the truth. I didn't do it to hurt you."

"Stop bickering," Roren said. "It no longer matters."

They were silent for a moment as Fenn fumed. Quiren watched him closely; he didn't trust Fenn. None of them really trusted one another and why should they? Fenn was unsure of Rogget's motives. Roren acted like he was lost and in shock, but there was something underneath his eyes that told Fenn he was smarter than he was pretending to be. Quiren had threatened to kill Fenn and now glared at him. And Fenn had to admit, he wasn't to be trusted, either. He'd lied about his mark as long as he could. And he'd kept his plans to himself, as well. Maybe if he'd talked to Sadie and Grayson about the stone earlier, instead of just telling them after he'd decided not to destroy it...maybe they'd still be there with him. Sadie would tell him what to do about Rogget. Sadie would still trust Rogget; Fenn was sure of that.

"What does the mark mean?" Fenn asked Quiren.

"Why would you believe what he tells you?" Roren said, still staring into the fire.

"I didn't say I would."

"You will believe. You will all believe—when the stone is set in its rightful place."

"Well, go on then," Rogget said.

The eis' smile deepened. He stood and pulled off his over-coat, then a long leather vest. He untied his tunic and pulled it down over his left shoulder. There was the mark of the faire on his arm, just like Fenn's.

286

Even Roren stared at Quiren now. "What is it?"

"The mark of the faire," Rogget said.

"Yes. And no," Quiren said, now pulling his overcoat back on and sitting again on the ground with them. "It's a fairy mark, given us at birth when they take our blood."

"They take our blood?" Fenn said. "Why?"

"For the stone. Those with the mark are bound to the stone and to the Rad—the council of the beast folk. We represent our kind there, when it is called. I am the consul for the eis."

Fenn let out a laugh and they all looked at him. "Who would I represent?"

"You are folk eis. You will represent those like you."

"But the folk have no consul," Rogget said. "Do they?"

"No," Quiren said. "The gathering was always for the immortals. There were never split folk represented before. But we have not had a Rad since the stone was stolen from us, many generations ago."

"What happens if a consul dies?" Roren said.

Quiren looked at Roren curiously, but Roren kept his eyes on the fire. "As the consul ages, a new bairn is selected of his kind."

"But what if he is killed suddenly?"

Quiren tilted his head and his brow furrowed. "Another would be selected."

"But they can be killed?"

"Why do you ask these questions?" Quiren said.

Roren shrugged and returned his attention to the fire. "I have lived my life in the west; we do not have such superstitious nonsense there."

"Ha," Fenn said with a laugh.

Roren looked at him, frowning.

"Sorry," Fenn said, trying to force the smile off his face. "But what about Rett?"

They all looked at Fenn while a cold wind whipped up and blew smoke suddenly into Rogget. He jumped up, coughing.

"Let's get some sleep, mind," he said. "We've still a long way to travel."

Chapter Forty-four

The next day they walked miles and miles through the wood until mid-day. They stopped to rest and have lunch and Rogget wandered off to find a rabbit or squirrel for the evening meal.

"Tell me, Fenn," Quiren said when they'd built up a fire. "What split skills do you have?"

"Split skills?" Roren said.

"He must have several odd things going on about him. They all do."

"How many folk eis have you come across?" Roren said.

"None. But the Hass is firm against them, even more so than against the beast. They say they possess unnatural talents. So, Fenn, what are your unnatural talents?"

They looked at him, smiling, waiting. Rogget reappeared carrying two dead rabbits by the feet.

"He can conjure fire, and toss it," Rogget said. "And he can read you when he touches you. He's got the eyesight of the eis. And when he was a small boy, he forced a playmate to eat a cricket with only his mind."

"How do you know about that?" Fenn said.

"I've been watching. And Father Treacher told me about the cricket."

"Darryl ate the cricket all by himself. I didn't have anything to do with it."

"Darryl said different, I guess. And don't you remember that was when you and Father came to live in Path? They had to move you around a couple of times because of that sort of behavior. It's a wonder you weren't branded the evil bairn when you were three."

After they ate a lunch of hard biscuits and jerky, Rogget was up and dousing the fire. "Let's pack up and move on. The animals were skittish. I'm thinking there might be some of the guard or the Hass roaming about. The sooner we get into the beast forest, the better, eh?"

They walked on until the sky darkened into a deeper shade of gray, and camped for the night in a thick wood where the wind was minimal. Rogget cooked the rabbits on wood spits over a small fire. Fenn wrapped his blanket around him and gathered pine needles into a pile to sit on, leaning against a tree not too far from the warmth of the flames.

And so they tramped for several days southward staying as far west as the forest would allow. At times, Fenn could smell the ocean and knew they bordered the sea. During the day, Quiren taught him and Koren sword and knife play, but each evening, they all grew more and more silent. Fenn was sure there was something wrong, but he didn't know what until one day, Rogget and Quiren returned from a brief hunt and had them pack up and begin moving again.

"Hurry," Rogget whispered. He pulled at Fenn's coat and together they darted through the trees.

290

They bolted, skirting thick trunks, jumping low shrubs, and batting at low-hung branches. Vines and leaves tore at Fenn's face and his feet caught roots and tangles of ferns. He got a glimpse of Roren, his face pale, scrambling to keep up; Quiren had disappeared into the trees westward. Cracks and thuds echoed around him, as if monstrous beasts plunged through the woods toward them from all directions. Turning back in search of Rogget, he felt something hard pitch against his legs and he was on the ground.

"Rogget," he screamed.

A shot rang out and Rogget roared. Soldiers of Hass, their heavy plum tunics emblazoned with a tree in flames, each one with a firearm, surrounded Fenn.

"Find the stone," one said as another pulled Fenn to standing.

He was bound at the wrists and feet, surrounded by guards, and marched through the woods alone.

Chapter Forty-five

Leah stood at the window of her upstairs room at the inn in Path, looking out on the center of the village. Soldiers of Hass paraded in the streets keeping watch on those citizens who had not escaped the Ruud before Kirche and his men took control. The villagers walked wide swaths around the soldiers, nodded politely as they tried to go about their routines. When she saw Dowling hurrying toward the inn, she backed away from the window and waited. She knew Dowling wouldn't come to her right away; that would arouse suspicion. So she paced and wrung her hands and worried.

When the knock at the door startled her, she hesitated so as not to appear eager. Finally, she opened the door and let the woman carry a tray into the room. The guard outside stood in the doorway and watched as Dowling set the tray on the table and left without a word. He watched as she picked at her food, ate a few bites, poured tea from the kettle into her cup, drizzled honey into it and stirred. He waited while she nibbled her bread, forced herself to eat as much stew as she could stomach. And finally, when she told him she was finished, he called for

Dowling.

The woman entered and lifted the kettle from the tray.

"Why miss, you haven't had but one cup of tea. I'll leave the kettle for you and be back in an hour or so with something sweet to tempt you. You really must eat more."

Leah nodded and watched Dowling leave before closing the door behind her, offering her guard an angry stare as she did so. Once alone, she finished the tea in her cup and poured the remaining water out of the kettle into it, then flipped the kettle upside down. As quietly as she could, she unscrewed the bottom of the metal vessel until it popped off. A piece of writing paper flitted to the floor and Leah scooped it up.

Dowling's note was scribbled hastily: Children alive, Steingefan. Signs posted, rally tomorrow, bairn of prophecy to be hanged. Lord Kirche's secretary asks after you.

At that last, Leah folded the paper over and ripped it again and again, fuming. How dare he? When she thought back to the last time she saw Prenalin, his face like a stone, his eyes cold, not that he would look at her, she shuddered with rage. And still, always that doubt. She hated herself for it, but it gnawed at her, bit at her dreams, unsettled her stomach and pierced her head with pain. Whose side was Prenalin on?

Kirche and Prenalin took to Michelruud castle, so Dowling said in one of her notes, while Leah was imprisoned with the ranking soldiers at the inn. She felt so helpless. She knew she couldn't let them hang Fenn; but what could she do? She paced the floor the rest of the evening, leaving the sweet cakes Dowling brought her untouched, until darkness filled the room. Without lighting a candle, she took to the bed and lay there. Eventually, she decided she'd have to try to jump from her window, just before dawn. It was her only chance.

294

When she startled awake some time later, she realized someone was in the room. Before she could move to scream, a hand slapped over her mouth and Prenalin whispered, "Don't shout; you'll rouse the guard."

Leah struggled against him, trying to tell him she didn't care, let the guard come in. Slapping at his arm, she managed to sit up in the bed.

"Listen quickly," he said. "Kirche plans to hang the boy. I wanted to warn you...prepare you."

Gasping for breath against his hand, without thinking, she rotated her face slightly and sunk her teeth into whatever skin she could manage to fit between them.

"Aargh!" Prenalin jerked his hand from her.

She scurried out of the bed and shoved him. "Get out," she seethed.

"You think I planned this," he said. She couldn't tell if his shock was true or feigned. "You think I gave you up to Kirche, that it was my plan all along."

"Wasn't it?"

He stared down at her in the darkness. The moon outside the window lit the left side of his face; his jaw was set hard and cruel. She could hear his breath soften as he tried to force a calm.

"He intends to hide you here in the Ruud," he whispered, "until your hair has grown back to its appropriate length. He then believes he can return with you to Ruhm, victorious. He has yet to learn of the uprisings there. Ruhm's ships, what is left of them, are due to arrive soon and then he may become desperate."

"I won't be here that long."

"Don't attempt an escape, yet; it won't work."

"Why should I listen to you?"

"There will be a battle, soon. The soldiers will be called on; there will be chaos. Then you can make your move."

"And let Fenn be hanged?"

"What do you expect to do? The courtyard in front of the castle will be filled with soldiers of Hass. You'll be taken away, or killed, and that won't help the boy."

"You apparently won't help him."

"My concern is you," he said. His voice was softer now, his brows knit together.

Leah hesitated, uncertain. "You swear to me—"

"I do. I swear I am not with Hass."

She nodded, but made it curt, and wondered if she would ever believe him. "What of Marigold?"

"They thought she was the laundress on the boat. She's at the Snapping Turtle Inn in Cold Sea Port, still working with the resistance."

"Can you stop him?" she said. "Can you save the boy?"

He shook his head and backed away; she moved toward him, anyway.

"Promise me you'll try," she said. Without thinking, Leah reached out to put her hand on his cheek. She took another step, lifted herself up on her toes, and put her lips to his.

Chapter Forty-six

When they drew the heavy metal cell door open, Sadie rushed in and fell into her mother's waiting arms, sobbing. The door shut with a clang and Sadie jerked in surprise.

"There, now, girl. All's turned out well. You're here now in Ma's arms."

Sadie shook her head against her mother's scratchy wool coat. How like Ma to see the world so simply. Sadie was there, with her Ma, so all was right. But all was so desperately wrong.

They walked to the corner where Sadie hugged her father and all three sat huddled over a candle flame, the only warmth in the room.

"They told me you were here and I kept asking and asking to see you and they kept saying tomorrow, tomorrow. I thought they'd never let me. I thought they were lying and you weren't really here at all."

"Aye," her father said. "Same for us. They told us when you arrived but wouldn't bring you to us."

"Why are they so mean?"

"I'm sure they wanted to question you first. Did they?"

"Yes. And Grayson. Over and over again. They hurt him."

"What about you?"

"They just scared me, only slapped me once." Her mother gasped. "But Grayson has a blackened eye and a split lip. Ma, it's awful."

"What did you tell them?" her father asked. "What is it they're after?"

"The kell stone. I told them we went into the mines of Galdred and we got lost and we found our way out and waited and waited but Fenn and the others never came out. So we walked to Port Lerringlass and came home."

She looked at her parents carefully, back and forth.

"Is that all you told them?" her mother said.

She nodded. "I only said that much because they told me they had proof that Fenn had the kell stone."

"Is that what happened?"

She stared at them.

"Sadie Pratt." Her mother laughed, but it was a strangled, frightened sort of chuckle. "You don't think your ma and da are spies for the Hass?"

Sadie tried to smile and wiped the tears from her face. "Well, maybe."

"Oh, dear gnomes underground," her father muttered.

"Go on, girl—" her ma gave her a squeeze—"it's all right. You don't have to tell us anything you don't want to. But I want to hear about all your adventures. For a time we were getting word from one of the king's spies. We heard about your travels in the hill country and that you were at the battle of the eis, but escaped unharmed. And then you disappeared from the wissenry at Cold Sea and that got us worried. I'm just so glad you're back with us."

"The wissenry wanted us to go north, but we went west."

"We heard as much yesterday."

"How do folk know?"

"There's a network of spies all over," her father said, "as it turns out. I'm afraid a battle is looming and we must be prepared."

"That's what I'm confused about. I'm not sure whose side I've been on."

"Were you not on Fenn's side?"

Sadie lowered her voice to a whisper. "I came home with Grayson because, well, I fought with Fenn over the stone."

"Fought how?"

"I lied to the Hass. We didn't lose them in the mine; we didn't even go there. I only thought of it because Leah was telling us about it on the boat. It was where Michelruud found the stone a long time ago."

"They told us you'd left with a young woman; was that Leah?"

"Miss Hallowsing, yes. She's from Ruhm."

Her father gave her a stern look.

"It's a long story, Da, but I promise she wasn't a spy or anything. At least I don't think so."

"Well, go on then," he said. "Why did you fight about the kell stone?"

"Fenn found it, beneath some sort of shrine. The wissenry wanted it destroyed. But Fenn—"

"He didn't?" her father said.

Sadie shook her head. "He said he was going to give it to the beast lord. I was so angry; I called him a traitor." A tear rolled down her cheek and she wiped it away.

"It'll be all right, Sadie, dear. You'll see."

"How can you be so positive? Fenn's here by now, with the stone. If he gives it to the beast folk, who knows what will happen? And if the Hass gets it...what if they use it against us?"

"All we need to know is that we will fight to get the Hass out of the Ruud," her father said. "That's all that matters to us at this moment."

"And we're together now," her mother said with a smile.

"But I need to get back to Grayson and make sure he's all right."

"No doubt they've sent him off to his da."

Sadie sighed. "I hope so. But something's just not right, Ma."

"What do you mean?"

"I don't know. I just have this feeling Fenn is in danger. And I think Grayson and I are in big trouble."

Chapter Forty-seven

Metal cuffs were clamped to Fenn's wrists, and the cuffs were chained to the floor behind him in a barred cell in the eastern tower of Steingefan. The light and dark from an unseen window took turns until Fenn no longer counted the days. He was hungry and cold and alone. Forced to lie on his side and grapple food off a plate with his mouth and slurp water from a shallow bowl, he grew weaker and weaker. Visions haunted him. When he slept, he saw his mother's hand, pale and trembling, heard her voice softer and softer until she whispered. Awake, Rogget's painful cry in the woods stabbed at him; he imagined the huntsman's face, eyes staring at nothing, mouth open but no words escaping. Roren, the fear in his eyes, lost in the forest. Was he dead, as well?

When Fenn thought he would go mad from loneliness, soldiers of Hass opened his cell, forced a potato sack over his head and detached his cuffed hands from the bolt in the floor. He was taken through the prison, outside, and put on cart. He lay down to keep from being jostled too much in his blindness. After traveling for half an hour, the cart slowed and Fenn heard a voice in the distance. The cart stopped and the voice was loud and nearby. Fenn sensed many people, their bodies shuffling about, a low hum of voices.

The loud, weasely voice called out, "The beast folk vowed revenge on your Ruud, and it was within their grasp. But the Hass has saved you. We have found him."

Fenn was forced to climb five wooden steps, shoved forward, and the sack was pulled from his face.

"The bairn of the prophecy is here."

Fenn looked out on the crowd. He was standing on a wooden stage erected outside the courtyard of Michelruud castle, and before him mingled what looked to be most of the villages of Path, Timber, and Town. At least, he was certain he'd never seen so many people in one place in the Ruud before, except Cold Sea Port, perhaps.

Behind the throng of quiet, dull-looking folk, a copse of trees shielded the road to Steingefan. Just north, through the wood, was the spot he, Sadie, and Grayson met Rogget and waylaid the carriage to sneak into the stone prison and rescue the children of Path. Behind him lay the King's Orchard and beyond that, the western wood and his best chance for escape.

"And we can thank our young heroes for helping us capture him."

The weasel voice belonged to Sorgood, King Welk's master of the guard. Fenn's first thought was that Welk had lied to him and was working with the soldiers of Hass to hold him captive.

There was mild clapping among the crowd as footsteps clomped up the stairs behind the stage; Sadie and Grayson walked forward and stood next to Sorgood.

Traitors, Fenn thought. Rage swept through him and he fought to push them away, but nothing happened. He was

302

drained and empty. Powerless.

"Without their help," Sorgood called, "we could not have found the bairn and saved your Ruud."

More lazy applause. Fenn looked to Sorgood; he, too, looked worn—unshaven, sweating, though it was cold enough for puffs of fog to exit his mouth when he spoke. Why did he keep saying 'your' Ruud? Wasn't it Sorgood's Ruud, too?

"They will tell you of their daring bravery," Sorgood said to the crowd.

Neither Sadie nor Grayson looked at Fenn as Sadie began to speak.

"We followed the new bairn across the Ruud and into the Great West until he found the kell stone in the mines of Galdred," she said. Her voice didn't carry nearly as far as Sorgood's.

"Yes," he said. "You say you followed him to the Great West and he found the stone. And you, innkeeper's son, how did you get the stone from the bairn?"

Sadie cast a nervous glance at Fenn and he saw despair and fear in her eyes.

Grayson said, "We waited until he was asleep and I stole it from his knapsack."

"That's not true," Fenn said.

From behind, someone grabbed both his arms behind him and squeezed them together, sending a shudder of pain through his body. A gruff angry voice whispered in his ear, "Keep quiet or I'll gag you."

Fenn glared at Sadie and Grayson, but they wouldn't look at him. There were more footsteps on the stairs and Fenn turned to see one of the Hass, in his purple robe; but this folk wore a tall, pointy hat on his head. He was blond and blue-eyed like the eis, frowning.

"It's true," Sorgood called out to the crowd. "We have the kell stone."

"Show us," someone yelled.

The Hass representative walked forward to stand on Fenn's other side and said, "Arrest that folk."

From the back of the crowd, a few folk pushed through toward the man who had dared to speak. Fenn suddenly realized the gathering was surrounded by Hass soldiers, dressed in purple tunics with the flaming tree emblem.

"Will you arrest us all?" someone else shouted. And suddenly the folk came alive as more Hass soldiers were drawn from their posts into the unruly mass.

"If you have the stone, show us."

"We demand to see proof."

"You can't arrest all of us."

"Very well." The Hass folk nodded to Sorgood.

Sorgood called for his guard and several soldiers in red approached the stage at Fenn's feet. The folk in the crowd hissed and booed. Fenn was suddenly struck with the urge to spit. How dare soldiers of the Ruud serve Sorgood and the Hass? Traitors. Not just to the king, but to their own folk. He leaned forward as if to move toward them, but his captor pulled harder at his arms.

One of the guard handed a velvet bag up to Sorgood and a hush fell over the gathering as Sorgood reached in and pulled out the smooth round stone.

"You see," Sorgood said. "The kell stone of legend is real. And we are now possessed of it."

Odd choice of words, Fenn thought.

"How do we know that's the one?" someone called from the back of the crowd.

Fenn looked wide-eyed at Sorgood, a smile erupting on his face. Sorgood seemed stuck for a moment, his brow furrowed and his head tilted and pushed back on his neck. He looked briefly to the folk standing beside Fenn and said, "Kirche?"

Kirche shrugged and said, "Arrest them."

Fenn smiled deeper.

"We can't arrest them all. We haven't enough room in Steingefan."

"Then answer them. I'm not used to such insolence. You folk of the Ruud need more authority. Ruffians."

Sorgood looked to his audience and said, "What other stone would be perfectly smooth and round? Do you think I conjured it out of air?"

"You could have made one," someone said.

"No one can make a stone like this."

"How do we know that?"

Fenn desperately bit his upper lip to keep from laughing. He never expected such skepticism from the folk of the Ruud. He took a look at Grayson, but his friend still shuddered in fear. They must have their parents, Fenn realized. Why else would they be so frightened? Maybe that's why they lied about stealing the stone from him.

"There is no other stone like the kell stone in this world," Kirche said.

"Then it must have some power," someone else called out. "Show us what it can do."

"We will use the power of the kell to control the beast and free you of fear. But first we must deal with the child of prophecy. How do you want him killed?"

Fenn's smile vanished as he cast his gaze over the crowd before him. His breath seized in his throat and his heart raced.

"You have the kell stone. Why harm the boy?"

"You have wanted him hanged," Sorgood said. "I have heard you call for his capture and death, myself. And now here he is. The Hass has found him for you and is willing that he should die as you wished."

"Aw, now, some of us, maybe. But I've never thought the boy ought to be killed."

"Maybe we were a bit hasty."

"Why kill him now? You've got the stone."

Sorgood looked past Fenn to Kirche. "You said they would cry out for his death."

"And you told me they wanted it."

"They did want it."

"Hear now," someone in the crowd called out. "What say we just lock the boy up at Steingefan?"

"Or the wissenry. He could be under house arrest."

The crowd broke out into a mumbling discussion of possibilities.

Kirche held up his hand for silence. "I have tolerated enough insolence from this crowd. If you wish to escape spending the night at your stone prison, there will be no more outbursts. We will hang the boy, as the folk of the Ruud have demanded."

Fenn searched the now silent crowd, fearful—his breath a shallow panting. Could he save himself? With his hands bound and his body hollow and empty of strength, could he escape this? The folk who had hold of him led him toward Grayson and Sadie. A beam stuck out overhead—he hadn't noticed it before—and Fenn watched as a noosed rope was tossed over it.

"No," he heard Sadie say. "You can't do this."

"You will stand there," Sorgood said to them, "and watch."

306

Everything seemed to pause when the noose was dropped over Fenn's head. If the crowd was making any noise, he could not hear it. He was aware of shuffling, jostling, and voices perhaps, but couldn't tell from where they came. Sorgood held the kell stone high above his head; folk rushed toward the gallows, furious; soldiers of Hass fought to the middle of the crowd and grabbed at folk, trying to force them away.

Suddenly, Sorgood sank to his knees and Fenn watched as the kell stone fell from his hands and rolled off the edge of the stage to the ground below. Sorgood froze, suspended mid-fall, an arrow piercing his chest just below his heart. His mouth opened and closed but no sound escaped.

Chapter Forty-eight

"Folk of the Ruud," someone shouted.

Fenn looked up, behind the crowd, as horses approached. King Welk sat astride his steed, a raised bow in his hands. "It is time for you to fight," he said. "Choose freedom, or choose the Hass."

There was a brief, shocked lull before chaos erupted and Fenn stood paralyzed for a moment as the world seemed to have begun again. The noose still hung around his neck and he struggled to escape from the folk who held him. Sadie screamed; Grayson rushed forward and grabbed at the noose. His captor was down, an arrow in his chest. Folk pulled Sorgood, still gasping for air, from the stage and trampled his body. Kirche had disappeared.

"We have to run," Sadie shouted over the din, lifting the noose from around Fenn's head.

"You run. Get your parents."

"Come with us," Grayson said.

"I have to get the stone. Uncuff my hands."

Grayson scrambled to the body of the dead soldier and dug

into his tunic pockets, pulling out a set of keys. He grabbed at Fenn's wrists and fumbled with one key after another.

"We don't have time for this," Sadie said. "Get off the gallows."

"No," Fenn yelled. "Do it now." He could see the kell stone beneath the feet of fighting folk in the crowd, kicked this way and that.

Finally his hands were freed and without a glance at Sadie and Grayson, Fenn scrambled to the front of the stage and leapt off it. Folk were fighting Hass soldiers with short swords, knives, and hatchets. Fenn ducked and dove to the ground; several folk tripped and fell over him. He caught another sight of the stone and grabbed for it as it rolled forward under someone's feet; they kicked it back and he grabbed again but it slipped away.

Scrambling to his knees, an elbow smacked Fenn's cheek and he fell. Another folk stepped on him; he screamed and rolled over, curling up, covering his head. Kirche appeared in front of him, crawling along the ground, blood oozing from the right side of his mouth; he was grasping for the kell stone.

Fenn got to a his hands and knees and threw himself into Kirche, taking the stone from him. Kirche pulled it from Fenn's grip and thrust a blade toward him, a furious rage on his face. Fenn glared at him, wishing he could force him to do his bidding—force him to let go of the stone. Gradually, Kirche's face relaxed. His eyes clouded over and he dropped the stone. The man fell onto his face and Fenn looked up to find Ma'am Hardy, with her cast-iron frying pan, standing over him.

"Get a weapon or get out of here, Fenn," Ma'am Hardy scowled and disappeared into the melee.

Fenn clambered to his feet and ran, bumping into Grayson. They had no time for greetings and without thought, Fenn followed him. Grayson led him through the trees toward Path until he stopped and Fenn realized they'd come upon Ma'am Dowling, Grayson's grandmother.

"This way." The woman grabbed Grayson and led him to a small stand of trees in the middle of the brief wood surrounded by shrubs. She told them to hide and went back into the fray. After a moment, Ma'am Dowling returned with Sadie and then led them all through the woods surrounding Path until they came to the back of the inn where she took them downstairs into the basement next to the alehouse cellar.

"You must hide here," Ma'am Dowling said. "The Hass has taken over the inn."

"Where's Da? And my brothers? Where's Mattie?"

"Mattie's off to Aaronland; she's safe. And the others escaped north to join the king."

"And left you here?"

"I stayed of my own free will and I have good reason."

"Yes Ma'am."

"And that reason will be down to see you in a moment."

They were left alone in the basement, one small lamp at the steps leading to the back door cast a hesitant light on their faces. Fenn realized he still had the kell stone in his hands and he lifted it; as he did so, it let off a green glow that lit the room below the inn. Shelves lined with tools, kitchenware, linens, and soaps filled the back of the basement. A pantry of canned goods, and the laundry, hemmed them into the small space at the foot of the steps.

After surveying the room, Fenn found Sadie and Grayson staring at him as if they were waiting for him to speak. Instead, he merely met their gazes, defiant.

Finally, Sadie said, "You don't think we wanted that to

happen."

And that was enough for the three of them to begin speaking at once.

"What did you *think* they would do to me, if you turned me in?"

"To Welk," Grayson said. "Not the Hass."

"You knew everyone was after me."

"But hanging?" Sadie said. "It's drastic, don't you think?"

"What else could you expect?"

"And anyway, we changed our minds before we got into port."

"But it was too late," Grayson said.

"Welk wasn't so bad, actually—" Fenn said.

"They took us to Steingefan!" Sadie said. "They tortured Grayson."

"—but he wouldn't let me leave; we had to escape."

"Not tortured, really," Grayson said. "More like bullied."

"We were on our way to the beast forest, when the Hass caught me and took me to Steingefan."

"And we only said those things on the gallows—" Sadie said.

"I still don't know what happened to Rogget, but I'm afraid he might be dead."

"—because they told us they'd kill our parents if we didn't."

"And the next thing I know, I'm going to be hanged and my two best friends are—"

"You were in Steingefan, too?" Grayson said.

"Rogget dead?" Sadie said.

"You didn't turn me in?"

"No, not exactly...but...Rogget?"

"We're your best friends?" Grayson said.

"Is that so surprising?" Fenn said.

"We *are* best friends," Sadie said, "and we always will be."

"What do you mean, 'not exactly?'"

"I told you before," Sadie said. "They questioned us. I know I shouldn't have said anything about the stone, but they tortured Grayson."

"They did not."

"You still have a black eye."

"That's from a fight. One of the Hass soldiers kept saying stuff and I punched him. He hit me back, that's all."

"You punched someone?" Fenn said.

"In the face." Grayson beamed.

"What was he saying?" Sadie said.

Grayson frowned. "I'd rather not say."

Fenn was sure he was blushing.

"Why do you think Rogget's dead?" Sadie said.

"He was shot...I think."

They were silent—Fenn watching them in the dim light of the kell stone, Sadie looking back and forth at both their faces, and Grayson refusing to meet her eyes. When the door opened and Leah Hallowsing came in, they all jumped. She rushed down the steps and took them into her arms, kissing each one on the top of his head.

"Oh, Fenn, you have no idea how glad I am you're safe. And the stone, you still have it."

"I was trying to take it to Dag Voorspeld; but I didn't make it."

Leah shook her head. "I'm afraid it will have to wait. The battles are begun—skirmishes in the villages now. Dowling says the Hass is rounding up the young; we fear they're going to ship them off to Ruhm."

"Why?" Sadie said.

"Ransom of a sort. It keeps the folk in line, knowing the Hass has their children. I've got to get you all north, where your King Welk is planning to draw the Hass...to Steingefan."

Grayson nodded. "My brothers and my da are there. They'll be fighting and I plan to join them."

"You're not quite old enough for soldiering," Leah said.

"Age doesn't matter so much right now, does it?"

"Of course it does. Your grandmother, your father...they wouldn't want you to fight. But you could help with the wounded, perhaps."

Grayson scowled.

"But what about the children of Path?" Sadie said. "We should take them with us."

"Dowling is spreading the word as she can—telling all the children to sneak out and head north."

"We should gather them up and *take* them."

"You three are being gathered up and taken."

Fenn thought Sadie would burst. She sucked in a breath and glared at Leah. "I don't want to be taken away while the others are left behind."

"They're not, Sadie. Trust me. Everyone is working to help them."

"Do you know anything about Rogget and Roren?" Fenn said.

"They've not been heard from, nor seen, not that Dowling's found out."

She left them again with the promise of returning. The three of them sat huddled in the basement listening to the muted sounds of their village under attack. Occasional shots from firearms prefaced screams and shouts. The smell of smoke and

314

burning wood filtered in through the cracks around the doorjamb and Fenn trembled, worried the Hass would burn the inn above them.

When Fenn woke from a restless sleep, Ma'am Dowling and Leah were standing in the darkened basement near the steps, fretting. As soon as he touched the kell stone, it let off a glow and he saw immediately that Sadie and Grayson were gone.

"Where did they go?" Leah asked him.

"After what you told me earlier," Ma'am Dowling said, "I think it's clear where they've gone."

Ma'am Dowling retrieved an empty flour sack from a shelf and placed inside it a small blanket, some food, and a flask of water for Fenn. When he put the kell stone inside it, its glow ceased and the room was darkened once again. He looked at Leah hopefully in the dim light of the cellar. They left him— Grayson to fight with his brothers, Sadie to help the other children escape. They knew he would have wanted to go with them, so they snuck out and left him. He was surprised at his lack of anger toward them as he lifted his brows at Leah.

She shook her head. "I know you'll want to find Sadie, at least, but you've got to think of the kell stone. We've got to get it out from amid the Hass."

The door above them flung open with a bang and a large figure stood silhouetted against the dim moonlight.

Chapter Forty-nine

Sadie made her way in the dark through the pines and stood just at the edge of the woods listening for their voices. Some time after dark, while Fenn and Grayson slept soundly in the basement, she'd heard kid folk at the back door to the inn collecting food from Ma'am Dowling. She waited for her chance, snuck out, and followed them as they took the path behind the inn and around toward the wissenry. When Sadie came upon it, she stopped and gaped. The wissenry building was a burnt out hull; brown smoke still billowed from its center.

Behind her, Sadie heard footsteps on the crisp pine covered ground and she turned. Jeopard Link, her father's apprentice, stuck a finger to her lips and pressed hard.

"Don't make a sound," he whispered and took her hand, pulling her back into the woods.

They walked hastily until Sadie's breath was quick and her heart pumped. He took her south to the high crossing where dozens of the young men and women of Path sat huddled in the cold night. She recognized Taylor and Winfred right away, and

Dora, the daughter of the smithy. They stared at her, their faces wide-eyed and alert. She remembered the last time she'd seen them—they were running through the orchard playing tag; it seemed so long ago.

"What are you doing here?" Jeopard asked her.

"Looking for you; I wanted to help the children make their way north, to Steingefan."

"We've already got the young ones out."

"Then what are you waiting for?"

"We're watching the Hass. There's a battalion stationed just outside Michelruud castle and as soon as they begin to move, we're going to alert Welk's guard."

"We should move on them ourselves," Eller said.

Sadie nodded at him. She barely knew Eller; his folks lived on the border between Michelruud and Aaronland and sold their vegetables at market every two weeks—the only time he came into the village.

"We should steal their weapons and use them against them," Dora said.

"That's not a bad idea." Sadie walked forward into the group. She sat on the ground among them and began to recognize more faces in the dark. Drew and Gettel who lived north in the woods by the pond; Cammie, one of Ma'am Hardy's daughters; the shoemaker's son, Kirk.

"We have our instructions," Jeopard said. "We're only supposed to watch."

"Are they drinking ale?" Sadie said.

Jeopard shook his head. "These soldiers of Hass don't imbibe like ours do. And anyway, the battle is on. No soldier would drink when they have to fight in the morning."

Sadie smiled. "You don't know much about soldiers, do

you?"

"Do you think they're drinking?" Milford, a young worker in the king's orchard said.

"I told you they are not."

"The inn is still standing," Sadie said.

"Their higher ranking officers are there."

"All right then. We'll sneak into the ale cellar next to the basement and take casks to the soldiers at the castle. What time is it?"

"Ten, I think," Milford said.

Sadie smiled. "Let's do it."

"What for?" Jeopard said.

"To let them have some ale of course. It's such a cold night. I'm sure we can persuade them. And the ale cellar's always open at the inn. The lock broke last year and Mr. Steppe hasn't a put a new one on."

"How do you know?"

Sadie shrugged. "How do you not?" She waited and, slowly, several of the others stood with her.

"How will we get it there? It's a long walk."

"We need carts and horses."

"The Hass has horses and carts in our stable," Kor Wolf whispered. "No one's guarding them."

"It's settled then."

At the inn, Jeopard snuck a look through the windows and reported that the soldiers downstairs were sleeping; ale mugs littered the floor around them.

"So much for your special Hass soldiers," Sadie told him.

They climbed into the cellar, one by one, and carried out the smaller kegs of ale and jugs of cheap wines imported from the west. They loaded up four carts and led the horses quietly around the outskirts of the burned town, onto the path through the wood and approached Town Village. The hanging stage still stood and soldiers of Hass had built small fires all over the grounds outside the castle walls.

Sadie and three others led the horses toward the soldiers' camp while the rest stayed hidden in the woods.

"Ho there, what's this?" One of the soldiers stood to greet them.

"We were told to bring you refreshment from the inn in Path," Sadie said. "A gift from your superiors who are encamped there."

"We do not drink ale," another said.

"They're drinking ale at the inn. They said they missed the Founding Day celebration while preparing to sail. They're celebrating late."

The soldiers gathered around, murmuring.

"We were told to leave it here and return quickly with the carts. We have more chores to do for the others."

"Very well." The first soldier waved them away.

Sadie smiled when she turned toward the wood. She and her three companions met up with the others several yards along the path.

"Now what?" Jeopard said.

"We wait. If they aren't used to ale, they'll sleep soundly and we'll go in and load the carts with their weapons."

Jeopard shook his head. "Your parents won't be happy to know I helped you with this."

"Well, then, don't tell them."

"Sadie Pratt," he said, his eyes wide. "You've got to be the worst behaved kid in the Ruud. And I couldn't be more glad of it."

And so they waited and watched from the woods while the soldiers of Hass enjoyed the ale, singing songs and staggering about. They fell into their fires and screamed and laughed. They shot their firearms into the air; they danced and tripped over one another until finally they settled down and dozed off.

The young people of Path followed Sadie into the camp and pilfered firearms, bows, arrows, long swords, short swords, and knives where they could find them. They snuck them back into the woods on Michelwood path and loaded them into the carts. Sadie crept through the darkness toward the castle wall on which soldiers of Hass had leaned their firearms. She picked them up, one by one, five in all, and struggled to cradle them in her arms. As she stepped over soldiers on her way back, she tripped and fell and found herself lying over a pair of legs. A soldier sat up and smiled at her in the darkness.

"Rutherford, what are you doing here?" he said.

"I...uh." Sadie looked around at the firearms lying about, one in particular lay across the soldier's lap. Sadie said the first thing that came to her. "I was trying to get home."

"Oh, aye," the soldier said. "You were always one for home. What's this?" He lifted the gun from his lap.

"It's my firearm."

The soldier laughed. "Rutherford, I'm going to tell Ma."

"No, don't tell Ma. I promise I'll put it away."

"What's this?" he said, looking at the firearms strewn about him.

Sadie still lay over his legs, her elbows resting on the ground. The soldier tried to move to reach for another musket.

"I can't move. Rutherford, help me."

He grabbed at Sadie and she began to roll over his feet. He pulled at her, dragging her forward. "Help me up," he said.

Sadie started to scream, but thought better of it. If she woke all the soldiers now, they'd be caught.

"Let me go," she seethed.

"Well, you don't have to be mad about it. I just, I can't...oh, all's well now. I can move my legs. See?"

Sadie stood and brushed herself off.

"Of course you can move your legs," she said.

But the soldier had already lain back to the ground. "Tell Ma I miss her," he mumbled and began to snore almost immediately. Sadie collected the guns. Her legs shook like jelly as she tiptoed through the sleeping men to the woods. Ma was right, she thought. Too much ale addles the brain.

Finally, one of the carts was heavily laden with weapons.

"Now for the hard part," Sadie said.

"What's that?" Milford looked at her sleepily.

"We have to get the cart through Path and out to the Steingefan road."

"They're so drunk, they wouldn't hear it if we drove a hundred horses through," Jeopard said.

Slowly, Sadie drove the horses along the edge of the wood, north, as the children walked alongside. She didn't feel secure until they were well into the trees. Soon, the wood would be behind them and Steingefan's towers would rise into the moonlit night.

"We've missed you in the village," Jeopard whispered to her in the dark. "But it looks as if your adventures have done you well. You've changed."

"Have not," Sadie shrugged, embarrassed.

"No," he said, "you have. You've found courage somewhere along the way."

"Maybe courage isn't found, so much as enjoyed."

Her father's apprentice drew his brows into a question; but he smiled.

Chapter Fifty

Leah gasped and stepped forward to shield Fenn as three figures stumbled down the stairs into the basement. When the larger folk tripped and grunted as he fell to his knees and his smaller mate barreled into him and landed on his backside at the bottom of the steps, she let out a chuckle. The third shadowy figure stood atop the steps, head tilted, hands on her hips.

"Knew it was a basement," Rogget said struggling to his feet, "and still didn't expect the stairs."

"We'll light candles," Leah said. "Marigold, take care on the steps."

"No time," Rogget said. "We come to fetch the young folk and get them north. Is that you, Fenn?"

Fenn stepped forward and hugged the large folk, then turned to Roren in the darkness, shaking his hand. "I'm glad you're all right. Rogget, I thought you'd been shot."

"He had been," Roren said.

"Aye, and Roren good enough to get me to the beast forest."

"They let you in?"

"Your young king there managed to persuade his lordship, yes."

"How'd you do that?"

"I'll let you know one day," Roren said. "But now we must—"

"But where are Sadie and Grayson?" Rogget said. "Ma'am Hardy said Dowling got you all from the skirmish."

"It's my fault," Leah told him. "I left them here alone and they've snuck away."

"But why?"

"Grayson wants to fight," Fenn told him. "I guess he didn't think Miss Hallowsing would let him. And Sadie's gone to gather up the other kids in Path, to take them north."

"Ard," Rogget rubbed his hands through his hair.

"Shall I find her?" Marigold said, making her way in the dark down the steps.

"Out of the question," Leah said. "She was my responsibility—"

"Let's just get Fenn north," Rogget said, "and then I'll come back for our firebrand, eh?"

Leah tried to dissuade him, but Rogget wouldn't allow it. Her stomach twisted itself into knots, as she vacillated between anger at the girl for putting herself in danger and guilt at not foreseeing it. She armed herself with her bow, even knocked an arrow, so deep was her fear at the girl's daring, and followed Rogget, now carrying a small firearm, and Roren with his bow. Marigold and Fenn walked between them as they snuck out from the basement—while Dowling made certain any soldiers who might awaken didn't find them out—and into the woods.

They hiked the path north, away from the inn, behind other buildings along the main road of the village, as far north as they could before having to leave the woods.

"We've got to go west," Rogget said, "behind Michelruud castle and make our way through the woods to the western side of Steingefan. Your Kirche's soldiers are already gathering on the plain in—" Rogget went silent, holding up his hand. He motioned for them to split up and Leah let him take Fenn while she and Marigold headed back into the woods and huddled there.

When she heard the smooth, snide voice in the distance, as if he were laughing, she launched herself forward, pulling out of Mari's grasp, and made a wide arc around the area in which his voice had arisen.

Through the trees, in a clearing, she saw Fenn and Rogget standing together—Rogget behind the boy, his arms around him protectively—surrounded by soldiers of Hass. She watched as Kirche moved forward, his smooth chiseled face lit up by the lanterns his aids carried.

He chuckled snidely. "It seems we play at cat and mouse."

"The boy's of no use to you," Rogget said.

"Drop your weapon."

Leah's heart raced as she saw Kirche raise his firearm at Rogget. The huntsman dropped his own small weapon to the dirt and one of his soldiers moved to take it.

"Let him go, and get back to your battle for the Ruud, eh?" Rogget said. "Capturing him's not going to do you any good."

Kirche shook his head and smiled. "Oh, I've no intention of capturing the boy, again. That proved too risky. Clearly, if I want him dead, I'll have to do it myself."

Leah let out a light gasp at the sight of Prenalin across the clearing; he looked into her eyes but no sign of recognition flickered on his face. It was dark, she reasoned; perhaps he couldn't see her hidden in the bushes. But would he stand there and let Kirche kill Fenn? She darted back, and made her way swiftly, silently, around the group, coming up to the trees behind Kirche.

"I won't let you do it." Rogget pulled Fenn behind him.

Fenn struggled against the man, cried out a mangled, "No."

Before Leah could hide, she felt the force of his power—a wall of wind left her splayed on the ground. Quickly, she told herself. She must get to her feet. Grabbing at her bow, she managed to nock an arrow as she clambered to standing and turned to the scene.

All were on the ground but Fenn, his fists balled tightly at his sides, his eyes raging at Kirche, now on his knees, now standing. Kirche chuckled, impatient, and shook his head. Leah watched his back straighten, his pride hurt, she knew. He raised his musket.

"Repel this," he said.

Leah didn't think about it; it didn't even enter her mind to hesitate. She raised her bow and let the arrow fly and when it hit its target, and Kirche dropped his firearm but stood for a few seconds, she could hear only her own breath. She'd pulled another arrow from her quiver, nocked it, and sent it deep into Kirche's back before she let herself care.

When Kirche sank to the ground, she expected a scene akin to the one at the gallows after Welk felled Sorgood, but instead, the soldiers of Hass fled, every one of them, scampering into the trees. Prenalin raced forward as Leah nocked another arrow; she moved into the clearing and aimed at him, expecting him to rush to Kirche. Instead, he came at her, his hand raised.

"Here," he said. "Do you see?" At his side he held a firearm. "If you had not done it, I would have."

She couldn't lower her bow, however, and kept it trained on him. "I don't believe you."

"Leah, stop it," Marigold said coming off the path from behind Rogget.

"It's all right," Prenalin said. "But come, we must hasten north. You shocked the soldiers well enough, but do not think this puts an end to Ruhm's plans."

"They will look to you," Leah said.

"No," Prenalin shook his head. He pushed Rogget and Fenn forward. "Where is Roren?"

"I am here," the young man whispered, scrambling to his feet.

"The mere secretary?" Pren continued. "No, they will find one of Kirche's commanders. Nothing has changed, I tell you. Leah, come."

She nodded to him and the others, lowered her bow and walked a few paces to where Kirche lay, his right cheek in the dirt. Kneeling at his side, she put a hand on his back, now soaked with blood. He was still breathing; he moaned at her touch.

"Are you sorry?" Prenalin said, standing at her side.

She nodded. "For myself."

Kirche's eyes fluttered open and he looked up at her. She drew her hand away.

"Pren," Kirche groaned.

"Quickly," Prenalin said, his hand on her shoulder. "They'll return any moment."

"Pren, help me."

Suddenly, Leah shuddered and cried out. She stood and put a hand to her mouth, then realizing it was wet with his blood, cried out again. Prenalin hurried her from the scene.

"It's not an easy thing," he told her as they fled, "to take a man's life. But Kirche was only too willing to take Fenn's, as he did your father's. You did the right thing."

But for the wrong reasons, she wanted to tell him. For she knew, even as everything in her seemed to deaden as she took the shot, there was a hard core of hate deep within her, and a terrible release of joy when Kirche reeled toward the ground. This would not make her father proud, she knew.

Chapter Fifty-one

Welk paced the open, dirt-covered ground that was once the old bailey behind the gate at Steingefan. They'd taken the dilapidated stone prison from the Hass soon after thwarting Kirche's plans for hanging young Fenn Foster. There, they'd gathered forces, sending out spies, and finally all was in place. The Hass would fight today, whether they wanted to or not. Word reached him the day before that all in the country north and east of Steingefan were poised and ready for the battle to commence. They awaited only word from Welk. As soon as he gave it, select members of the king's archers would leave the castle on horseback through the front gate and engage the Hass. Hass muskets would be no match for his archers, who could fire upon them from a safe distance.

A thousand folk stood just over the bridge, facing the Hass army, many clad in leather armor in hopes of withstanding musket fire. But while the Hass had more firearms than the king's guard, they still had only one for every ten of their folk. And their supply of gunpowder, and their slow reloading gave the Ruud folk all the advantage they needed to dash toward them and engage them hand to hand. Clutch would sound the alarm and the people of the hill country would come at the Hass from the east, while Hargodt and the northerners, joined by the able from the wasteland, would attack from the western side of the stone prison. The Hass had another few hundred men coming from Path this morning, as his scouts had informed him; and their ships had made port from which more folk would embark. The Ruud seemed already in the hands of Ruhm; Welk wished only to live long enough to see this battle won and his folk safe.

The sky eastward glowed in a pale bronze light as the sun rose over the horizon miles away. It was time. Welk raised his hand to the lead rider of his mounted archers, and nodded. The gate was raised and they crossed the bridge over the moat and rode out, kicking up dust. Welk turned to the castle behind him. The gentler of the ladies and several of the elderly peered out of the windows. Welk shrugged; these noble folk women were not well suited to battle. But the folk women of the Ruud were willing to fight. And those who were too small for battle were ready to tend the wounded or care for the children and frail wherever they found them.

He looked about him at the folk who had managed to find refuge behind the walls of Steingefan after the initial battle the day before. Snuck in right under the noses of the Hass who were too busy singing and sipping the spiced bitters of the Ruud to see them making their way through the tall grasses all around and swimming the moat.

Suddenly he heard the shouts. It had begun. The archers on the stone roof of the prison fired arrays of arrows while the crowd of folk, carrying whatever weapons they could find, surged forward. Welk climbed the stone steps to the top of the barbican and looked out at the scene. Folk rushed forward from

Steingefan, across a span of the plain, into a throng of Hass. Spats of musket fire resounded and black smoke billowed. The mounted archers remained on the outward edges and continued their attack, being reloaded by folk children running back and forth from their positions along the outer edge of the castle moat. Hundreds of folk ran in from both sides, hacking at the Hass. As he predicted, their few muskets were abandoned for the sword once the folk were upon them.

Welk spied Hass reinforcements coming from Michelruud Castle on foot. So soon, he thought. Something, he was certain, was amiss. But there was no time to consider what—the battle was engaged. It was time for him to make his way off the barbican and into the fray. He took a deep breath, winced slightly at the pain from his wound, and gazed once more to the Ruud, his beloved homeland. It was as he predicted after all—he would leave Michelruud without an heir. But this was not his worry any longer, not his Ruud. She belonged now to those who came after.

As he turned to start his climb toward his own end, he caught sight of angels in the distance, east; they hovered, focused on a folk running along the outer edge of the battle toward the prison. Welk sucked in a sudden breath. Fenn Foster. The angels swooped down at him, but the boy waved his arms at them and they were thrown back, as if he'd hit them hard.

Chapter Fifty-two

With the sounds of Kirche's men returning to the scene, perhaps suffering guilt for having left their posts, or more likely caught by a superior and herded back, Leah and the others fled north. Leah lost Rogget and Fenn first, then Roren. Soon enough, Marigold was into the woods ahead of her and vanished. Only Prenalin kept pace with her. She led him west, behind Michelruud castle, just as Rogget had planned, and they came out at the edge of the battle, where she caught sight of Sadie Pratt atop a horse-drawn wagon heading toward Steingefan followed by a group of young folk.

She called to the girl as she and Prenalin ran forward. The battle was on, and there sat Sadie, out in the open, daring herself to be shot.

"Miss Hallowsing," she shouted with a smile. "Climb aboard. But be careful, I think they're all loaded."

Leah peered into the back of the cart. "What have you done?"

Sadie beamed. "We stole them. And we got the soldiers drunk on ale. I don't think but half of them will make it to the battle today."

Leah found a seat next to her while Prenalin preferred to walk.

"Very well, then," she said. "I suppose the folk of the Ruud could use some extra firearms."

Sadie swatted at the horses and they broke into a trot, while Prenalin ran alongside the wagon with the young folk. With every sound of musket shot, she and Sadie ducked low on the seat as if that would save them. But the archers on horseback rode some fifty yards from them and Leah knew they must at least be mildly skilled at staying out of musket range. Still, every shot brought her head down, her shoulders hunched. She forced herself to sit upright again as Sadie courageously whipped wildly at the reins. Faster; they must ride faster.

Finally, Sadie turned toward the old stone prison and they raced across the plain where the tall grass, browned and brittle from the cold, folded easily under the horses' hooves. Before they pulled up to the side of the castle, folk were bridging the moat with thin wide planks of wood for them to cross.

"Firearms," Sadie shouted. "We have muskets and powder."

The cart was taken over by folk and driven toward the field of battle. Leah stood with Sadie and watched them race into the throng.

"I fear the others are already out there," she told the girl. "Marigold, Rogget, Roren...perhaps even Fenn."

"My parents are out there, too," Sadie said.

"Are you sure? They could be in the castle."

Sadie shook her head. "We've never known a battle like this. At least, I've never heard stories of such. But the stories we do tell...no, all of our folk who can be, are out there in the smoke and clang, fighting for the Ruud."

336

Leah pulled her bow off her shoulder. "Well," she said to Prenalin, a tremor of a smile at her lips. "Shall we?"

Chapter Fifty-three

Fenn ripped holes in the sides of Dowling's flour sack and slung the bag, with the kell stone safe inside it, on his arm as best he could. He ran, with Rogget and Roren, through the forest and onto the plain, where they found themselves behind the Hass battle lines. They made their way eastward to where the folk of the hill country were advancing into the melee. They lost Roren there, who'd picked up a sword from an early wounded, or more likely a Hass deserter, and joined the folk, darting into the fight.

He and Rogget almost made it to the moat, when the angels, sensing the stone, he imagined, found them. Each time Fenn flung them away, nearly falling to the ground from the force of it himself, they came at him again. Rogget fired on them and for that, one of them grabbed him and carried him off toward the center of the battle; Fenn was now alone. With each thrust of energy from his hands he was weakened and the angels gave him no time to recover before they came at him again.

Still, he made progress, finding himself near the eastern side of the old stone castle, where the remains of the outer wall stood, broken and in disarray, just on the other side of the moat. Folk rushed this way and that inside the bailey, carrying swords, hatchets, and pitchforks. Some carried wounded soldiers and laid them down. Wounded already, he thought.

Urgency spurred him on and he stepped forward, looking into the murky waters of the moat. He struggled to breathe cleanly. Turning, he saw another angel swooping down at him. He threw his arms up at it, repelling it. The angel let out a shriek as it tumbled in the air. Fenn rushed forward, slid down the hill and fell into the water. He swam as best as he could, struggling to keep the flour sack secured on his arm, and turned again, flinging his hands upward, forcing the angel away once more; but the energy pushed his face under water. He struggled for the surface and found his way to the steep slope on the other side. A hand grasped at his and he looked up to see Grayson reaching for him; he pulled Fenn up and out of the water.

"This way." Grayson led Fenn into the crowded courtyard where he could hide.

Fenn looked up at his friend and smiled. "You're filthy."

"War is a dirty business, it seems."

"Your father and brothers, are they all right?"

"I can't say."

"I'm sorry."

Grayson put a hand on Fenn's shoulder. "This isn't your fault."

Fenn nodded.

"I've got to get back out there."

"I should go, too. I can hide the stone—"

"No, Fenn. You know you can't."

"But why?"

"The mark. You know what it means, don't you?"

"Do you?"

"Sadie's da told mine. You've got to stay here with the stone. When all of this is over, then you can do whatever it is you have to do. But now, stay safe."

Fenn watched as Grayson ran into the crowd of folk crossing the bridge, making their way out into the battle, and disappeared. A woman screamed and Fenn turned to see the angels, three of them, surging toward the folk as they scattered. He knew there was no safety, not truly. They would find him and they would hurt a lot of folk in doing so. Fenn knew it was crazy, but when he saw King Welk on the old barbican that stretched over the fractured prison gate, he ran through the folk to the stone steps and climbed, taking himself closer to the angels.

When Fenn pulled himself atop the barbican, Welk gasped.

"I'm sorry," Fenn said, panting and watching the skies. "They're after me."

The three angels caught sight of him and raced forward. Fenn threw his arms at them and they fell back, tumbling through the air, their faces filled with rage. But the force of his own repel left him flopping backwards. King Welk grabbed him by the shoulders, dragging him back, keeping him balanced.

"Get down from here," the king demanded. "I'll take care of them."

"They'll follow me," he said. "I can't let them near the folk."

Suddenly an angel swooped up from behind them and grabbed at Fenn's long coat. King Welk raised his sword and slashed at the angel's arm sending it shrieking away.

"Get down, I tell you."

Fenn ducked as another angel came at him. The king raised his sword, but too late, the angel knocked him down and off the edge of the barbican where he dangled, fighting to hold on.

"Look out," Welk yelled as he struggled back onto the stones, groaning with pain.

The angels dove at Fenn. The largest swatted at him with a short, icy blue blade. Fenn ducked again, this time falling flat to the stone, while the king lunged toward the angels. Fenn rolled over onto his back and threw his hands at them again, forcing them higher into the sky.

"How are you doing that?" King Welk asked.

"I don't know, but I'm tired. I don't think I can do it much longer."

Fenn lay on the stones looking up at Welk. The king's hair was wet with sweat—his dark eyes gazing down at Fenn with a mix of concern and anger. Fenn's charm throbbed heatedly against his skin in time with the king's heavy breathing—even the amber stone could do nothing to alleviate it.

"You need to get down," Welk said.

"I can't. They won't leave me alone. I have to do something."

Suddenly an angel swooped at Fenn and King Welk threw himself in the angel's path. Fenn watched, horrified, as the short blue blade pierced the king's back tearing through his tunic. The angel shrieked, triumphant, as Welk, limp as a rag doll, disappeared over the edge of the barbican. Fenn rolled and looked down—his charm and the amber stone, dangling out of his tunic, pulled hard against him, reaching out to the king as he landed with a splash into the murky moat below.

"No," Fenn screamed and searched the sky for the angels.

He scrambled to his feet, pulled the flour sack from his arm and reached for the kell stone. Anger rose through his legs, to his stomach, and into his throat. His breathing came so heavy spit flew from his mouth with each heave. The angels approached once more, this time smiling with anticipated victory.

Fenn glared at them and waited. *Let them come.* When they were mere feet from him, he thrust the stone above his head and held it there, repelling with all his might.

For several seconds, everything blazed a shocking white. There was no sound; the battle silent, the shrieking of the angels muted. He heard no horses, no firearms, no screams of the wounded. And then pulsating waves, like drumbeats, echoed from the stone—both outward, away, and at the same time, into his arms, to his chest, throughout his body, threatening to crumble the barbican under his feet. Circles of white heat flew against the angels, hammering across the sky. The first wave hit the trees of Michelruud far in the distance and bent them toward the sea.

The angels had flown a hundred yards, thudding to the ground amid the battle, before the stone stopped emitting its thunderous power. Fenn screamed in rage—at what he wasn't sure—and tossed the stone hard at the bridge below him; he watched as it crumpled into the moat. The waters bubbled and fizzed and spewed and the ground began to quake. Fenn fell to the floor of the barbican as it shook violently.

He saw King Welk climbing weakly out of the moat below. The ground all around began to break up; in the distance, trees buckled and fell. Quickly Fenn scooted himself to the steps and climbed down. He let King Welk lean on him and they hobbled away from the barbican as it crumbled and fell. People ran from the castle as its walls caved.

"What's happening?" Fenn shouted over the din.

Everywhere people were running and screaming, except the wounded, who lay on the ground reaching out with bloody hands, calling for help.

"Get low," the king said, his voice filled with pain. "Get

low."

King Welk pulled Fenn to the ground and they lay there while the earth shook all around. Fenn's mind raced frantically. Rogget. Sadie. Grayson. Where were they? Were they all right? His charm burnt against his chest but he couldn't move to pull it away. The amber stone sought to cool him, but failed. He fell onto his back and lay staring up at the blue, cloudless sky. What had he done?

Finally, there was silence and the ground only trembled like a purring cat. Fenn stood on shaky legs and looked out across the moat. The kell was in upheaval, cracks and crevices spread across the land like a spider's web. The moat had drained. Few trees stood in the distant Ruud.

The battlefield began to stir. The soldiers of Hass stood, found their weapons and the folk of the Ruud did the same. Horns sounded in the distance, from Michelruud.

"What is it?" King Welk asked him, struggling to sit up.

"Someone's coming."

Screams echoed from the battlefield, from both the Hass and the folk and in unison they all began to back away, toward the castle. Fenn walked forward and climbed some of the stones that remained of the barbican. Suddenly he caught site of a centaur, then a troll.

"It's the beast folk," Fenn said, turning back to the king. "The beast folk are here."

Fenn looked again as the folk of the Ruud took up their swords against the Hass once again. Now the Hass was caught between them and the beast.

"The eis," Welk said and Fenn looked eastward. A sea of pale green robes rushed forward battling both soldiers of Hass on the ground, and angels in the sky.

344

Chapter Fifty-four

The folk of the Ruud were divided on the question of Michelruud Castle, the only castle in the Ruud left untouched by the shattering of the kell stone, or the burning scorn of Hass. There were those who insisted it was simply a matter of superior construction; and some who charted out the force of the upheaval and claimed location mattered. But there were those who believed its ability to endure symbolized Michelruud's dominance and whispers of a united Ruud spread folk to folk and village to village.

Marigold oversaw the return of the soldiers of Hass, in the few ships left unburned, to Ruhm. They were humbled, both at their defeat and the kindness shown them by the folk of the Ruud. Kirche's death was taken as a sign of vulnerability, a sign of change.

Fenn was allowed to walk beside Welk's cot as he was carried home. Aware of the folks' stares, he kept his gaze on the ground, his jaw set firm and determined; he would not cry. When the king's hand lifted from where he lay and one of the guards nudged Fenn, he glanced at the dying folk and saw him smiling.

"Look," Welk told him. "See."

And so Fenn lifted his eyes to watch the line of folk from Path and villages beyond as he moved among them. There were none on bended knee, nor bent, as Welk had spread word that there would be no more of that in the Ruud. Tear-stained cheeks, rounded and plumped by smiles. Worn, tired, dirty from their work in rebuilding and putting their homes back to rights. When they were not gazing worriedly at the king, they eyed Fenn kindly, offering him nods of encouragement. All was well, he realized. Perhaps he hadn't destroyed the Ruud, though it was by all measurements quite ruined; instead, he seemed to have strengthened it.

While the dead were being buried, orders for lumber being sent north and south, requests sent to stone quarries in the west, and considerations made for some show of thanks to all the beast, Fenn waited in the lobby of the castle, told to remain there until summoned by the king. He could not sit still so he paced in front of one of the hearths, letting its warmth compete with the heat from his charm—pulsing with every beat of his heart.

"Well..."

Fenn heard Grayson's voice. He and Sadie, with the king's new master of the guard, walked toward him, smiling. Grayson's dark hair was stuck to his face with sweat and Sadie's tunic was riddled with stains of grass and dirt.

"...you managed to destroy the Ruud, after all."

Without thinking, he grabbed them both and they stood in a tight circle, laughing, crying, relieved.

"I didn't know it would happen; I didn't even know what I was doing."

346

"You don't have to know," he said. "It's a prophecy. It's not like you could help it."

"The Ruud isn't completely destroyed," Sadie said.

"Are you kidding?" Grayson laughed. "The ground's uplifted. The trees are down. And the Hass burned just about everything."

"You can't blame the fires on me," Fenn said.

The doors flew open and Clutch and two of his gang trudged in. Fenn stepped back and looked to the master of the guard.

"What are they doing here?"

Clutch nodded at him, but walked past, to the back of the room and into the king's chambers.

Fenn turned to Sadie and Grayson, shocked. "I knew they were acquainted, but—"

"The king has summoned you," Dunham said, standing at the back of the room. "Your friends may join you, if you wish."

Fenn nodded. "Will you come with me?"

Sadie took his hand and together they let Dunham, solemn and grave, lead them through the small sitting area, into the bedchamber, to the king's bed, where Welk lay, frail and gray. Clutch was kneeling at his side, one hand clasping the king's, their faces only inches apart; they whispered. Fenn struggled to hear their words, to make sense of them, but he could not. Confused, he reached to the charm at his neck, lifting it from his burning skin. Clutch looked at Fenn, and then nodded to Dunham, who put a hand on Fenn's back, giving him a gentle push.

"You will approach the king," Dunham said.

Fenn looked to Grayson for some support, but he and Sadie only stared at him, wide-eyed. He walked slowly to the bed and looked down at Welk with a slight bow. But the king, he realized, wasn't looking at him; instead, his gaze was locked on Fenn's chest and his charm.

"Where did you get that?" Welk whispered.

"It was my mother's."

Welk shook his head and winced in pain. "That's not possible."

"My mother was as eisen."

Welk looked at him carefully. "My brother," he said. "The charm, Dunham." Each word seared with pain and Clutch put a hand to Welk's chest as if to quiet his suffering.

The king's aide snapped his fingers and a guard, hidden in a darkened corner of the room, approached Fenn and held him, firmly, but gently, by the arms while Dunham took his rope from around his neck.

"It's mine," Fenn protested, squirming to free himself from the guard's grasp. "It was my mother's."

"It was not your mother's," Clutch said quietly.

"It was!"

Dunham handed the hemp rope, with the gold charm and the amber stone strung on it, to Welk who grasped it to his chest. "Rue-Anna," he whispered and closed his eyes.

Fenn struggled to free himself but a look of warning from Dunham calmed him. The room went silent and all eyes were on the king. His face was serene, a slight smile at his lips, a tear rolled out of the corner of his eye toward his ear. As the seconds passed, the smile faded and the king paled. Dunham moved in front of Clutch, reached for Welk's wrist and held it for a moment, then placed his ear at the king's mouth. He stood and nodded mournfully to the guard, who let go of Fenn.

"The king is dead," Dunham said, choking on a sob. "Long

live the king."

"But," the guard mumbled, "who is king?"

With a ragged sigh, Dunham looked up at the small gathering. Three young women, dressed in silk, cousins of the king, if he remembered Father Treacher's lessons correctly, huddled tearfully in a corner. Their brothers, younger still, stood sullenly near the fireplace. King Arnot lounged on a divan, wounded in the leg, and Queen Felisha of Damon Wall, mourning her husband's death in battle sat stiffly in a soft chair. The new master of the guard and three of his men—no doubt they were close to Welk—stood aside, near the door. Servants, Dunham, and Clutch. An odd assortment.

Dunham moved away from Welk's bed and Clutch stepped forward, looking down at the king's body. No one spoke, no one dared cough or cry. Clutch pulled the hemp rope from Welk's grasp, pulled it apart with a snap, removed the amber stone and retied it. He unclasped the kings fingers, replaced the charm, folding his hand around it, then—startling the gathering of folk—Clutch bent and kissed Welk's cheek.

Dunham sank to his knees. "Elrundt, King of Michelruud. King of the Ruud."

Whispers and murmurs flew through the group as the folk sank to the floor. Only Fenn remained standing, staring at Clutch, the thief.

"I want my charm back," he said. He tried to sound brazen, but his voice cracked with anguish.

Clutch looked at him peculiarly—a mix of sadness and joy. He reached into a pocket on the side of his trousers and held his hand out to Fenn. In his palm lay the stone charm the children of Path had carved for him after he rescued them from Steingefan, along with the amber stone Fenn had taken from Clutch's tent.

Fenn moved forward a few steps and took them both. "But I want the other," he said. "I want my mother's charm."

Clutch waved his hand at the folk in the room. "Leave us," he said. They rose and moved to the door. Clutch looked at Sadie and Grayson. "You may remain," he said. The rest, all but Dunham, filed out of the bedchamber. When they were alone, Clutch put his hand on his brother's, still grasping the charm against his motionless chest.

"That is not your mother's charm," Clutch said. "It belonged to Rue-Anna. She was a daughter of the eis, as was her sister, your mother."

"I don't believe you. My nurse Clara said my mother had it."

Clutch nodded. "Aye. Rue gave it to her, on the eve of her wedding. A tradition of the eisen. One is wed free of jewels and charms. Aliara would have returned it to her after the ceremony. If she'd survived..."

Fenn shook his head, confused.

"Welk carved the charm for his betrothed, and braided for her that rope. But he never married Rue-Anna; she was taken from us before the day arrived. She never had a child. It was Aliara who married the prince. Aliara...had a child?" Clutch's voice drifted into a hollow silence.

Fenn looked carefully at Welk's graying face, at Dunham standing at the door, his head bowed, and then back to Clutch. There was confusion and doubt in the thief.

"May I touch you?" he said.

Clutch held out his palm, and Fenn put his hand atop it. He looked at Clutch, who smiled weakly, his eyes brimming with tears. At first, instead of visions or memories rushing at him, Fenn felt only trust, devotion, and that sadness and pain he'd known long ago when Clutch had first stolen his charm from him. Then came a rush of images—the woman, his mother; he was sure of it. Smiling, laughing. And Clutch.

"Tell me what you see," the thief said.

"My mother."

His smile deepened. "She was taken from me, before our child was born. Or so I thought."

Dunham cleared his throat. "Sire," he said, "we can call for the wissendes and find the truth."

"No need," Clutch said, pulling his hand from Fenn's.

"Who are you?" Fenn said.

"Have you not guessed? I am Elrundt, second son of Evan the Fearsome. And now—" he shrugged—"king of the Ruud."

"He's your father, Fenn," Sadie whispered from behind him.

"My father?"

"It would appear thus," Clutch said. "Come, my son. We have much to discuss."

Clutch wrapped his hand around Fenn's, engulfing it. Together, they left Welk's chambers, walked through the lobby and out the huge double doors into the courtyard where a thousand folk had gathered. A cheer rang out among them.

"Long live the King! Long live the King!"

"I must confess," Clutch told him, giving his hand a squeeze. "I've no mind to be a king."

Chapter Fifty-five

While Damon Castle and the wissenry building at Cold Sea Port had been burned, the port city itself was largely untouched by the kell stone, and Leah was grateful for Wanda's hospitality. She'd prepared a grand lunch and sectioned off a small corner of the dining room for their last meeting. Leah fluffed her hair, bringing out a laugh from Wanda, and determined to leave it uncovered even when she set foot in the palace at Ruhm. A rush of daring tingled in her chest at the thought and she blushed.

"You'll be sure to come visit again, won't you?" Wanda said as they walked downstairs to the lobby of the Snapping Turtle Inn.

"Indeed. I'll miss the Ruud while I'm away. I think Pren and I will embark on a project to restore the forests of the west."

"And invite the gnomes and trolls to explore, no doubt."

"No doubt." She laughed. "I've already got a brownie begging for a ride on our return trip."

"Watch him," Wanda said. "He'll take root in your house and do terrible mischief."

"Pren." Leah took his hands when she reached the bottom of the stairs and let him kiss her cheeks. "Are they arrived?"

"They are."

She slipped her hand through the crook of his arm and walked with him into the dining room where she was nearly knocked over by Sadie Pratt's hug. Leah tousled Grayson's hair and gave Rogget a kiss on his beard, for which he blushed and offered a deep thanks.

"What became of you at the battle, Mr. Reynold? I imagine you'll be telling heroic tales for a month or two."

"You've no idea," Rogget gruffed. "It was chaos, o'course. But chaos and me, we got an understanding."

"And what of Darnit?"

"He's out back, miss, waiting for a visit and a scratch behind the ears."

Leah laughed, but stopped suddenly when she saw Fenn standing with Marigold and Roren at the long table now set with plates and utensils. She moved away from the group and went to him, smiling.

"Your Highness," she teased and bowed low.

When she stood and looked to him, for a moment she feared she'd insulted him—he was prince of the Ruud, after all. Instead, he bowed as well, rose and said, "Lady Hallowsing of the Hass?"

"You've heard?"

They all laughed and sat, and let Wanda's waiters bring out trays of roasted fowl, potatoes, turnips, and greens. She told Sadie and Grayson that Prenalin was not yet discovered as a spy and would return to Ruhm, with her as Kirche's widow. Together, they would work toward change in the Hass.

"But the soldiers saw you in the woods," Rogget said. "You

killed Kirche."

"It's not likely they'll remember her," Pren said. "They'll be easily convinced it was just another folk of the Ruud."

"But I thought you two would marry," Marigold said with a smile.

Leah blushed and hissed at her, "Hold your tongue, or I will take back my offer to make you Stationer to the King."

Marigold held up a potato stuck onto her fork. "Tell me you have plans to marry and I will keep quiet."

Prenalin coughed and Leah caught his face reddening.

"Very well," Leah said to the now silent table, "we have plans."

"More wine," Rogget called out and they all cheered.

"And tell me," she said. "Grayson and Sadie, what are *your* plans for the future?"

"Please don't talk as if we'll never see one another again," Sadie said.

"You're right, of course," Leah reassured her. "Still, humor me."

"I'm going to start a university," Grayson said.

"Is that so?"

"What a wonderful idea," Wanda said, bringing in another tray.

"I agree," Rogget said.

"Maybe you should start the wissenry all over again," Fenn said. "The way it used to be, all about facts and learning."

"That's what I was thinking," Grayson said. "But, open to anyone who wants to learn."

"And what about you, Sadie?"

She shrugged. "I'm too young to have to decide my future."

Laughter echoed all around.

"It's true," she protested. "But I have an idea I'll be exploring. Maybe I can lead tours all over Kell for Grayson's students."

"That's a great idea," Grayson said.

"And Rogget?" Leah said.

"Ard, miss. I'd like to be Fenn's guard."

"Done," Fenn said.

"Just like that?" Rogget said.

"Just like that."

"You'll make a great king," Sadie said.

"I don't plan on being one."

"No king?" Roren said.

"Ruhm had one in name only," Fenn said.

"Too true, and look what took the king's place—the Hass."

"I'm thinking of something different. Well, my da is, anyway."

"It's lovely to hear you say *da*," Sadie said.

"It's not lovely," Fenn said. "It's powerful." He grinned at her.

"You're saying King Elrundt hasn't a mind to be king?" Wanda said, taking her seat at the table.

"About time you let yourself eat," Leah needled her with a smile.

"That's right," Fenn said. "But please don't go talking about it, yet. He's got some weird idea folk ought to decide on who they want to be in charge. Committees or something."

"Why that's right interesting," Wanda said. "Word of it will not pass my lips afore your father speaks of it, I promise."

"I think Ruhm would want to know more about this," Marigold said. "We'll need someone here, an ambassador, to keep us abreast of the news."

"Aye," Rogget said. "And the Ruud should have one in

Ruhm as well."

"It sounds as if we're making progress already," Pren said, smiling at Leah.

"I'm going to miss you all," Fenn said suddenly and the group quieted.

"You can come to Ruhm, anytime," Leah told him. "And you'll have Sadie and Grayson and Rogget, still."

"And me," Roren said.

"You're staying in the Ruud?" Fenn asked him.

"For a while, at least."

"But," Leah said, "what will you do?"

"He could be our new ambassador," Pren said.

Roren shrugged. "I think perhaps I will tell my secrets at a later time. This gathering is for remembering how we came to be together and how we have each changed one another's lives."

"No, no, hold on," Fenn said. "There's one secret that has to be told. Grayson."

Grayson looked up from his plate of food, still chewing. "I have no secrets," he said.

"Oh, yes you do. Tell us what the guard at Steingefan said to make you hit him."

"What's this?" Rogget said.

"I thought they'd tortured him," Sadie said. "But as it happened, he'd just got himself into a fight."

"Our Grayson?" Leah said. "Studious and smart...fighting?"

Grayson blushed and Leah winked at him. *Poor, sweet child.* But she still wanted to hear his secret.

"Go on," she begged. "Tell."

Grayson put his fork down and took a drink of cold tea from his glass. He wiped his mouth with a napkin and looked around the table at them all.

"Very well," he said. "I will not give you the details—"

"Aw, come on," Fenn said.

"If you'll be quiet, you'll understand."

"Yes, Fenn," Sadie said. "Let him talk."

"If you must know, one of the Hass guards said something unkind about our Sadie. He hinted she wasn't as brave as one might expect."

The table was silent. Mouths fell open, into smiles. Ripples of giggles broke out and were quickly shushed. Finally, they all turned to Sadie. She sat, her eyes wide as saucers, her gaze on her roasted fowl and potatoes, her cheeks flushed pink.

"And so you hit him," Fenn said.

"Thank you," Sadie whispered with a smile, "waiter boy."

Grayson laughed and Fenn stood, his chair groaning against the wood floor as he pushed it back. He raised his glass. "We must drink to Sadie's champion. Grayson, defender of her honor."

"Hear, hear!" They all sang out.

Leah couldn't help feel this may be the last time she would experience such warmth—at least for a very long time. She would sail with Pren and Mari in the morning. She'd only been able to send a message to her mother, in the care of Madam Always, across the hill country. She'd see her eventually, she knew; but the delay wore at her day and night. She and her mother must comfort each other in the face of her father's hanging, but it would have to wait. A kingdom must be reset, freedoms restored, a community of folk not used to thinking for themselves must be guided. Leah had no time at present to think of herself alone. She could feel the weight of the truth on her shoulders—its telling a matter of saving Ruhm—and knew her father must have felt it, too. She smiled at his memory, though her eyes were filled to the brim.

Chapter Fifty-six

When Rogget rustled him awake before the sun tipped at the edges of the horizon, it took Fenn several seconds to remember. He was still at the Snapping Turtle Inn in Cold Sea Port. Leah Hallowsing was sailing west to take Ruhm and rework her into a kingdom in which the beast and folk could learn to accept each other. The folk of the Ruud were rebuilding, already working with the beast folk to ensure villages were welcoming to them. His charm was gone—buried with King Welk on the plain of Nergens where he lost his betrothed. Clutch, the thief, was Fenn's father. He opened his eyes.

"Aye," Rogget said, smiling at him. "It were no dream."

Rogget helped him dress in the fine silk tunic and pants Wanda had pressed for him and as he wrapped the oiled leather belt around his waist, he heard a light rap on the door. Instinctively, he reached to his chest for the gold charm. In its place, on a hemp rope his father wove for him, hung the stone charm from the children of Path, and the amber kell—Clutch told him he'd have given it to him, anyway.

"Before we let him in," Rogget said, "I should prepare you."

"Who is it?"

"Name's Budden. Representative of the gnomes, so he says. He's got the kell stone."

"What?" Fenn cross the room in an instant and pulled the door open to find a squat, greenish brown folk, tall as Fenn's waist, with a broad, rugged smile on his rough, lined face and thin wisps of gray hair dancing about his head. He held the stone out to Fenn with something of a nod.

"But...?"

"Wen groeven hetuit," Budden said. "Means...sorry, I have not spoke folk in many an age."

Fenn took the stone and beckoned Budden into his room where the old gnome looked around and whistled.

"Fijne accom," he said. "Ard, I done again. Nice room."

"Where'd you get the kell stone?" Fenn said.

The stone glowed and its green color leaked into Fenn's fingers, traveled up to his wrists, just as it had done when he first found it.

Budden nodded. "Yes, see. It is yours. We dug it out. The gnomes."

"I thought I'd lost it. I thought the kell had taken it back."

"The beast lord summons you with the stone. The young king of Ruhm is to...how do you say? He must travel with us."

"Roren?"

"Aye."

"Wanda's already had a pack made up for me to carry," Rogget said. "Blankets, a lantern, food."

"Can Sadie and Grayson come?"

Budden whistled again. "Into the forest, I say yes. But not to Rad."

360

Fenn looked to Rogget and the huntsman shrugged.

They said their goodbyes to Leah, Prenalin, and Marigold, and set off that morning with Roren, who didn't seem surprised at the invitation. Sadie's ma was against the trip, but after some negotiation with Rogget, finally allowed it. Grayson's da was in Path helping with the restoration of the village and Grayson acted rather grown up about being on his own.

When they all reached the edge of the forest later that morning, Grayson turned to Rogget and said, "You start counting and you'll see. It'll only take one day to get in, see the beast lord, and come back out."

Rogget's brow creased and Sadie laughed so loud a flock of roster fiends squawked and lifted off the tops of the trees into the sky. Once in the forest, the daylight dimmed and only shimmered in dusty rays through the trees.

Rogget whispered, "The forest still brings a touch of fear out of me."

"Nothing to fear," Budden said. "We have the stone."

As they traveled, they were joined by many others. Talkative fairies followed, flitting above their heads. Brownies, both woodland and displaced, skipped along beside them. Wolves and felidae prowled on either side. When the centaurs plodded into view ahead of them on the path, Rogget stopped and gawked. The largest of them stepped forward and glared, his rusty orange coat and wild brown hair and beard glistening in the sun's rays.

"Huntsman," the centaur said. "It was you who shot me many years ago, on orders from your superior, I am told."

Rogget stammered but couldn't manage to form the sounds into anything resembling words.

"He thought he killed you," Fenn said.

"Aye," Rogget managed to blurt out, "and Dag Voorspeld let me think it."

"Such was your penance."

Rogget huffed and snorted along the path for some minutes after the meeting, but eventually calmed down. "I suppose I should be glad the creature lives."

"He's not a creature," Sadie said. "He's a folk."

"He is Red Lichen," Budden said. "Very wise. Most respected."

"It's going to take the folk of the Ruud a bit of getting used to," Rogget said, "this fraternizing with the beasts."

The trek was much like the last time Fenn had ventured to the lord's lair. They crossed the river, but no troll demanded payment on the bridge. They hiked until after lunchtime and stopped to eat, with little discussion, as if they all had worries none wished to share. When they finally approached the lair, in what seemed the darkest part of the forest, Kwitcher bounded into the group and grabbed Sadie's kneecap.

"Scared and Bitten," he said. "Pretty. You are now Grown Wise. So good to see you once again."

"What is your name now?" Grayson asked him.

"I remain Kwitcher. Catch much anger and trouble. But is new trend. All the best displaced brownies taking names."

"And what are you going to call me now?"

"You are also grown wise; I will call you Learned, today. Nearly Orphaned!" Kwitcher squealed and hugged Fenn's knee.

"Hello, Kwitcher."

"But you are no longer nearly orphaned, are you?"

"How did you know?"

Kwitcher breathed in deeply. "You smell of comfort and finding home. Come, come, friends of my friends. I will take you all to the lair."

"I am guiding the bearer of the stone," Budden said.

"Very well, then," Kwitcher said with a bow. "I follow Budden of the gnomes."

When they arrived outside the lair, Rogget nervously tousled Fenn's hair and punched him lightly on the shoulder. "Go on, then," he said. "Make us proud."

"How exactly do I do that?"

Rogget roared with laughter. "I haven't any idea. Maybe, it would be best if you simply be yourself. Ard, yes. That would make us proud."

"The stone," Budden said.

Fenn dug the stone from his knapsack and held it, watching its glow permeate the skin of his wrists.

"You and the young king," Budden said, "will follow me."

"Why Roren?" Fenn asked.

"That is a question only the lord can answer."

Fenn smiled at Sadie and Grayson. "I'll be out soon."

"Try to remember everything," Sadie said. "I want the whole story on the way home."

He nodded, turned, and carried the kell stone into the lair of the beast lord where he was enveloped in cool, damp air. Several beast folk sat in a semicircle on stone benches, looking at Fenn and Roren—a troll, a displaced brownie, and a woodland brownie. One of the wolves sat nearby. Red Lichen stood at the edge of the trees, his arms folded at his chest.

"Take your place," a purring voice said.

Fenn looked up to the beast lord's throne and stumbled back two steps. "Lucas?"

Chapter Fifty-seven

Lucas nodded and pulled the hood of his velvety black robe from his head.

"But, you're dead," Fenn said.

"I am."

Fenn shook his head, trying to find some sense in Lucas' words. "Then why are you sitting on the throne of the beast lord?"

Lucas chuckled, a throaty, cat-like sound. "I suppose because I am the beast lord. I am Dag Frieden. Day of Freedom."

"How'd that happen?"

"Being felidae helped. Did Father Treacher not tell you, at least after I was killed?"

"The wissendes never told me much of anything useful."

"I'm sorry for that. Felidae are conceived and born as folk. Long ago, we lived our first lives as folk. But when the folk invaded our lands, we shunned the form and turn our young to felidae shortly after birth; it is a grisly business. I am told my parents wished me to live as folk in honor of the ancients, and so when the choice was offered, I felt it already made."

"So, when you died, you didn't die all the way?"

"My form only changed to shiftling. And I have the mark, as

you do."

Lucas bared his right shoulder and there, on his pale thin arm was the mark of the faire.

"The beast lord has the mark?"

"It is how we are chosen."

"Didn't the guards see it in Path, when you were taken to Steingefan?"

Lucas shook his head slowly. "Folk can be easily persuaded."

"By felidae," Red Lichen said.

"We have the gift of seduction," Lucas said, smiling, "but I could not have remained undiscovered long. Fearing I would be harmed, my brethren took me from the danger."

Fenn sighed with relief; events were starting to make sense. "So, Quiren told the truth."

"Truth?"

"About the Rad and the mark meaning I'm consul for split folk."

"You thought it meant you were the child of prophecy?"

Fenn nodded. "I didn't want to believe it; but what else could it mean?"

"None, neither immortal nor mortal, can foretell the future. The mark is shared by all who will enter here this day."

Fenn looked around at the beast folk until finally his gaze fell upon Roren. Every folk present, he realized, was concentrated on Roren.

"The woodland brownies demand an explanation for his presence," the little brownie said.

"So do we," the troll said. "What is *his* kind is doing here?"

"Show them," Lucas said to Roren with a nod.

Roren, looking perplexed and fearful, pulled off his overcoat and bared his shoulder. There, Fenn saw the same mark. Three long tapered lines tipped with dots.

"You never said anything," Fenn said.

"I was unsure of its meaning."

"But, Quiren told us."

Roren shook his head. "I was still uncertain of who to trust."

"Do not blame the folk," Lucas said. "We have never had a folk consul. They have no tradition to help them along."

"Nor split consul," the troll said. "Soon the Rad will be overrun with splits of all sorts."

"The kell stone decides."

Fenn looked at the stone, still in his hands.

"That is not an explanation," the brownie said.

The other beast folk nodded.

"If the fairies have decided the folk deserve a seat at the Rad," Lucas said, "we dare not shun them for no reason."

"We shun the harpy and the doppelganger consuls."

"I said for no reason. And the fairies tell us none of the harpies or doppelgangers have been marked."

"But these folk are not beast."

"That's not what the wissendes would say," Fenn said. "That's the whole reason we came to the Ruud in the first place. Michelruud, the first king, was a wissende in Ruhm. He discovered beast and folk are all...just folk. We're kin."

"The folk forced us off our land," the troll said. "If they be part of the Rad, trolls will not participate."

"It's true," Lucas said. "The folk have dealt wrongly with us. But we must put it behind us and move forward."

"We have the kell stone again," the wolf said, more of a growl than actual speech, though Fenn understood him well enough. "We can force their retreat, now. All the way back to the southern continents where they belong. Already we feel its power."

"You don't own the land," Fenn said. "Mountains and rivers, the plains, the forests. They belong to all the creatures of Kell."

"Put the stone in the basin," the troll shouted. "See if those two are cast out."

"Yes," Lucas said. "We will consult the Rad. Fenn, you wield the stone. You must deliver it to its rightful place."

Lucas pulled the staff from beside his throne and carried it to the stone basin, where the water dripped over the face of the rock into the pool below. Fenn joined him there and when Lucas lowered the claw end of the staff toward him, Fenn pushed the kell stone into the claw until it set with a pop.

Lucas lowered the staff into a small hole in the pool of water and pushed it down deep until the kell stone sat just above the water's surface. The huge boulder began to tremble and the water stopped running over its face. Fenn stepped back and watched as the trees surrounding them shuddered. Roster fiends shrieked. Lucas pulled him away from the basin and he watched, stunned, as Quiren, the eis, appeared, as if from nothing, before the rock.

Quiren nodded at Fenn and moved to the stone benches where he sat with the troll. A feeorin, larger than a fairy of the Ruud, but clearly, to Fenn, a fairy, appeared next. Her wings fluttered, she blinked several times, and flitted off to find a spot to perch with the brownies. A duergar raged through, shouting what Fenn thought could possibly be obscenities, flitting off to sit as far away from the feeorin as she could get.

Fenn gasped when Brenna stood before him and seemed to float across the lair to stand with him. She looked around briefly before turning to Fenn and taking his hands.

"It is good to see you again. I've been worried about you."

When an angel fell through the portal, stumbled, and stood,

fluttering his wings, the gathering grew noticeably cold and several beasts shouted.

"The angels sided with the Hass," the troll cried out. "We must not allow them a representative at the Rad."

"He is Durahn," Brenna said and the others hushed, "my ally. Part of a new coven of angels, looking for peace."

A grumbling rippled through the gathering but Brenna glared at them each in turn until they quieted.

"Greetings, all," Lucas said. "The kell stone has been returned to us after many generations of absence. It would have passed into legend had it not been for the bravery of Fenn Foster, a folk eis of the Ruud."

"It is a shame on our history that a split had to restore the stone," the woodland brownie said, angry.

"It didn't need to be so," Brenna said. "Any of us could have retrieved it."

"Not so," the brownie said. "We are not all capable, and therefore not all culpable."

"The beast face certain death in the west," the troll said. "And you propose we could have simply traveled there and searched for it?"

"I contend we use the decorum of meeting and speak only when called upon," Red Lichen said.

"Don't be foolish, Lichen," Lucas teased with a smile. "It has always been speak as desired in the Rad."

"We do not run centaurian meetings in such chaos."

"Freedom is chaos," Quiren said.

"And chaos freedom?" the troll said. "I think not."

Lucas raised his hand and all were silent. "We may speak as we wish, but at least let us keep on topic."

And thus began the first council of the Rad in generations.

Fenn sat with Roren and Brenna and he was keenly aware of the way they eyed each other, trying not to smile. He shook his head, but couldn't help smile himself.

When the meeting ended, hours later, and little had been decided, but much discussed and argued over, Lucas approached him outside the lair where he'd met Sadie, Grayson, and Rogget.

"What will you do now?" Lucas asked him.

"I have to get back to Path, to Clutch. I mean, Elrundt. I mean...my father."

Lucas nodded. "I will come with you and offer him my condolences on the loss of his brother. And after that?"

"My father—" the words were coming easier and easier to him—"wants to leave the folk to govern themselves and venture southward."

"And you will go with him?"

"He says he won't go if I don't want him to."

"And so you will go with him."

Fenn sighed. "I think I will."

"They say there are dragons on the southern continents," Grayson said. "*If* they exist," he added with a smile.

"And a different sort of kell in the south, I'm told," Rogget said. "Amber."

"I hope there aren't any prophecies about that one," Fenn said.

"So, it's all over then," Sadie said. "No more bairn of prophecy. No more running."

"But Fenn did destroy the Ruud," Grayson said, looking hopefully at Lucas.

Lucas shook his head. "There is no such thing as prophecy; the future cannot be foretold."

Roren left Brenna and joined them. "We have been invited

to visit the ice realm," he said. "I do hope you all will join me."

"I will," Sadie said. "I'd like to see inside the palace, not a prison tower."

And so it was settled. Fenn, Rogget, Sadie, and Grayson let Lucas lead them along with Roren out of the forest on a path northward that would take them through Timber. As they hiked, surrounded always by some group of beast or another, Fenn couldn't help catching glimpses of Roren. Something nagged at him—a truth he dared not say aloud. How could Dag Frieden be wrong? How could the wissenry be wrong?

And yet, there it was. The young king of Ruhm, destined to die of starvation in the mines of the Great West, marked as a consul of the Rad by the fairies. As if they knew...as if it had all come to pass as it was meant to. And then there were the dragons! What was it the prophecy said? The dragon flies above him. All laid waste below.

"I think I will," he blurted out. "I'd like to see this southern kell for myself."

Books by this author

Fantasy by Dana Trantham
Children of Path: The Kell Stone Prophecy Book One
The Wretched: The Kell Stone Prophecy Book Two
Mark of the Faire: The Kell Stone Prophecy Book Three
The Kell Stone Prophecy: Complete Trilogy

Story Runners: Awakening

Women's, Literary, Romantic Comedy, and Young Adult
by Dianna Dann

Camelia
Always Magnolia
Bookish Meets Boy

Paranormal Humor by by D.D. Charles
Zombie Revolution

Children's fiction by Dana Trantham
Zombie Cats (middle grades)
Wayward Cat Finds a Home (children's chapter book)

www.waywardcatpublishing.com
Dianna Dann   Dana Trantham   D.D. Charles